FRIENDS *No Longer*
By Cinda Brea

I0618489

Copyright© 2014 Cinda Brea

This book is a work of fiction. The names, characters, and incidents are the products of the author's imagination or are used fictitiously.

All rights reserved. No part of this publication may be reproduced, stored in a retrieval system, or transmitted in any form or by any means (electronic, mechanical, photocopying, recording, or otherwise) without the prior written permission of the copyright owner, except for brief quotations in printed reviews.

The scanning, uploading, and distribution of this book via the internet or via any other means without the permission of the copyright owner is illegal and punishable by law. Please purchase only authorized electronic editions, and do not participate in or encourage electronic piracy of copyrighted materials. Your support of the author's right is appreciated.

Acknowledgment

I dedicate this novel to my very creative and humorous sister, Freddie Jacobs, who I truly wish could read "Friends No longer" and give me her honest feedback and to all the past and current residents of Seaside, California. Thank you to Brenda Smith and Gay Bellamy for previewing this novel and providing me with the feedback my sister, Freddie, can no longer give.

As always, thank you Judy Bullard at customebookcovers.com

TABLE OF CONTENTS

Chapter 1

Monia Phillips sits across the table from her mother, Clarissa, enjoying a late afternoon lunch at Saritas, a local family owned restaurant. Monia appreciates the sense of relief that has slowly creped over her since she completed the one hundred and ten mile trek to the Monterey Peninsula and her family home in the small coastal city of Seaside. Loading a U-Haul truck and then driving it to Seaside with her beloved 2004 Volvo wagon hitched behind has resulted in an exhausting morning.

Watching Clarissa, Monia has seen little evidence that the woman is pleased about her only child's move back home. *You'd think she would be more grateful. After all, I made this move because of her.*

"Why are you watching me like that, Monia. I don't need you here to keep an eye on me; I'm not that old yet," the sixty-four-year-old Clarissa Phillips declares. "When did you say your place will be ready, anyway?"

"Mom, I just got here a little over an hour ago. Are you tired of me already? You always told me to be gracious to house guests. I haven't been here long enough to start stinking up the place yet." Monia makes reference to the old proverb about house guests, like fish, starting to smell after only three days.

Finally, Clarissa smiles and reveals her true feelings about her daughter's return to the area. She had no idea how happy Monia's move back to Seaside would make her. Over eight months ago, when Monia first declared her intentions to return, Clarissa had chalked the declaration up as sheer bravado. Her daughter had a great life in Frisco. Monia's job as a physician's assistant to an orthopedic surgeon was both challenging and rewarding, paid well, and was far from too demanding. Monia loved the work and liked the people she worked with. Her only complaints about her life in the city were that the cost of living was so high that she feared she would never be able to afford her own home in the Bay Area and the traffic was atrocious.

Monia had; however, found a very reasonable apartment not far from her job, living above a family in the Castro District. She and her landlord family had little interaction and were so satisfied with their landlord – tenant situation that the landlord raised the rent only slightly over the years. So Monia continued living above the Aleman Family and gave them no cause for complaint.

Clarissa had often visited her daughter in San Francisco, usually accompanied by her soon to be ex husband, Darnell, and it was not out of the norm for Darnell to visit Monia on his own. As an only child, Monia was as close to her father as she was to her mother. Both parents stopped visiting over a year ago and now, with Monia back home on the Peninsula, there will be no more cozy home-like excursions to San Francisco for Clarissa. Her trips to the city will be like they were before Monia became a city dweller – rush up, shop or take care of whatever business necessary, and drive back home the same day or shell out wads of cash for some over-priced mediocre hotel room. Of course all the inconvenience the occasional trip to the city will once again entail is worth it because her daughter will now live only ten minutes away. Clarissa had told herself she didn't want Monia to give up her life in the city. It was too much of a sacrifice from her child and it was not necessary, but Monia had been determined. Now here she sits, watching Clarissa, and getting on her nerves already.

"You won't need to house me long, Mom. My place should be ready in a couple of days. The tenants are out and the place needs some cleaning and a fresh coat of paint. I'll have so much more room than my last place. I can't wait to get settled in. I hope you'll help me decorate. I still can't believe you refused to let me live with you, at least for a while," Monia tells her mother as she takes on the air of one truly offended and she is, though only slightly.

Clarissa simply grunts and digs into her refried beans with a corn tortilla.

When Monia made the decision to move back to the Peninsula, she believed her mother needed her near and she wanted to be close enough to keep her mother company on a regular basis. Monia's parents had been married for thirty three years and always seemed like the best of friends to Monia. She thought they were inseparable. She remembers answering her phone early one Tuesday morning and hearing Clarissa speaking loudly on the other end. "I just thought I'd better call and tell you that your father is gone."

"Gone where? What do you mean dad's gone?" Monia had felt panic as she thought about the disappearance of a family friend years earlier. The man has not been heard of since and many believe he is dead.

"I put the son of a bitch out and he's not coming back!"

"Mom, what happen?"

"Your father has a girlfriend he's been seeing for a while now. Do you believe this shit? Why didn't the asshole just leave instead of screwing around? I can't believe he thought I wouldn't find out and then the motherfucker had the nerve to think I was going to let him stay here. It will be a cold day in Hades before I stoop that low."

"Mom, let me call you right back. I need to call the office."

"You ain't got to call me back. I just wanted to tell you before you found out on your own. You're grown and need to know what's going on."

"I'll call you right back."

Monia hung up the phone and had to take a seat and a breath before she dialed her office. She felt like she was falling down a deep well. Her loving parents could not be in this situation. They were her foundation for everything, always so stable. She had seen this with her friends' families, mothers left alone while fathers started new lives with younger wives and little children; trying to determine which parent to spend a holiday with; not able to invite both parents to your house for dinner at the same time. Although there may be young children involved in early divorces, it seemed to Monia that late marriage divorces were much more difficult. Of course the children of long term marriages were usually on their own or close to being so but the horror of having to become so involved with a parent's life because she or he is devastated by the betrayal of their best friend and longest love. This could not be happening, but it was and did.

Monia had taken a few days off and showed up at her parents' home in Seaside two days later. It was late evening when she arrived and she hadn't bothered telling her mother she was coming. She tried the front door and found it open. Her parents were notorious for not locking the door during daylight hours. The house was dark, with all the blinds and curtains drawn, and completely quiet. Monia found her mother sitting on the back patio listening to music, drinking wine, and smoking a joint. "Mom, are you getting high?" Monia had asked in complete shock.

Clarissa had just taken a long slow drag off the joint. She looked at her daughter without the slightest bit of surprise or shame, then looked at the joint as if to make sure she was indeed smoking reefer and replied with complete calm. "I sure am."

Monia had convinced her mother to put the joint out but Clarissa refused to give it to her or turn over her stash. That was a year ago and Clarissa still will not give up her marijuana. Monia does not get the impression that her mother indulges excessively but wants her to quit the illicit activity. Clarissa won't even discuss it with her daughter.

That weekend was spent talking to both her parents separately because Clarissa refused to allow Darnell back in their home. She declared she could not stand the sight of the man and had not heard his voice since six days earlier when she had the locks to the house changed and a new security system installed. Darnell had been so ashamed and deflated. He stated that he wanted Clarissa to forgive him and wanted to move back home. He could hardly look his daughter in the eye as they talked over dinner at the Embassy Suites where he was staying. Looking back, Monia believes he couldn't look her in the eye because he hadn't broken off the relationship with the thirty-eight-year-old dental hygienist he was seeing.

Darnell pleaded with his wife and may have actually remained on the straight and narrow if she had allowed him to return but Clarissa was as tired of him as he was of her. It wasn't that they didn't love each other anymore but they were both just plain bored and thought their lives together played a significant role in their boredom.

"Mom, dad is really sorry and wants to come back home. Won't you give him another chance?" Monia had begged on Darnell's behalf.

"I don't want your father back. He made his bed and now he can sleep in it. I like it here by myself. I don't have to worry about feeding nobody but me. If I don't want to clean, I don't have to, and I know you don't want to hear this but here it is, after all you are grown now. I don't have to worry about spreading my legs if I don't want to. Our entire marriage your father complained that I was not interested enough in sex, always wanted me to initiate or be more active. I'm a woman and I'm five years older than your father. I figured he'd get tired and leave eventually because he felt so sex deprived. Here I am sixty four years old and got to be trying to have sex twice a week. I'm too old for that shit. Now he's got him somebody that can satisfy him and I'm happy for his sorry ass. Let's see what he finds to complain about now. I guarantee you he'll find something, but it won't be me." Clarissa shut Monia up about letting Darnell return home with that very open and honest statement.

It had not taken long for all to realize that Monia's father had accepted his fate and settled in with his lovely hygienist. Monia felt certain that her mother needed her near and had not expected Clarissa's flat refusal to allow her daughter to move in with her. "You're a grown woman and I'm sure you have grown woman ways. You're not going to want me telling you anything, but I'm your mother and refuse to keep my opinion to myself when it comes to you. If I don't tell you the truth, who will? We'd just get on each other's nerves. And what about that on-again-off-again boyfriend of yours? I'm sure he'll want to slip down here and spend the night sometimes when you two are on good terms. No, it's best if you have your own place when you move here so that way we can stay friends. I won't feel the need to fuss at you too much and you won't have to ignore me as much. Besides I might want to get me one of those on-again lovers."

Monia had no rebuttal for her mother's matter-of-fact soliloquy. She did; however, make a futile attempt at denying her relationship with Marcus. "Marcus is not my boyfriend, Mom. We're just friends that date occasionally."

"Yeah, when he wants to have sex."

"Mom, that's not true. We've been friends a long time and sometimes we want to spend time together. Sometimes we go out or vacation together. Our relationship is not all about sex. We're just comfortable with each other; that's all."

"Well you keep telling me there is no love involved," Clarissa said and then got quiet for a moment before asking, "Does Marcus date other people?"

"I guess he does. Yes, yes he does," Mona had reluctantly admitted.

"Well, tell me this, does he ever get involved with any of those women or does he come and go with them like he does with you?"

"Listen Mom, I don't keep track of who Marcus is seeing. I've told you we don't have that type of relationship."

"I'm not blind, Monia. I know exactly what type of relationship you and Dr. Marcus are having but maybe you need to figure it out. If this is what you want in a man then I'm happy for you. I'm of the old school, as I'm sure you can tell by the situation between me and your father, and I don't believe in sharing no..."

Monia cuts her mother off. "Okay, that's enough, Mom! Let's change the subject. You're not going to make me mad and get me to change my mind about moving back home. I've already got two job offers. I've given notice at both my apartment and my job. I'll be there next month. Love ya. Gotta go."

Considering all the arguing her mother and she had endured about her move, Monia can hardly believe she is back in Seaside with their relationship intact and stronger than ever. Now if they can just live within ten minutes of each other and maintain their independence and sanity, the move will be worth the effort.

Chapter 2

Sleeping in for a few days before she starts moving into her new home is high on Monia's agenda until Clarissa starts talking about how excited she is about her daughter going to church with her on Sunday morning. "When was the last time you attended services at New Life? Everyone's going to be so glad to see you."

"I wasn't planning on going to church service tomorrow. I've got all my stuff packed away in that U-Haul," Monia responds.

"You don't have anything you can get to? I sure would like you to go with me. You know once you get settled into your own place, it'll be like pulling teeth to get you to go."

Monia doesn't answer in hopes that the discussion is finished but quickly realizes that the discussion may be over but the issue is not. Clarissa has gone all passive aggressive and gotten quiet on her. As happy as Clarissa seems much of the time, Monia understands that the breakup of her thirty-three-year marriage has taken an emotional toll. This sullen behavior is something Monia has never seen coming from her mother.

Feeling guilty, Monia gives in and goes out to buy an outfit for the next day's church service. She had not expected to spend her second evening in Seaside out shopping. This is her first time at her old shopping haunt in years. She loved shopping at Del Monte Shopping Center when she was a girl and is surprised to see how little the retail center has changed. Yes, the store names have changed and there is some revamping and modernizing but basically the place is as beautiful and serene as ever. Monia strolls through the stores at a leisurely pace, taking in the relaxing environment and comparing it to the hustle and bustle of shopping in and around the city. She purchases a simple skirt and dressy top. She really does not need shoes because she and Clarissa wear the same size shoe and exchange footwear regularly but a pair of heels that she cannot resist catches her eye.

Monia finishes her shopping just before the stores close and has to think hard to remember where she parked her car. It takes her so long to find the vehicle that she begins to fear it may have been stolen. Her relief at finding the car is soon replaced with anger when, after several attempts to start the engine, it will not turn over.

Fortunately she spots a mall security vehicle and waves the driver down. The security patrolman hooks up a portable battery charger to Monia's vehicle and allows it to idle for a while, but the vehicle will not maintain a charge on its own. The car battery is new, so Monia is fairly certain it is not the battery alone.

A call to her insurance agent, her mother, Clarissa, is her next option. Clarissa offers to pick her up and says they can worry about the car later.

"I've got to get her towed home or to a garage. I don't want to leave her here overnight."

"Girl, that car will be fine until tomorrow. They've got tons of cameras at Del Monte," Clarissa tells her daughter. Sensing the concern Monia feels for her nine-year-old vehicle, Clarissa puts on her agent's hat. "Let me get you a tow service. I'll call you right back."

The security patrolman very kindly remains with Monia and talks nonstop until he sees the large flatbed tow truck approaching.

"How you doing?" The patrolman greets the tow truck driver as he exits the cab of the large truck and renders only a slight nod of the head in response. Monia tries not to look at the driver too hard but he is quite spectacular. The man has shoulder length dark chestnut brown dread locks that hang loosely around his chocolate face. He is long, lean, and athletic looking. There is something oddly familiar about him.

"How are you?" the driver walks a little closer to her and speaks with so much warmth in his voice that Monia tries to get a better look at his face, even leaning in closer but it is dark out by this time and she still can't see the man well.

The brother goes through his ritual of loading her car up on the flat bed of his truck before getting any information or asking her to sign any paperwork. Monia makes a mental note to discuss the man's lack of professionalism with her mother. Finally, after securing the vehicle, the tow truck driver approaches his customer and gets near enough for her to see well. "Jeremiah!" Monia yells, unable to hide her joy and surprise at seeing her childhood friend.

"How you been, Moanie? It's been a long time." Jeremiah Sumuels stands in front of her as he removes his gloves and watches her with that same sly smile he flashed when she was ten and he was fifteen. Monia remembers what a crush she had on that long lanky boy back then. Although Jeremiah's mother and Monia's parents are close friends, it has been nearly eighteen years since she last saw him. She had no idea he was living in the area. As far as she knew Jeremiah had dropped off the face of the earth when she was fourteen years old. Now here he stands before her more beautiful than she remembered, a tow truck driver. *Don't be so damn bougie, Monia. As long as the brother is alive and makes a decent living, legally, be thankful.*

"No one has called me that in years." Monia smiles at her friend as she gets closer and gives him a long hard hug. "God, Jerry, I haven't seen you in so long. I had no idea you were back living here. When did you get back?"

"I've been here over nine years now. I returned just about the time you started working EMS. I been keeping up with you. Your mom throws a nice bit of work my way. Hop up in the cab. We'll stop by the garage to leave your car and get mine. I told Clarissa I'd drive you home."

"What's up with the dreads? When did you go all ethnic?" Monia asks.

"You like? I read somewhere that I may not go bald as fast wearing the dreads." Jeremiah gives a light chuckle. "Clifford is clean. I mean serious chrome dome. I haven't seen him in years but my mother showed me a picture. I figure there may be some validity to the claim since I'm the older brother and I'm still holding on. Besides, the women love 'em," Jeremiah grins.

Clifford is Jeremiah's younger brother and Monia's childhood nemesis. He picked on Monia nonstop when they were kids. They attended the same elementary and middle schools and both went to Seaside High. He was two years older though only one grade ahead. Monia remembers when he and his friends taunted her with names like "snaggy" when she lost her teeth and "bucky" when the teeth grew back in. When she got to junior high, Clifford was there waiting with his bullying friends. He started calling Monia "piggy" because she had filled out a lot. Jeremiah was the one who put a stop to the harassment. That was when her tiny crush on him had become full blown.

It was one of their family get-togethers and the young people had been banished to the family room. They didn't mind the banishment because it gave them complete control over the television and the Nintendo game system. The adults were in the front of the house playing cards, drinking, talking shit, and listening to music. Clifford decided he was safe badgering Monia whose breasts seemed to be growing a cup size a week.

Jeremiah was quite a bit older than the other children and had, a year or two earlier, stopped attending all the family gatherings. He was doing his own thing which rumor had it entailed hanging out with the wrong crowd, doing drugs, skipping school, and getting laid. On this particular occasion he was in hot water with his parents so they had made him come along to the Phillips' home for the party. Monia had been pleased to see him and he kindly bestowed that deliciously sweet smile upon her, causing her to blush all over her eleven year old body.

Clifford had become angry after Monia beat his pants off in a game of Super Mario in front of Linda Barry, another young girl who was watching them play. After fuming for a few moments, Clifford started in on Monia with "I don't think I'll call you 'piggy' anymore. I think I'll call you 'tittie'." Monia had been embarrassed to tears and was about to leave the room to hide her watering eyes when Jeremiah grabbed her by the arm and stopped her. Jeremiah dipped his head down to look Monia in her face and said, "You know why he teases you so much, don't you, Moanie?" He smiled that ever present smile he held for her alone. Monia didn't answer but stood there and gave Clifford the stink eye.

"Shut up, Jerry!" Clifford had yelled in protest.

"He wants you to be his girlfriend. That's what little boys do when they like girls. They tease them and pick on them because that's the only way they know how to talk to the girls they like." That piece of information had done more to boost Monia's self-esteem than all the confidence boosting speeches her parents had delivered over the years.

Monia smiles remembering that time as she rides in the cab of a tow truck with a man she has not seen in nearly two decades who feels like the long lost brother she never had if you overlook the long standing crush.

"So what brought you down this weekend -- just checking on your mother?" Jeremiah asks.

"No, I'm moving back. I've got a job and a place down here."

"Wow, I heard you were doing really well up there in the Bay Area. What happened?"

"Nothing happened. I just want to be closer to my mom. She's all alone now, you know."

"Yeah, I'm sorry about your dad. I know that was a real shocker to her, you too I imagine." Jeremiah looks over at her as he drives down Munras Avenue toward Fremont Boulevard.

"It was. Mom's actually taking it better than I am. She and dad talk on the phone and handle their business affairs as if there is nothing to it. I don't think I would be so nice if my husband of thirty three years just up and started playing around with a co-worker."

"You sound madder than Clarissa. Have you talked to your dad?"

"Mom was scary mad at first and who could blame her but now I wish she would show a little more anger. She seems perfectly happy to be rid of my dad. I talk to dad just about every day. He calls me more now than he did when he and mom were together, sounding all pitiful." Monia's anger at her father is apparent in her voice and manner of speaking. "I'm sorry but I just can't feel sorry for him. I have to worry about my mom. She's alone now. Dad has someone and he kept lying to me even after he was busted. It'll be hard for me to ever trust him again."

The more Monia talks about her father the angrier she becomes, so Jeremiah is quiet for the remainder of the drive. Once he off loads Monia's Volvo, he locks up the garage, directs Monia to a little Fiat, and heads off to Clarissa's home.

"I wouldn't expect you to drive this little thing," Monia laughs.

"Well I'm cheating. We use these to do a lot of running around for the shop. They have saved a bundle on gas. I occasionally take one home."

"Your boss doesn't care or is that what you mean by 'cheating' – the boss doesn't know?"

Jeremiah glances at Monia with a big smile now. "The cheating is for tax purposes. The boss is more than happy for me to use the Fiats. I am the boss."

"Nice! It must feel good to own your own business. I knew you were into cars but I never thought of you as an entrepreneur."

Jeremiah gets serious for a moment and asks as he exits the little Fiat in front of Clarissa's home. "You probably never thought of me at all, did you?"

Monia is surprised by the question and starts to answer but Jeremiah doesn't seem to expect one. She's even more surprised when they enter her mother's home and she realizes that Clarissa and Jeremiah are pals. "Hey baby! Thank you for dropping everything and going to rescue my girl. Where's the baby?"

"She's been with her grandmother since last week. She'll be home tomorrow."

"That's the other grandmother you're talking about, right? I know Sharon doesn't like that. She loves that grandbaby. You want some coffee. I got the strong stuff like you like it," Clarissa offers her friend.

"No thanks, Clarissa. I'd better take a rain check on the coffee. This late it'll keep me up all night and I've got to get my rest. I've got to drive down to Pismo to pick up my girl tomorrow."

"Oh, so your baby's mama lives way down there. How often does your daughter visit her?" Monia asks, hiding her surprise at hearing Jeremiah is a father.

"Not too often because of the drive. Her grandmother lives in LA but she has a sister in Pismo Beach and we use her home as a meeting spot. Erin is getting to the place that she doesn't like visiting that much. There are no other children and she's pretty restricted to inside the house. Sometimes I take her so I can check things out and see who else is living there. I'm afraid I may have to stop the visits. Seems that neighborhood gets worse each time I go down."

"Well you have to consider the baby's safety and yours too. It can be very dangerous in a lot of these neighborhoods if people don't know you, especially in the LA area. They are gun happy down there," Clarissa chimes in.

"I know. I've tried to work with her grandmother because I don't want her mother coming back for custody. Veronica is a good woman and she loves Erin, so I hate to deny her but I may have to." The subject of Jeremiah's young daughter and the visits to her mother's family has weighed heavily on him for some time.

"How old is your baby now and where is her mother?" Monia asks.

"Erin is six going on sixteen." Jeremiah laughs and Clarissa nods in agreement. "Her mother is up in New York trying to make it big in show biz, I think. Listen, I've got to go, ladies. Moanie, it's good to see you after so many years and I'll give you a call before noon on Monday about the car. It probably won't be too bad, maybe just the starter."

"Oh, do I owe you something now for the tow?"

"Nah, tow's on the house. I'll pad your repair cost to make up the difference." Jeremiah laughs, gives the ladies each hugs, and leaves.

Both mother and daughter are rejuvenated after spending time in the presence of their family friend. When the two women notice each other's smiles, they crack up laughing. "Mom, I hope you're not trying to flirt with Jeremiah. You know he's trouble. I hope he's not your contact," Monia chastises her mother.

"Don't you worry about my contact. And what do you mean Jeremiah is trouble? Why would you say that? When was the last time you saw him?"

Monia thinks for a moment and becomes sad when she recalls the last time she saw her old crush before this very evening. "I was about fourteen and me and my girlfriend Ja'Niece were up at Mal's Market headed home. Jeremiah came out of the store and we begged him for a ride. He told us 'no' and told me I shouldn't be asking grown men for rides. I remember telling him 'you ain't grown and you better give me a ride or I'm going to tell Miss Sharon and my mom too.' He gave us the ride and came into the house to say hello. Dad was so mad about me getting in the car with Jeremiah and he told him so. Later, me and dad had an argument. I think that was the first and last time I talked back to him. I thought that was so mean. Mr. Trotter was missing and their family was having a hard time. Jeremiah just said 'I understand Mr. Darnell. It won't happen again.' He still smiled at me and said 'See how much trouble you got me into, Moanie.' Dad just looked all stern and didn't offer him a seat or anything. Jeremiah made a little small talk and finally left. It was painful and I was so mad at dad. You know Jeremiah was my first crush and he was always nice to me. Even then I knew dad would not have treated him that way if Mr. Trotter was still around."

"Your father was just trying to protect you, Monia. You know Jeremiah went through some rough times back then. Drugs, girls, doing poorly in school and." Clarissa checks herself. "We'll let the past remain in the past. Let's just be glad for Jerry. He's doing well in his business and loves his daughter."

"I was surprised to see him tonight. He seems happy with that business. He was always good with cars like his dad. I am glad to see him doing so well. Why didn't you tell me he was back living here?"

Clarissa is a bit ashamed. Darnell had asked her not to mention Jeremiah's return to Monia and she respected her husband's request without pursuing the matter. Both parents knew that Monia had a childhood crush on Jeremiah and both wanted to get a good feel for the man before facilitating a meeting between him and Monia. Jeremiah had often asked about Monia and Clarissa and Darnell would smile and tell him tidbits of Monia's life but never encouraged the friends to reengage each other. Not long after Jeremiah's return to the city, he became involved with the mother of his child and soon his questions about Monia became less frequent. "I guess it just slipped my mind. It wasn't that we were keeping it a secret from you but there didn't seem to be a good reason to tell you he was here."

"God, I can't believe he's been back here for nine years and I didn't know it."

"Well, Monia, you know you seldom visit us here except for a few days at a time. You might have seen him if you had spent a little more time here on the Peninsula. He's got quite a reputation as the person to go to for high end car repairs." Clarissa changes the subject. "And you listen, Miss, I meant what I said about my contacts."

Chapter 3

Jeremiah could hardly wait for the clock to strike noon so he could head out on the drive to Pismo Beach to pick up his six-year-old daughter, Erin, from her maternal grandmother, Veronica. Since Veronica's sister lives in Pismo, she takes the longer stretch of the drive when they meet between their two cities to make the visits possible. The fifty-five-year-old Veronica usually has her husband, youngest daughter, nephew, or some combination of the three rides along on the drive from her home in Los Angeles to Pismo Beach. Jeremiah always makes one leg of the trek alone.

These drives afford him much needed quiet time even when the traffic is hellacious. He likes spending time with his own thoughts and planning for his life with his child and his business. The business has far exceeded his expectations but he does work hard at it. He finds himself downright jubilant when a customer likes his work. The car sales are an absolute phenomenon. His crew works with him to restore older cars and make them special and customers are begging for them. He's got customers calling and asking him to work on their classics and to find cars for them. He never expected the sales to take off like they have.

What a gift his knack for cars has become – a gift from his father, Trotter Sumuels. As pleased as Jeremiah is about learning auto work under his father's tutelage, thinking about the man stirs up so much pain that there are times when the son wishes he had never met his father.

Trotter Sumuels disappeared twenty years ago when Jeremiah was seventeen and his brother Clifford was fourteen. Trotter and his wife, Sharon, had been married just over twenty years on the day he went missing. The couple would have celebrated their fortieth wedding anniversary this year. Nothing about life for the Sumuels family has been the same since the disappearance. Sharon had become a functioning shopaholic who over indulged in alcohol and loved gambling more than her other addictions combined. Clifford had abandoned his mother and brother as soon as he got old enough to do so. When Clifford finished school, he moved to San Diego, married and had children, started a thriving dental practice, and spent all his time and effort pretending there were no skeletons in his family closet or elsewhere, not even under the skin of those he left behind.

Jeremiah had, without question, suffered most of all. He was the last known person to see his father alive and since he and "Trot," as Trotter was often called by those close to him, were on bad terms, many assumed Jeremiah had done something sinister to his father. The police had questioned him relentlessly. His mother had tried to protect him but even she had her doubts. One evening after cursing the police out and telling them to leave her "goddamn son alone" she had sat Jeremiah down, looked him square in the face with tears streaming down her own, and asked, "Jerry, did you do anything to your father? I understand if you did, son, and I will protect you. To my death bed I will protect you, but I need you to tell me the truth." To learn that his mother doubted his story hurt as much as being accused of hurting his father. No one, it seemed, believed him. The sad truth was that Jeremiah did not know the truth himself.

Trotter Sumuels was an enigma of a man. He had left his family back home in Louisiana and joined the Army when he was only seventeen years old. Five years later he was married with a child on the way. His military career field was supply but like many young inductees he was a grunt or infantryman while serving in Vietnam. He had been stationed in Fort Ord, California, on several tours and he and Sharon made their home in the adjacent small town of Seaside. Trotter retired from the Army in the early 1990s and started working as a full time auto mechanic at Del Rey Auto Repair for his long time friend Gilbert Salas.

Trotter had been a hustler his entire life. He was a gifted musician who played piano, trumpet, some guitar, soprano, tenor, and his instrument of choice, alto sax. The alto sax was the instrument he considered manly enough for a manly man like him. It was a tossup as to which skill Trotter was best at or held most dear, auto repair or music. The music provided the most glory and allowed him to spend time around the people he enjoyed most, other hustlers and women, but his skill under the hood of a car paid him well. If he would have dedicated himself to working on cars he could have made a good living in that arena, but Trotter needed the glamour, the women, and the drugs. For those things, he used his remarkable ability to play music.

After losing the shackles of a military life, Trotter began spending more of his free time away from home. Very likely, if Sharon had been willing to share him with all his many talents life would have continued to run smoothly in the Sumuels household. Trotter was the type that could have easily burned the candle at both ends for another fifteen or twenty years. He was full of himself and stamina, but Sharon soon put her foot down and started demanding that he give up the music gigs and, oh yes, the gambling. Sharon was a gambler also but never neglected her home or family to gamble. She preferred casinos; whereas, Trotter frequented the card games often found in a number of Seaside homes. For the first time in their marriage, the couple started to have physical fights. At first Trotter just tried to keep Sharon off of him but soon the fights escaladed and Trotter was hitting back.

It was not long after Trotter started spending so much time away from home that Jeremiah started spending time away from school. After a year of skipping more classes than he attended, Trotter got Jeremiah on part time at the garage. Sharon didn't agree with her son dropping out at sixteen but Jeremiah was out of control. They could not make him participate in school, so when he wasn't somewhere getting high, sleeping, eating, or getting laid, he was at the garage working on cars. Gilbert, the owner of the garage, didn't take no crap, so Jeremiah could not show up on the job high and he never did, at least not visibly. He did all his damage in the evening after he got off work.

With all the cash he was making and no one making him save it or checking to see what he was using it for, Jeremiah soon moved on from marijuana to coke and from there on to crack. There were other drugs too; there wasn't much he hadn't tried. His father, Trotter, could do any drug and put it down and walk away. Trotter was the epitome of a recreational user. His only addictions seemed to be excitement and risks. When the father learned that the son was delving deeper and deeper into the world of habit forming drugs, he pulled his son's coat and demanded that he stop but it was too late. Jeremiah was hooked on crack from his first hit. In a way he was more fortunate than many because he had plenty of money to support his habit and less fortunate for the same reason.

The last day Jeremiah, Sharon, and Clifford saw Trotter, Sharon had refused to give him the keys to any of the three family vehicles.

Loaded and impatient Trotter slapped his wife hard across the face. Sharon lit into him like a crazy woman. When Jeremiah heard the commotion, he ran into the living room and tried to break up the fight. Before long, he and his father were wrestling. When they broke apart and got to their feet, Jeremiah told his father, "If you hit my mother again, it will be the last thing you do." Trotter threw a jab and busted his oldest son's upper lip. Jeremiah was hurt and his mouth bled profusely. He nearly lost a tooth behind that jab. His parents stopped fighting long enough to get a towel for his mouth to try and slow the bleeding while Jeremiah fought to hold back his tears. Clifford had watched the entire fight and cried through it all.

"I need you to leave this house and never come back," Sharon told Trotter. "I mean it this time."

"I pay for this mothafuckin' house. I'll leave here when I get good and ready. Give me my goddamn keys. I'm taking Jerry to the hospital to get that lip sewed up."

"You're not taking my son anywhere."

"Give me the keys, woman."

"Mom, please give him the keys," Jeremiah mumbled over his bloody swollen lip and through the bloodied towel.

Sharon surrendered and handed the keys over. "I'm going with you," she announced.

"Drive your own car and meet us at Community." Trotter had snatched the keys from his wife so hard she nearly lost her balance. He then pushed Jeremiah toward the front door and slammed the door behind them, not saying another word to his wife or youngest son.

Sharon never showed up at the hospital. Trotter gave the staff some bogus story about Jeremiah getting into a fight with another kid. Father and son were out of the hospital emergency room in record time with a recommendation that Jeremiah visit a good oral surgeon if he wanted to keep his front left incisor and not walk around looking like the drug addict he was.

Instead of Trotter taking Jeremiah home, he took him to a small apartment in the heart of Seaside on Olympia Avenue. Jeremiah had no idea who the apartment belonged to and his father did not tell him. The men sat down and smoked a couple of joints together. It was the strongest reefer Jeremiah had ever experienced. Trotter let his son consume a couple of glasses of a cheap wine he found in the refrigerator and it wasn't long before Jeremiah stretched out on the sofa and fell fast asleep. That was the last time Jeremiah saw his father.

Later that morning when Jeremiah woke up, it took him quite some time to recall the events of the day before and figure out where he was. Trotter was nowhere in sight but the car keys were on the scratched up coffee table and the car was parked out front. Jeremiah had waited several hours but he was scheduled to work at noon, so he left the apartment, drove home, showered, and went in to work as usual. His father should have been on shift also. When the boss, Gilbert, questioned Jeremiah about his father's whereabouts he couldn't tell him.

Jeremiah placed a check-in call to his mother at the dress shop where she had worked for years. He didn't want to upset her or cause her to worry unnecessarily so he did not mention Trotter but hoped Sharon would say something about his father. When she didn't, Jeremiah shrugged it off and thought Trotter was probably shacked up with some woman who had picked him up at the apartment. At least that was what Jeremiah had assumed.

Five days passed before Sharon, at the insistence of Gilbert and Darnell Phillips, filed a missing person's reports. It was weeks later before the police started investigating the disappearance of Trotter Terrell Sumuels, husband and father of two.

It took a while but the police had eventually honed in on Jeremiah as the last person known to have seen Trotter before his disappearance from the whole known world. Once the investigators got their feet wet in the muck that constituted the lives of the Sumuels family, they waded in deeper and deeper, causing even more havoc in the three lives that had been turned completely upside down.

Sharon was certain Trotter had run off with another woman and as damaging as that scenario was to her pride, she shared it with anyone who would listen, even perfect strangers. The fact that the mysterious apartment was leased in Trotter's name added credence to her take on his disappearance. Sharon needed to get the focus off of her child. She was not certain that Jeremiah had not caused Trotter's disappearance but if he was responsible he was justified. After all, he had been defending his mother.

Clarissa and Darnell Phillips had stood with Sharon and her boys like no one else. In public, Darnell had stood shoulder to shoulder with Jeremiah and embraced him as if he was his own son. After six months and when all the circumstances leading up to Trotter's disappearance became known, Darnell, never said as much but, withdrew his support for Jeremiah.

Clifford, who had always idolized his father, was so angry at Jeremiah that he physically attacked him on more than one occasion. In opposition to his mother, Clifford told anyone who would listen every sordid detail about his older brother. To this day, Clifford hounds the Seaside Police Department about the cold case that surrounds his father's disappearance. Jeremiah has not seen Clifford in more than sixteen years, not since Clifford left their mother's home for college. The brothers were never close but had loved each other. Now Jeremiah only feels sad when he thinks about his brother and Clifford feels only anger when he thinks of Jeremiah.

If there had been any way for the police to pin a murder or manslaughter conviction on Trotter Sumuels' eldest son, he'd be in San Quentin right now. The circumstantial evidence had been entirely too thin. Also their investigation indicated not only did Trotter owe gambling debts but he owed several drug dealers. The drug debts were minimal but everything about Trotter lead police to believe he could have been killed by anyone or could still be alive leading a life elsewhere. Trotter had a reputation for being nothing if not resourceful.

The tragedy was the cloud that hung over Jeremiah's head. Many people in Seaside and around the Peninsula spoke of him in the same way as one local resident, "that boy who murdered his father and did only God knows what with the body." The loss of his father caused Jeremiah to mature quicker than he might have. The son stuck to his normal routine of getting high after work and partying for the first few days after his father's strange disappearance, but once his mother began to worry, Jeremiah did also. When Sharon looked at him with red rimmed eyes, more from the lack of sleep than crying, and told him, "Jeremiah, Son, it looks like we have lost your father, I don't think I can live if I lose you too. You have to keep a clear head about yourself, Son, or neither of us may survive this." She had not raised her voice or spoken angrily but the words chilled him to his core and he knew she meant them. From that point on, Jeremiah started fighting his drug use. He worked as much overtime as he could at Gilbert's garage. He took GED preparedness courses to finish school, and after a great deal of resistance he got professional help. It was a long hard battle but eventually he believed he was clean.

Sober or not, much of the citizenry of Seaside had little use for the young man. He was not welcomed in the homes of friends he had known most of his life. On two separate occasions, acquaintances of dubious character solicited Jeremiah's participation in criminal activities. One proposed he act as the inside man and allow the theft of tools and equipment from Gilbert's garage. Jeremiah soon became a loner. After much discussion with his mother, he decided to leave Seaside and attempt a living in Los Angeles with some distant relatives. It took him all of two days to find part time work in a garage. He was such a dependable worker that the boss brought him on full time after the first month. Soon he found a better position in another repair shop and got the opportunity to do customization work. He loved it. After only a few months Jeremiah felt the urge to move on. He joined the Army on a deferred enlistment and was sworn in six months later. Seven years and two traumatizing tours in Iraq later, Jeremiah rejoined the ranks of the civilian workforce and returned to his old garage.

During his years in the military, Jeremiah honed his skills as a customizer. While stationed stateside, he kept a side job doing auto repairs and customizing work. He kept to himself, did very little partying, and saved every dime he didn't need to live on. All of his fellow noncommissioned officers relished the day they were allowed to move into off base housing, but Jeremiah remained in the military barracks his entire career. His fellow noncoms often teased him and questioned his reasoning. He didn't understand it himself, but he saw no point in spending money he could save on housing that was provided for free. Sometimes he spent a little time off post with a woman he was dating but he never shacked up, though he was made welcome on more than one occasion. Jeremiah was not looking for a wife or a family. He was trying to survive the uncertainty surrounding the broken family he had left behind. That family was all consuming.

Based on the incidents of violence he had lived through during his military deployments and the loss of his father, Jeremiah had no choice but to seek counseling on a regular basis. He wanted to be healthy but was so weighted down with guilt over his father's loss and the loss of fellow soldiers that he didn't rest at night. Through counseling, he concluded that he had nothing to do with his father's disappearance. Once he exonerated himself of that deed, his sleep returned and his life took on some normalcy. He gained in confidence and stature and managed to complete the requirements for his bachelor's degree in industrial design. Jeremiah stood up in his tiny LA apartment one morning and realized he was living an empty isolated life. He had friends but no one truly close. He had lovers but no one he actually loved nearby and he wanted to go home, so he did. That was nine years ago.

Chapter 4

Jeremiah arrives in Pismo beach just over an hour and a half before his scheduled meet time to pickup his daughter, Erin. He had thought about driving down the night before but the call from Clarissa made him rethink the idea. His shop had been closed for three hours when she called him on his cell and told him she needed him to tow a vehicle right away. Jeremiah had not hesitated.

He'd do anything for Clarissa except be her contact with the dope dealer and, actually, he was considering even that. She had surprised the hell out of him with that request. He wouldn't do as she asked and refused to give her the name of anyone who would. He did; however, tell her to stay away from certain people whose names she called, even one of her own cousins. He confirmed the name of one person he knew to be fairly trustworthy, at least as trustworthy as a dope peddler could be in his line of work. Jeremiah also encouraged Clarissa to ask her doctor for a prescription for the drug. It seemed to him that marijuana was good for whatever ailed you, though he was not sure how much help the reefer would be in mending Clarissa's broken heart and disillusioned mind.

With all the mystery surrounding his father's disappearance, it seemed to Jeremiah that his own mother, Sharon, never had the leisure to nurse her heart over the loss of her husband. By the time she became certain the police would not throw Jeremiah in jail, Trotter had been gone nearly two years. Sharon was too confused and tired for a broken heart. Since she lived in denial of her husband's death, grieving his loss was not an option. Sharon remained far to pissed off at Trotter to grieve for him.

--

Sitting in his parked car in front of his long-time friend Leslie's Pismo Beach home, Jeremiah ponders going inside. He and Leslie have dated for a little over three years and he must admit their relationship is the best he has ever had. Leslie befriended him long before they climbed into bed together. Sadly, their friendship has become strained over the past year. Jeremiah had felt their relationship was fine, if not perfect. He had been surprised when she started asking him to bring Erin and spend the night with her and her children or wanting to drive to the Peninsula with the children and stay over with him and Erin. In short, Leslie wants them to start behaving more like a family unit; whereas, Jeremiah wants to keep "family" out of the equation. He and Leslie have spent a good bit of time together but seldom sleep together when her children are at home and never when Erin is under the same roof. Now the relationship is being tested. Though Leslie has not said as much to Jeremiah, he understands that she is ready for a full on commitment.

Other women have continued to be a part of Jeremiah's life over the years. He has never lead Leslie or any woman to believe that he sees her exclusively. Up until the past three months, Leslie dated Jeremiah only. He, admittedly, was surprised and disappointed when she told him she was seeing other men. The most surprising thing about her revelation was that Jeremiah was not jealous, disappointed when he couldn't see her on his trips into Pismo to drop off or pickup Erin, but not jealous. At first he chalked the lack of emotion up to his maturity. Soon he had to admit that the absence of jealousy was because he did not love Leslie in that way. The friends never talk about love. Neither Leslie nor he are needy people, so moving on will certainly not be difficult, but he does not want to end the relationship with his friend. Leslie is his best friend and his confidant. He finds it hard to imagine life without her.

The humming of Jeremiah's phone awakens him from his thoughts. "Are you coming in or are you just going to sit out there for the rest of the day?" Leslie asks with mirth in her voice.

Jeremiah enters Leslie's modern hillside home which overlooks the blue of the Pacific and finds her preparing a large arugula and orange salad. "Where are Jake and LisBeth?" he asks as he looks around for the nine and eight year old who usually run to greet him upon his arrival.

"They're with some friends on a play date. I thought it would be nice if we had some time alone today. I could use it. I was expecting you last night." Leslie's statement has no terseness or accusation. She is simply stating a fact.

"Yeah, Clarissa had an emergency so I had to change my plans. Her daughter, Monia, is back living in Seaside and her car broke down last night. They needed a tow. I've got Moanie's car at the shop now so we can work on it first thing Monday. But hey, I didn't know you were looking for me. Hope I didn't ruin your evening."

Jeremiah walks up behind Leslie and kisses her on the side of the neck. Leslie turns and moves into his embrace. They stand there holding each other for a few moments before she asks, "Monia is the one you haven't seen in years, right?"

Jeremiah doesn't remember mentioning Monia to Leslie who has always amazed him with her remarkable memory. "Right, she's the closest person I have to a sister. I missed her. It'll be good to have her back in the area. I don't remember mentioning her to you."

"I remember you mentioning her in a couple of your Clifford stories. I got the impression you and she were very close, even closer than you and your brother. Have she and Clifford stayed in touch over the years? What was that you called her?

Jeremiah smiles thinking about Monia. "Moanie. I gave her that nickname when she was about three or four years old because she used to whine and cry so much. Damn that was a long time ago. I doubt that she and Clifford have much contact. They didn't care much for each other growing up. I'm pretty sure that was because Clifford had a crush on her and teased her all the time."

Leslie holds Jeremiah a little closer before asking, "You hungry?"

"Not especially. That salad looks good though."

"Let me put it in the fridge." Leslie escapes his grasp and moves the beautiful spread of greens into her large French door refrigerator. "Want a little wine?"

"It's too close to the time for me to meet Veronica. I'll take some coffee later, if that's okay."

Leslie shrugs and moves back toward him at her kitchen island. "I went down to the Tiki last night after I realized you weren't coming and met some friends. It was nice." This is her way of telling Jeremiah that she had a date the night before.

"Anyone special?"

"No, no one special. I only have one special man in my life," Leslie tells him with a look he has come to know well. She moves closer to him. "Now where were we?" she asks as she starts removing Jeremiah's shirt. "How much time do we have?"

"Just over an hour," Jeremiah tells her as he lifts her onto the island and realizes she has nothing on under her oversized shirt.

--

The coffee-to-go Leslie provided for Jeremiah comes in handy on the ride back to the Peninsula. Erin talks nonstop for the first thirty minutes of the drive.

When Erin first came to live with Jeremiah he had no intentions of making so many trips up and down the California coast. Veronica had promised to visit Erin in Seaside on a regular basis so the child would not need to travel so often. Jeremiah had mentioned Veronica's plans to visit Seaside to his mother who expressed reservations. "Where will Veronica stay during these visits?" Sharon had asked.

"At my place. Where else would she stay?"

"You realize that once you start letting her come up and stay, it's going to be very difficult to stop. Is she coming alone?"

"I doubt it and why would I want to stop her from coming up to visit with her granddaughter, Mom?"

"Because, Jeremiah, you and Tina are no longer a couple. I understand that you are a generous man, but if you get too involved with your ex girlfriend's family, you will live to regret it; that I can guarantee you. I like Veronica but she has already shown a propensity to take advantage of your generosity. She and her family will visit more often than you will want and she will expect you to help her with the costs of her visits and to feed and entertain them when they are here. How will you feel about going off and leaving your ex girlfriend's family in your home on Saturday's while you're working?

"And one day, as hard as this may be for you to fathom, Son, you're going to have a serious relationship with a woman and no matter how understanding that woman may be, she may not like Tina's family staying in your home. If Veronica wants to visit Erin up here, she should take responsibility for her own accommodations and her own travel expenses. If you start this and then decide to stop it after you become involved with someone, Erin may resent the new girlfriend and fault her if you no longer allow Veronica and her family members to stay in your home. You need to work something out with Veronica that does not involve you footing the bill for their visits or providing them with a place to sleep, because I guarantee you five years from now that will be a problem."

"Five years from now is a long time, Mom," Jeremiah had made the mistake of speaking his mind.

"Do you really think five years is a long time, Son? Do you really think it is, because I'm here to tell you, it isn't?"

"You're talking about something that may happen in five years and I'm just trying to get my daughter a visit with her grandmother."

"Okay. You do what you want, Jeremiah," were Sharon's last words on the subject.

Jeremiah had known his mother was being opinionated and sticking her nose where it belonged only if he allowed it. Sharon always gives her children her opinion on matters she considers important. She is a typical mother in that regard and Jeremiah is a typical adult child. He dislikes his mother giving him advice before he shows the good sense to act independent of that advice. He had known his mother was right. He had his own concerns about whom and how many people Veronica would bring to his home each time she came. She never travelled alone and usually had two or more family members accompanying her. He had to admit that as much as he liked Veronica, he was not particular about having her or Tina's other family members as overnight guests on a regular basis. He knew the family well enough to believe that if he made his home too available, they would visit every time they had an opportunity.

His mother's words were confirmation. So Jeremiah very tactfully made it clear to Veronica that she could not stay at his home during her visits. Veronica seemed to take no offense at Jeremiah's decision and if she did, it did not show. Jeremiah had always been kind and generous with Veronica and her family. She had no desire to alienate him and thus make time with her granddaughter less possible. So Veronica made plans to stay at her sister's home in Pismo Beach several times a year and Jeremiah takes Erin to visit her grandmother during those stays. On other occasions, like this one, Veronica meets Jeremiah at her sister's home in Pismo and takes Erin back home to LA for a visit and then meets him back in Pismo at a designated time for the child's return home.

"Daddy, you should stay with me when I go to Grandma Vera's house." Erin tells her father as if she has been reading his thoughts.

"Why's that, Pumpkin?"

"Because I bet Uncle Luis would not talk to grandma so bad if you were there. He'd be fraid to."

"Afraid."

"Afraid, yeah." The child corrects her speech. "Uncle Luis is mean to grandma and all he does is sleep and yell at her about stuff like what's for dinner; he's tired of picadillo; he wants some money cause he knows you gave her some for me. He even told grandma 'the word you told me to never say' school."

"He told her to 'f' school?"

"Yep. Poor grandma. I feel bad for her. I don't think she likes my uncle very much."

"I feel bad for her too, baby." Jeremiah thinks about this situation and wishes he had followed his first mind and not taken his daughter for this week-long visit. Over the past year, Luis, who had been such an easy going kid, has gotten out of control. Jeremiah decides this is the last time he will allow Veronica to take Erin back to LA and he will only take his daughter to Pismo when he can stay in the area with her.

Chapter 5

Monia is relaxing out on her mother's deck and taking in the marvelous view of the Monterey Bay when Jeremiah calls. He tells her the problem was her starter as he suspected but since the car is so old he is having his guys perform a thorough check of the various systems. Monia says she doesn't want him to go through a lot of trouble but Jeremiah explains that both he and one of his master mechanics have driven and completed visual inspections of her car and the only check remaining is the computer diagnostics. "You know if anything happens to this car now that I've worked on it, Clarissa will never forgive me. I'll have to keep it up and running for you now that you are in the area. We rotated your tires and changed the oil because it was past due. I can tell you, it's nearly time to invest in a new set of treads; these are getting pretty worn."

"How much longer do you think I have doctor?" Monia jokes.

"You've got a few more thousand miles but I wouldn't put it off too long. I don't carry tires here; but I can get them for you at a good discount and put them on at no cost. Just let me know when you're ready to put them on."

"You're treating me like the big brother I never had."

"Yeah, okay." Jeremiah laughs. What time do you want me to pass by to pick you up? Are you free for lunch?"

Monia hadn't thought about getting cleaned up and out of the house at all, but she does need to get her car. "Just call me when you're on your way. We can do lunch if you let me treat."

"I'll be there at about one thirty; be ready."

Jeremiah is glad Monia is back in town. There is a vibrancy about her that he loves. He thinks about her sitting on his knee when he was thirteen and she was eight while they played video games or watched television. He wonders if she can help bridge the gap between him and some of the black populace in Seaside. He has been back on the Peninsula nine years and feels more isolated than ever from the now diminished black populace of the city. Nearly all his friends and associates that are near his age are either white or Hispanic. Many of these people are unaware of his story and others don't seem to care, but the black folks care. Even blacks who had moved to the city in more recent years, long after Trotter's disappearance, deal with Jeremiah with a long handled spoon. His father had made many friends in and around the city. He had fixed cars for free, played for fundraisers, and partied from house to house. Someone needs to pay for his loss and Jeremiah is that someone. He hopes none of the black Seasiders dissuade Monia from her association with him. He hopes she will continue to be his friend.

--

The food at the Fish Hut proves better than Monia had expected and she and Jeremiah have a blast laughing about old times and all those family parties. They reminisce about what a brat she had been, how mean Clifford was to her, and what a rotten thug of a teenager Jeremiah once was. Monia is respectful of Jeremiah's feelings and he of hers but both are relieved that they don't need to tiptoe through a conversation filled with minefields.

"So tell me, how does Clarissa seem to you?" Jeremiah asks with a look that shows his genuine concern for Monia's mother.

"Well." Monia hesitates. "She seems fine. Every time I talk to her she seems better. I do have a concern though." Monia keeps her eyes on Jeremiah as she tries to figure out the best way to ask, "Are you my mother's contact for reefer?" She spits it out just as Jeremiah is taking a sip of his ice tea causing him to actually spit the tea across the table at her.

"I'm so sorry, Jerry, but I don't think she should be smoking marijuana."

"I am not providing dope to Clarissa. She asked me and I told her flat out no. I did; however, tell her who I thought she should stay away from and that included your cousin, Rodney."

Monia's eyes turn to saucers. "Thank God. I hope she wasn't considering him."

"Yes, she was. She needed something to help her cope and to be honest, I'd say it's better than using alcohol or even prescription meds." Jeremiah takes on a guilt ridden look. "I may have also suggested she get a script for the stuff rather than buy it illegally."

"Jerry!"

"Hey, I didn't want her combing the streets looking for reefer when she ran out. If she has a script she can just go buy it legally. To be honest, I'd prefer to get it for her but I was hoping if I refused that she'd forget about it. I guess I was wrong." Jeremiah leans back in his seat and gives Monia a thoughtful look.

Monia leans back also and folds her arms across her chest. "Why you looking at me like that. What's on your mind?"

The question makes Jeremiah's mind go to places that make him feel slightly uncomfortable. He gives Monia a disarming smile and asks, "So was it very difficult for you to give up your life in the big city and move back here to lil ole Seaside? That's some sacrifice."

"No, I'd been working on my job almost since the day I got out of PA school. That's over five years and as much as I liked my old job, I was getting too comfortable and needed a change. This situation with my parents just lit a fire under me and made me do something that was long overdue."

Jeremiah has been watching her as she explains her situation and can't help but shake his head. He still thinks of her as that fourteen-year-old he had to tell guys to stay away from because she was so fine and overly-developed for her age. Though she appeared more mature back then, once she opened her mouth, you knew she was just a kid. He remembers her mother telling a twelve-year-old Monia to close her legs and sit like a lady as he averted his eyes from her exposed underwear and later having to remind her of her mother's words.

"Now what?" Monia complains at his stare and ever present smile. It's that same smile he gave her all those years ago but now it appears more personal. She had loved it when he smiled at her back then and she always blushed and joked with him. She is finding it a little harder to joke now.

"So, what about your personal life, your friends, boyfriends, anyone special? Wasn't it hard to leave them behind? I know you're not that far but long distance relationships are hard to maintain?" Leslie immediately creeps into Jeremiah's head. He has been hanging on to a long distance relationship with her for years and she is just about finished and he knows it.

"That won't be an issue with my friends. I only have a couple that I'm close to who live in the city. The rest are just casual friends. It gets hard to make good friends as you become older, at least for me. The guy I was dating or should say am dating is far from clingy. We could use some time apart. We'll see what happens there." Monia hates to admit that she gets plenty of time away from Marcus and only sees him when he has time for her.

"Not a love match, huh?"

"Well," Monia averts her eyes, dips her head, and drags out the word.

"You don't have to explain to me about open relationships, Moanie. I've had my share of those."

"So, why haven't you gotten married, Jeremiah? I would think the women here would be all over you. Not many brothers in Seaside anymore. I'm surprised one of my old girlfriends from school hasn't called me crooning over you. You know we all had killer crushes for you back then."

"You had a crush on me?" Jeremiah asks with just a bit of a blush showing through his rich chocolate skin.

"Oh God, yes and don't you dare pretend like you didn't know it. I used to be up under you all the time when our families got together. Mom used to always tell me to get off your knee. You could hardly sit down before I'd plop my behind on that left knee of yours. Finally, my mother sat me down one evening and told me I was entirely too big to be sitting on yours or anyone else's knee and she had better not catch me doing it again."

Jeremiah has to laugh at this. He had no idea about the crush but he does remember a time when she camped out on his knee and having to ask her to move for a minute so he could do whatever. Those were good times back then when their families got together and celebrated life. Both he and Monia long for those times to return.

They sit there quietly for a few moments with Monia now watching Jeremiah and waiting for him to talk about his romantic life. "Well?" she nudges.

"Well what?"

"Who are you dating, brother? Anyone I know?"

Some of the joy leaves Jeremiah's eyes as he tells her "I date and I'm not going to say 'no one special' because that would be an untruth. Dating the sistas in Seaside hasn't worked out for me. I've still got a pretty bad reputation around here, even after all these years. I guess people think I'm a rehabilitated killer or something. I don't even approach women in Seaside."

"So who the hell you datin'?" Monia asks with sista-girl ilk.

The smile is back.

"Can I get you guys anything else?" the waitperson asks, giving a gentle nudge for the couple to finish their catching up elsewhere.

Monia looks at the woman with a smile and shakes her head but Jeremiah's eyes turn to steel as he looks at the woman and says, "We're good." He knows the woman was rushing them for no good reason. There are no customers waiting on a table. The restaurant does not close between lunch and dinner and Monia and he still have fresh drinks sitting in front of them. He never gets rushed or bothered when he is with a white, Asian, or Hispanic male and seldom gets bothered when he is with a female of another persuasion but whenever he is having a leisurely good time with another black person, white wait staff seem to feel a need to control the situation, especially older white women.

"She's just doing her job," Monia tells him, noticing his perturb.

"Yeah, right. Maybe I should do mine as a customer and leave her a sorry-assed tip."

"Forget about her and tell me the juicy details of this love life of yours." Monia now has a conspiratorial look on her face and really wants to know about Jeremiah's love life.

He is no longer interested in the conversation. "Like I said, I date."

Monia knows he has decided not to share and she will not press him. It's none of her business anyway and Jeremiah is definitely irritated.

"Tell me about your daughter. Is she a handful?"

Now Jeremiah gives her a full blown smile as he talks about Erin. "She keeps me hopping. It's not easy being a single parent, but my mother helps me a lot and I've found a good lady to come in and help with the housework, do some cooking, and most importantly take care of Erin. She's six years old and one of the smartest kids in her class but man she talks nonstop sometimes. When I can, I pick her up from school. She eats, takes a power nap, and then it's on. She'll keep me company while I'm cooking and talks the whole time. I have to remind myself not to tune her out. Sometimes your kids are telling you some important stuff so you've got to pay close attention. I have to say, my life would be pretty empty without my girl."

"Wow, Jeremiah is a father; how nice." Monia smiles at him before asking, "So she's a little genius, huh."

"Moanie, I kid you not, she's a whiz kid. This kid comes up with some stuff that really makes me think. Check this out. One

Sunday when she was four, we were driving back from Pismo and we were talking and for some strange reason, I started talking about animate and inanimate objects. For the life of me, I cannot recall what made me start talking to her about something like that. Erin asks me to explain what inanimate means. So I tell her the best way I know how and start giving her some examples of animate objects and inanimate objects. Then I start pointing out different things and asking her to tell me if they are animate or inanimate and she does pretty good. I mean, I'm impressed at how fast she catches on, right. She gets quiet for a moment, so I know she's thinking and then she asks me, 'What about the wind?' the wind, Moanie. I swear I was stumped. I've asked a number of people that same question. I even asked a science professor from CSUMB. He came in and had us do some customizing on his Camaro. Dude cracked up when I told him my four year old asked me that question. He told me he'd get back to me. Now it's a running joke between us whenever he comes in. She's something that girl of mine."

"So when do I get to meet the brilliant child who has taken my place on your knee?" Monia gives Jeremiah a smile that touches him deeply and he likes it. She makes him feel warm, really warm.

"Soon. Maybe I can add you to my list of backup babysitters. My mom and yours top the list. I can probably make room for you somewhere near the top."

Monia laughs. "She must be a really special child if people are on a waiting list to keep her for you. It's great you've got so much help."

"Yeah, but even with a few people on my list, sometimes she ends up at the shop with me. You know our mothers like to leave town on occasion and play the odds and please don't try to get them on a Friday night."

"You are kidding?"

"No, I'm not. Thank God Gilbert's wife, Irma, helps me with her. I have used their eighteen-year-old, Inez, also but I have to be careful with that girl. I use her to watch Erin very seldom and only during early hours. The last time I had her babysit late at night Gilbert was supposed to pick her up. When he hadn't showed after a half an hour, I started bundling Erin up so we could drive Inez home. That girl looks at me and says, 'I could spend the night you know.' I mean, do you know how tempting shit like that is to a man living without a woman – to any man really. To have this gorgeous eighteen-year-old talking about she could stay the night. And meant it, Moanie, meant it. So I don't even have her come over except emergency situations and only during the day and only if she can drive herself. I mean, I've got all kinds of stipulations before I use that hammer. I'm not trying to get killed behind young stuff."

"Jeremiah!"

"Just keeping it real for you, Moanie."

Monia has to laugh at Jeremiah's honesty. "What did you tell her, Jeremiah? What did you say?"

"I said 'girl, your daddy would kill me!' and she looked at me and said, 'I know you not scared of my daddy.' I told her 'Yes, I am scared of your daddy and those big ole brothers of yours too."

"She got big brothers?"

"Yes she does. She's got three brothers but that oldest one is a big fellow."

"Bigger than you?"

"Hell yeah! Cat's got about a hundred pounds on me and I'm talking muscle not fat and he's not as tall as me. He's a big boy and he stays in the gym. Name's Chewy. He comes by the shop every once in a while to help out. I use him because he is good at what he does. Cat ain't friendly at all, never has been, and I look at him like I ain't friendly either."

Monia is cracking up laughing now. "So she probably started thinking you were wimpy wimpy wimpy after that, Jeremiah."

"That's okay. I don't care if she thinks I'm a wimp if it will keep me from getting my ass kicked by one of those hefty-assed brothers of hers. I'm telling you, Seaside may be small but these dudes around here don't play. There's some tough old dudes around here. These gangs here are serious because you know there's that whole wannabe dynamic."

"Do you think her brother's are gang bangers?"

"I don't know what those cats are. I just know I stay out of their way and try to look like I eat bullets for breakfast. They've made me step up my time at the gym, that's for sure."

"You spent a few years down in the LA area didn't you? You didn't get involved with any of the gangs or anything?"

"Nah, some of the cats I worked with maybe, just like now – gangs, drugs, and shit. When my dad disappeared, Monia, I was in a bad way. I'm not going to lie; I was strung out. Once I got straight, I had to try and stay as far away from anything or anyone who would pull me back into that lifestyle. Some things you just have a weakness for so I have to be careful when it comes to drugs. I let the guys at the shop know, if they're doing any type of drugs, they had better make sure I don't detect it. I don't piss them but they know they better not show up looking or acting high. I better not see a sign of it. Once in a while some of their boys roll up and want them to work on their rides. I tell them it's regular price. Family is different. I try to make concessions for close family. But if I let them start working on Joe Joe's ride for a little of nothing, the next thing you know my garage is a hangout for all types. They stay away because they know ain't nothing they're interested in happening at my place." Jeremiah looks startled all of the sudden. "We had better get out of here. You made me forget all about the time. I've got a business to run."

Chapter 6

After her extended lunch with Jeremiah, Monia decides to stop in at her new workplace for a quick visit with Dr. Navya Singh and her staff. Dr. Singh's specialty is bariatric surgery and her Munras Avenue clinic is co-located with the offices of Dr. Daniel Sloan, a plastic surgeon, and only a mere four miles from Monia's front door. The drive to and from work each day will be a huge advantage over the trip she made to work each day when she lived in San Francisco.

Dr. Singh's billing specialist, Susan Teeter, greets Monia and shows her around the suite, ending with Monia's personal office, which is twice the size of her previous office. Monia tries to hide her excitement as she walks over to the large plate glass window which overlooks a well maintained greenbelt.

"Hi and welcome." Monia is startled by the greeting of her fellow physician's assistant, Pamela Whitehall. Monia had hoped to meet the young woman whose praises Dr. Singh had song so enthusiastically and indicated would provide Monia invaluable training in her new position.

"Hello," Monia returns the greeting and matches Pamela's smile with one of her own.

"Pam, this is Monia Phillips, our new PA. I guess you two will be working together closely," Susan tells the women as she looks from one to the other.

Pamela extends her hand and gives Monia a strong warm handshake and a direct look. "I've been looking forward to meeting you. You're in good hands with our Susan here. She'll handle you with kid gloves. I tell you, I'm sure glad you are here because we need the help."

So far so good on the staff. Monia does not want to get too excited about what appears to be a great group of female coworkers, but she is pleased. Susan, who is a petite fortyish white woman, appears competent, friendly, and more than helpful. Pamela, who Monia guesses is about her age, is pleasant and willing to share her knowledge. The one other office staff member Monia has met is Shirley Conrad, the office manager, who is without a doubt a southern-born sister. Shirley is reserved in her manner but also impressively efficient. Shirley had called Monia several times to make sure every detail of Monia's employment was covered. When Monia had suggested Shirley email her as a way of communication, Shirley replied, "If you have no objections, Ms Phillips, I prefer to get the details of your employment clarified over the phone. I will send you a confirmation email of all we discuss and, if you like, a letter via the postal service."

"Whatever works for you is fine with me, Shirley."

Monia had felt the woman's proper exterior begin to melt during that call. She had even received a welcoming smile from Shirley upon her arrival in the office earlier.

"I'll leave you two to talk." Susan turns and leaves Pamela with Monia.

"So when do you start?" Pamela asks.

"Exactly two weeks from today. Oh and thank you for all that recommended reading. It has been very helpful."

"Good; I'm glad. Of course the best way to learn is on the job, but that material will get your juices flowing for the work; what we do here is very rewarding. I hope you like working with Dr. Navya as much as I do. I have learned so much. She is an excellent teacher and a caring physician. Her patients are more important than the big bucks. You'll like it here; I'm sure. Where are you living?"

"I've got a place not far off of Fremont Blvd in Seaside."

"Ooh, I hear it can be kind of rough over there. That's where Shirley lives."

Monia laughs. "Yeah Seaside has always had a bad reputation. It's no more dangerous than Monterey. It may be a little safer, but the media really plays up crime in Seaside. Of course compared to PG and Carmel most places in California are rough. I grew up there and that's where my mother lives. I took this position to be close to her."

"I hope your mother isn't ill," Pamela tells Monia with a concerned expression.

"No just life changes. She and my father recently separated, actually it's just over a year and I'm the only child. I just wanted to be here for her. I got the sense that she needed me, but now I feel this move is more for me than her." Monia smiles as it dawns on her that the words she just spoke are true.

"Does your father live in the area also?" Pamela the PA asks.

Monia can see the curiosity in the woman's face and comes clean; better to die by a lethal dose than get eaten alive with small bite questions. "Yes, but he has someone. I'm all my mother has." Monia hesitates at this moment as she thinks about Jeremiah and the host of other people who love Clarissa. "That's not right. She has other people in her life. Like I said before, it is starting to look like this change is more about me than her. She's doing just fine," Monia adds with a quirky grin. "What about you? What brought you here and how long ago?"

"Girl, I've been here six years. I had no intentions of staying when I came. My boyfriend was at the Naval Post Graduate School. When Navya's PA position came open, I jumped on it. I thought sure he was the one and that we were getting married. I may have been here six month when we called it quits. Now, you couldn't pry me away from this little piece of heaven with a crowbar. I love it here. It's expensive but what place isn't these days. I've got a friend that jumped up and moved to Austin last year and her mortgage is higher than mine. You know they keep telling us Texas is the place to buy cheap but don't you believe that about Austin." Pamela stops abruptly and says, "I'm sorry; I'm rambling."

Monia laughs. "No you're not. I notice you and the other ladies refer to Dr. Singh as Navya."

Pamela smiles. "Oh, she prefers we call her Navya or Dr. Navya. She's pretty laid back. Listen, let me know a day or so ahead when you want to start shadowing me. I think the plan is for you to shadow both Navya and me. I'll confirm that with her. You're going to enjoy working here; I promise." Pamela squeezes Monia's arm and starts to leave the office. Before she reaches the door, she turns around with her cell phone in her hand. "Oh, give me your number so I can send you mine."

Monia calls out her number with a smile and says, "Thanks, Pamela."

Pamela is a sista. Due to her bone straight hair and olive skin tone, Monia had not been certain of the woman's ethnicity when she first walked into the office, but Pamela's speech and demeanor are clear signs of her black heritage, be it biological or environmental. Monia feels an instant kinship with the women of her new office, everyone from Susan to Dr. Singh feels like family, especially old surly Shirley. Monia smiles thinking about that nickname for

Shirley, Surly Shirley. She can hardly wait to become close enough to the woman to use that name to her face.

Doctor Singh is tied up with patients so Monia leaves the office without visiting with her. She schedules a short visit on the doctor's calendar for the Wednesday prior to her start date and she asks both Susan and Shirley to let the doctor know she came in and will stop back periodically over the next two weeks. "Thank you for stopping by; It was nice meeting you," Susan says with a smile.

"Nice meeting you guys too."

"Let us know if there is anything you need." Surly Shirley responds without the hint of a smile and not bothering to look up from her busy work.

"I will, Shirley, and thanks for all your help getting my paperwork set up."

Shirley looks up and affords Monia a glimpse of her beautiful deep dimples and says matter-of-factly, "You are welcome. See you soon and don't forget to let us know if you need anything."

--

When Monia enters her mother's home later that evening she has a glow on her face accompanied by a big smile.

"You must have had a good afternoon. What have you been up to today?" Clarissa asks her daughter.

"I went by my office and met the other PA. Her name is Pamela Whitehall. I also met with Shirley, the lady who helped me with all the information and paperwork for the job. She is reserved but actually seems pretty warm and another coworker, Susan, showed me around the place. It was a good visit but the doctor was busy so I didn't get to talk to her today. I really think I'm going to enjoy working with this group of people."

"Good, baby. Were you there this whole time? You've been gone a while."

"Well no, Jeremiah and I sat and had a long lunch together. We had fun talking about old times. It really feels good to spend time with him. It's been so long that I thought I'd never see him again."

Clarissa gives her daughter a somewhat skeptical look as she gets up from her sofa and heads toward her kitchen. "You know Jeremiah has a reputation here."

"I know about Jeremiah's reputation. You don't need to warn me off Jeremiah. There's nothing going on between us." Monia sounds agitated.

"Ooh missy, don't get so defensive. I didn't say there was anything going on between you and Jeremiah. Sounds to me like you have Jeremiah on the brain. I'm just making conversation. He's got a reputation and it's a damn good one. His business is growing leaps and bounds. You know I insure him, all the cars and everything, and that has given me a nice little premium share. That boy is meticulous when it comes to that business. He has had one vehicle badly vandalized. They tried to steal the car but Jeremiah had just installed a top grade security system. He had records of every man hour and each piece of equipment installed on that vehicle. If he has a loss, he doesn't need to worry about a thing. I've been impressed with that young man. People are beating down his doors to do business with him. So when I say he has a reputation, I'm not talking about that old bullshit."

"Your mouth has sure gotten nasty," Monia complains. She doesn't remember her mother using such foul language before her separation.

"Well, I'm just telling you. I can't believe you're still talking about that old bullshit. That boy didn't have anything to do with his father disappearing. People need to let that mess die. He can't help it if his father cared so little about his family and was so irresponsible that he took off like he did."

"So Mom, you actually think Mr. Trotter just took off? You don't think something sinister happened to him?"

"Let me put it like this, Monia. Something may have happened to that old tired-assed man since he left because it's been – what, twenty years now. I believe that old scum bag left because he was tired of all the responsibility and had debts with some bad people and needed to get out of Dodge. That's what I think."

"What does dad think?"

"Who cares what your dad thinks. Trotter could have been around here robbing banks and your dad would have thought his shit didn't stink. He and Trotter were thick as thieves."

"But dad was never like Mr. Trotter." Monia's statement sounds more like a question.

"What do you mean by 'never like'?"

"Well, I mean Mr. Trotter had kind of a reputation for being a player and liking women and stuff."

"Where did you hear that? You were pretty young when Trot disappeared."

"Ja'Niece and I have talked about it a couple of times and you know people around here have never stopped talking about Mr. Trotter like he was a big deal."

"Yeah, well, a lot of people liked Trotter and I'm sure that included a number of women. I don't know how Sharon turned a blind eye the way she did. As for your father, he never gave me any indication that he fooled around on me until I found out he was fooling around on me. But I'm not talking about Darnell or Trotter Sumuels. I'm talking about Jeremiah. Jeremiah has been a rock this whole time, through all this mess. He may have left but he always tried to take care of his mother. Even when he was making a little of no money, he still sent her something every month. There were times I know she was making a lot more than him, especially after they put her over the management of that second shop in downtown Carmel. That doggone Clifford left here and it is just recently that he started sending Sharon a little money."

"When was the last time Clifford visited with his mother?" Monia asks.

"He hardly comes anymore, not since Jeremiah moved back. Sharon goes down and visits with him and the boys occasionally. She'd give anything to get those two boys back together so that her grandchildren can bond and they can all be a family again."

Chapter 7

Walking around her own condo fills Monia with satisfaction. She may still owe several hundred thousand on the place but she can legitimately call herself a homeowner now and she likes her new home. The condo is far from extravagant but it is nicely situated in a quiet neighborhood with quick easy access to Fremont Boulevard and her job. It should take her no more than fifteen minutes to get to work on a bad traffic day. She has three good sized bedrooms, two full bathrooms, a closed in garage, plenty of storage and from her upper floor she can see the bay. The more she walks around the place the more satisfied she becomes.

Now she faces the daunting task of unpacking and setting up her new home. Her mother had suggested she ask her cousin Rodney to help her unload the U-Haul but Monia does not trust him. Her girlfriend Ja'Niece has promised to drive down from San Jose and give a helping hand and her on-again-off-again kinda-boyfriend, Marcus, has committed a full day and a half to the project. Monia spoke with him last night to make sure he would show and called him again first thing this morning to get him up and on his way.

Marcus is a doctor of internal medicine but it was not difficult to get one of his partnering physicians to cover the time he had promised Monia. She had been pleased and touched by his offer of assistance, especially with his steadily growing practice.

Monia's got a full pot of coffee going, all the fixings for cold sandwiches, and a nice array of fruit and juices. She also plans to treat her crew to one or two hot meals out. She is so thankful for the help that she is willing to bend over backwards as repayment.

Not waiting for her help to arrive, Monia starts the heavy work. She's expecting a furniture delivery and an appliance delivery in the late afternoon, so she wants to get as much done as possible before her new sofa, bed, dresser, washer and dryer, and refrigerator arrive. She has a good start off loading boxes from the U-Haul into the garage when she spots Ja'Niece's little green Beetle pull up in front of her driveway, blocking the U-Haul in.

"Hey girl, looks like you're on a roll," Monia's life-long friend tells her. "It feels good being back here in Seaside. God it changes so much but stays the same." Ja'Niece stands and looks around as if she is taking in the entire city. "This is a nice neighborhood. Didn't Fremont Junior High used to be around here somewhere?"

"Yep, right where you are standing."

"Umph, my mama went to Fremont. Well are you going to show me your place and can I get a hug?"

Monia closes up the truck and garage before giving Ja'Niece a hug followed by a grand tour of her new home.

"Monia, this is cute. You got lots of room to spread out and can fix it up however you want. Ooh, this makes me want to buy my own place," Ja'Niece groans as the ladies make their way out to the terrace. "Nice view of the bay. You know I'll be visiting you more often now. This'll be like coming home and much better than making that drive to Fresno."

"Well, you know you are always welcome. How could I turn you away after you invest your sweat equity in my new home?"

Ja'Niece pushes Monia in the shoulder. "Ooh, girl say sweat equity. Speaking of sweat, where is old stinky Marcus? I thought he'd be here by now."

Ja'Niece and Marcus do not get along well and constantly pick at each other; so much so that Monia did not plan to tell either that the other had volunteered to help her. She did not want Ja'Niece or Marcus to back out because the other would be on site. Normally, she does her best not to bring them together. Monia never enjoys herself when the three of them are in the same place at the same time, but she needs their help and will suffer the bickering for the greater good of getting that U-Haul unloaded and all the boxes upstairs and unpacked.

"How did you know Marcus was helping me? I thought I was being sneaky?" Monia gives her friend a confused look.

"You told me, silly. Did you forget?"

"I guess I did. You two fight so much I was scared to let you know he would be here because you might have backed out."

"Girl, I wouldn't leave you hanging like that because of that imbecile. Let me drink a cup of coffee and get started. How's your mom?"

"Great. I feel a little weird when I tell myself or someone else that I moved here because of mom. She seems better than I've ever seen her."

"I'm glad to hear it. She's tough, your mother – someone to emulate. Is she stopping by? I'd like to see her."

"She may."

Monia and Ja'Niece work for nearly an hour before Marcus calls and tells Monia he cannot make it to Seaside until late evening.

"What happened? Did you go back to sleep?" Monia asks, though she knows the man well enough to know he never oversleeps.

"It's one of my patients. I just can't get away today. I'll try and make it tonight or first thing tomorrow; okay, Hon."

Monia hates for him to call her "hon." It is so impersonal and she has told him so any number of times, but he still does. Monia does not argue or complain because she does not want to make Marcus angry, not yet, not now; she needs him. He has pledged not only his body but the use of his truck to move a bedroom set from her mother's home to her new home. She needs him to show up tomorrow. "I guess I'll see you later then. I hope everything goes well with your patient."

"Listen, Hon, I'm really sorry about this; it just can't be helped." Marcus sounds sincere.

How pathetic. Monia puts the phone down, thoroughly disgusted with Marcus. She has asked so little of him over the years of their "friendship" and he has given even less. She wonders if there is really a patient or if he just has something else he'd rather do with someone other than her.

"So where is Dr. Sorry, M.D.?" Ja'Niece asks, entering the room with a box of kitchen ware.

"A no show, at least until tonight or tomorrow."

"Oh well, what'd you expect?" Ja'Niece turns and goes back down to the truck for another box.

The ringing of Monia's cell phone stops her from offering up a defense for Marcus. "How's it going over there with the unpacking, Sweetie?" Clarissa asks but before Monia can answer she adds, "Jeremiah asked for your address. He only lives a couple of blocks away from you on Kimball, just around the corner. He said he was coming over to see your new place. Did all your help show up?"

Telling a half truth, Monia tells her mother, "My help is here."

Clarissa can tell by the way Monia answered there is something wrong but decides not to delve. Her office is busier than usual for a

Thursday. Monia is a big girl and she will work it out or ask her mother for help, if she needs it.

Monia gets off the phone and sits down on a box for a moment and thinks about Jeremiah stopping by. She expects Ja'Niece to have something negative to say about Jeremiah and Monia does not want to get into a pissing contest about him. In the long history of their friendship, Monia and Ja'Niece have had one serious argument which caused them not to speak to each other for several months. That disagreement was about Jeremiah's guilt or innocence in the long-ago disappearance of his father. Ja'Niece had told Monia that her father was certain Jeremiah had done away with Trotter. Everyone knew the father and son had a fight the night of Trotter's disappearance and that Jeremiah had lost that fight and ended up in the emergency room with stitches in his mouth. Monia had told Ja'Niece that her father should not talk about situations he really had no firsthand knowledge of and that she was surprised that a school principle would gossip like an old bitchy woman. The friends had angrily gone their separate ways and not spoken again until Christmas day that year.

"Am I working by myself here?" Ja'Niece asks with ever present attitude as she enters the house and walks to the cooler for another bottle of water.

Monia stands up from her seat and announces, "Jeremiah is on his way over."

Ja'Niece stops in her tracks and slowly turns around to face Monia with shocked disbelief. "Jeremiah, that guy who?" She catches herself quickly as she remembers how Monia defended Jeremiah years earlier and nearly ended their friendship over him. "He's back in Seaside?" She asks, showing as little rancor as possible.

"For a long time now. He owns Del Rey Auto Repair on Del Monte."

"And a mechanic!" Ja'Niece has gone from dismayed to critical. *And I thought I was bougie.*

"Hey, anybody here?" They hear Jeremiah climbing the stairs and announcing his arrival right on cue.

"Hey, Babe, come on in," Monia yells with much more warmth than she feels. Between Marcus's failure to show; her mother telling Jeremiah where she lives; Jeremiah inviting himself over; and her anticipation of beating Ja'Niece down if she is the least bit nasty to her beloved Jeremiah, Monia is ready to climb in her not-yet-delivered-bed and close out the world.

"Moanie, you got a nice crib here, girl. We're neighbors, you know." Jeremiah enters holding a large brown restaurant bag. He stops and looks at Ja'Niece as he tries to place her. "Hello," he speaks to her in his rich deep voice. He seems surprised to find someone else with Monia and it is apparent that he finds Ja'Niece attractive.

"Hi," Ja'Niece returns the greeting like an awestruck teenager and blushes.

Monia wants to tell her friend to stop staring and close her mouth. Jeremiah is a good looking brother. He has on his casual work attire but looks as if he is on a photo set advertising high end outdoor wear. Monia knows of no other man that could make a pair of steel toed work boots, jeans, and a tee shirt look so good. She tells herself that his good looks have no effect on her because she spent so much time with him and Clifford and they are both like her brothers. She is surprised to observe Ja'Niece's reaction to the man's exceedingly good looks and charm. Jeremiah has probably caused many a woman to do a double take on a clear day. Even in his casual work clothing he looks better than most men would look in a custom made suit. The chestnut dreads against that smooth chocolate skin, his unbelievably clear light brown eyes, the perfectly edged up facial hair, all on a long lean muscular six foot two inch frame simply cannot be ignored.

"Jeremiah, do you remember my friend Ja'Niece. It's probably been years since you two have seen each other."

"Yeah, yeah." Jeremiah gives Ja'Niece one of those long subtle thoughtful looks that make a woman melt as she wonders what exactly is on the man's mind. There is just the slightest hint of a smile on his mouth. All of Ja'Niece's guards are blown. She is a complete sucker for a good looking man. Jeremiah could be a coyote known for abandoning women and children in the hot Arizona desert to die without food or water and Ja'Niece would be willing to give him a shot at this point, just so long as there is a real penis represented by that bulge in the front of his pants. "Hey, you know my mind's not what it used to be; I'm getting old." Jeremiah sounds frustrated as he tries to place Monia's girlfriend.

Ja'Niece is not slighted in the least. She blushes even more, if that is possible, extends her hand to Jeremiah, and tells him in a low sultry voice, "You may not remember me but I remember you. It's nice to see you again, Jeremiah."

"You still here in Seaside?" Jeremiah asks

"No I'm up in San Jose but I expect to be spending a lot more time here now that Monia's back down this way."

"That'll be nice. I get up to San Jose on business every once in a while." Jeremiah and Ja'Niece stand there grinning at each other as if they are in the room alone.

"What's in the bag, Jerry?" Monia asks by way of breaking up this stare fest.

"Oh, I brought you some lunch." He now looks at Monia as if he is seeing her for the first time and has been caught with his hand in the cookie jar.

The ladies thank him for the food but declare they are not ready to eat yet.

"That's cool. I'm going to help you get this truck unloaded. With the three of us it won't take long. Then we can eat. Sound like a plan?"

"Okay, but you really don't need to do that, Jeremiah. We can manage and I know you've got a business to run." Monia answers unappreciatively.

"Sounds good to me," Ja'Niece responds with far more enthusiasm and another alluring smile at Jeremiah.

Monia is ready for Jeremiah to leave. She tells herself she does not want to be in the middle of an affair between these two friends, mainly because Ja'Niece can be quite the drama queen and always becomes obsessed with the man in her life.

Jeremiah gives Monia that special smile he holds for her alone, pushes her in the shoulder and tells her, "I'm good. They know how to call me if they need me. Got my gloves and my belt out in the truck. Besides, my lunch is in that bag. I'll be right back."

"Monia, I remember him and his brother being cute but, my God. Does he have a woman?"

"I'll tell you like he told me – he dates." Monia folds her arms across her chest and watches Ja'Niece who is staring at the open doorway like a dog waiting on a treat. "I guess you're no longer concerned about what happened to his daddy or bothered by him being a mechanic."

Jeremiah enters the kitchen carrying a large box. Ja'Niece leans forward and whispers to Monia, "I'd have conjugal visits with that brother on death row if they'd let me," before she flits her perfectly round size eight butt out to the truck to haul in a box of her own.

"Secrets?" Jeremiah smiles at Monia."

"No, my friend thinks you're hot."Monia says with obvious disgust.

Jeremiah's grin grows as he drops the box. "Wow, I'm flattered. You don't have a problem with that do you? You've got a scowl on your face. I hope you don't find me repulsive."

Although Monia and Jeremiah have always harassed each other and she is certain he is not serious, the statement surprises her. "Why would you say something like that?"

"Just asking. You look upset. What's the matter? Is it that your guy didn't show up?"

"What do you know about that?" Monia knows Clarissa is the culprit. "That's alright; I already know the answer and no," Monia moves toward the stairs. "It's got nothing to do with him," and it doesn't.

Jeremiah follows her out to the truck. He is almost positive that Monia's bad mood is because of his little flirtation with Ja'Niece. He can't wipe the smile from his face.

By mid afternoon the truck is unloaded and all the boxes sorted. Monia wants to return the truck but has no desire to leave Jeremiah alone with Ja'Niece. She tells herself they might decide to go at each other while she is away. She is determined that she will be the first person to have sex in this home under her ownership. Jeremiah senses that Monia is ready to be rid of him. He takes his leave but offers to return to take the ladies to dinner. Monia wants to decline his offer but knows Ja'Niece will go without her, so she agrees. Also she has acted too much the part of the jealous girlfriend and wants to dispel that illusion from Jeremiah's head and her own.

"Don't forget about us, Jerry," Ja'Niece yells and gives Jeremiah a pretty wide faced grin as he pulls away from the house.

Monia forces a tight-lipped smile also and waves her hand goodbye. *Who is this cow to be calling my friend "Jerry?" Family are the only ones who call him that.* Jeremiah always corrected those who chopped his name to "Jerry." He much prefers "Jeremiah." As far as Monia knows, his family and hers are the only people he allows to call him "Jerry." She wants to correct Ja'Niece but knows it is not her place.

"Girl, you been so quiet this afternoon. I hope you're not still upset over that tired Marcus."

"No. Jeremiah asked me the same thing. I'm fine. I'm sorry if I've been too quiet. I really appreciate you coming to help me, Ja'Niece. I've got to do something really special to repay you."

"It's no problem. I was planning on being on my way back home by five but I'm going to wait until after we go to dinner with Jerry."

"Good! I could use the extra help," Monia laughs and makes an attempt at appearing unfazed by Ja'Niece's interest in Jeremiah. "I hope you come down for Tasha's wedding. I won't have a problem attending since I'm living here now. We'll be able to see all our old friends. The reception will be at the Embassy. It should be fun."

"I haven't sent my RSVP yet but I think I'll plan to be there. Visiting Seaside is becoming more and more promising with each passing moment." Ja'Niece declares.

--

The delivery trucks come and go, bringing Monia's brand spanking new items. She and Ja'Niece move the sofa around the living room no less than six times, plopping down on the new piece in exhaustion and deciding it works best where the delivery men first placed it.

Jeremiah calls and bows out of dinner due to an important situation at the garage. Monia tells him she understands. She is pleased he had to cancel and that he didn't ask for Ja'Niece's cell number or ask Monia to pass his number to her friend. Ja'Niece does; however, ask Monia for Jeremiah's number. Monia gives her the shop number without hesitation and lies about having his home phone or personal cell number.

"We can still go to dinner. Where would you like to eat?"

A sad Ja'Niece tells her, "Nah baby, I've got to get home; I'm tired."

Monia stands there and watches her friend in disbelief as she gathers up her belongings to leave. *This is so typical of her—always letting men get in the way.*

"I'll probably be back in a couple of weeks. Are you sure you're not going to be able to make it up next weekend for my birthday?" Ja'Niece asks.

"I've already got your present picked out on Amazon. You should get it a day or two before your big day. I told you my mother's got a welcome home thing planned for me and she won't budge on the date and that's just two days before I start the new job. I can't be partying like a rock star with you next weekend. You'll like your gift though. I made it extra special to make up for my absence."

"Okay, but I'm going to miss you. I'd much rather have you than some old present."

"I bet," Monia says sarcastically.

The friends hug and part company and only a short time later Marcus calls to tell Monia he'll be down first thing the following morning. Monia takes pity on him and unhooks him from her line. "I think I can handle it from here. We got a lot done today and a family friend says he'll move the bed for me this weekend," she tells him, sounding pleased with herself and her team.

A relieved Marcus asks, "How bout I drive down Saturday evening to see the new place, take you to dinner, and spend the night." His voice has taken on a deep slow mellow tone now. This is without question a request for sex. The lowering of the voice in both pitch and volume is a dead giveaway. Monia is not interested. Her mama didn't raise no fool. Dude was a no show when she needed him. "Sorry Marcus, me and mom have a full weekend planned. I'll call next week, okay, Hon." To Marcus's surprise and disappointment, Monia ends the call without waiting for a response.

Late the next morning, when Clarissa and Jeremiah show up to help Monia, they find Marcus there also, on his knees wiping out kitchen cabinets and laying down shelf paper. After introducing Jeremiah and Marcus, Monia pulls Clarissa to the side and tells her, "Just so you know, we have a full weekend laid out. If he asks you what we've got planned, throw bingo in a couple of times. That should send him on his way."

Clarissa looks at her daughter as if she has lost her mind. She considers telling Monia that she will not lie for her but since she is not particular about her daughter's relationship with the flaky doctor, she agrees.

Jeremiah works for only a couple of hours before taking his leave but promises to come back and help whenever Monia needs him and confirms that he will pick up the bed from Clarissa's for Monia. Clarissa finishes unpacking and putting away the master bath, Monia's closet, and the linen closet before she takes her leave. No sooner than Clarissa leaves, Marcus wants to get amorous but Monia refuses. She tells him she has to get cleaned up so she can pick up her mother and take her to bingo.

"You mean you'd rather go to bingo than go get in that big beautiful new bed with me. I can't wait to break that thing in. I love making love in a new bed."

Monia wonders how many new beds he's made love in – never with her, that's for sure. "Marcus, I moved here for my mother. I can't very well back out on our first official date."

"I'll make it quick."

Son of a bitch. It's always all about you. Fuck me. I guess that is the point. Instead of cursing him out like he deserves, Monia simply starts walking toward her front door to escort him out. It had crossed her mind that he might attempt to stay, wait for her to return, and maybe spend the night, but she quickly dismissed that concern because her cable and internet won't be on until Monday. That's far too much of a sacrifice for Marcus to make to spend time with Monia. He does not find her that exciting and Monia knows it. "I would invite you to stay but you know there's no cable or internet."

It is as if that realization slaps him across the face. If he stayed, he'd have to use up entirely too much data to keep himself entertained before and after the quick romp in the bed. Marcus gives Monia a quick peck on the mouth and throws in a, "Oh, nice place, by the way," on his way out the door. Monia will not likely hear from him until he's got nothing better to do. Clarissa has been so right about Marcus. Monia figures he'll text in a few days, call her in a week or two, and try to visit in a month or so. Whether she allows him to visit will depend on how lonely or sexually deprived she feels when he calls. *How pathetic!*

Later Monia's father, Darnell, stops by with a housewarming present, a nice card containing a hefty check. He settles in on a bar stool and seems to want to stay for a while so they order a pizza. Monia does not know why but she feels more at ease with her father than she has for some time. They eat their pizza, drink beer, chat, and laugh.

Darnell has had a hard time talking openly with his daughter since his separation from his wife. At first it was clear Monia was as angry with him as Clarissa was. She had, eventually, called her father and resumed their relationship but not with the same sweetness as before. This is their best time together in over a year. "Monia, why didn't you tell me you were moving down here? I wish you would have discussed this with me before you made such a drastic decision."

"I felt like mom needed me here. I don't think there was anything you could have said that would have changed my mind. Anyway, I'm here now?" Monia tells him as she hunches her shoulders.

"Did you get the impression that your mother was in such bad shape that you needed to quit a good job so that you could move here and take care of her? Every time I talk to her she seems fine – great, actually. Is she putting up a front for me?" Darnell doesn't look up at his daughter as he asks this question. He does not want Monia to see how much he hopes Clarissa still loves him.

"No, she seems the same way to me. I wish I felt half as good as she acts."

Darnell grunts at this news and shakes his head.

"Dad, I'd think you'd be happy I moved back home. You seem downright deflated. What's wrong? You look sadder every time I see you."

Darnell leans back in his seat and throws his napkin on the counter. "Monia, I just wish you would have told me about these big changes in your life. I'm still you father and one of your closest friends. Don't let this mess that's going on with me and your mother come between you and I. I've been feeling bad enough as it is. You're not trying to get rid of me are you?"

"Come on, Daddy." Monia seldom calls her father "daddy" any longer but feels he needs some intimacy. She gets out of her seat and gives him a long hug and sees his eyes are wet when she pulls back. "Dad, what's the matter?"

"I remember taking you to college, then moving you up to Frisco, and later to your new apartment – well I guess old apartment now – up those narrow stairs. Now you don't even bother to tell me you're moving back to Seaside and don't ask my advice about buying your first home. I would have helped you. I hope you didn't do all this alone." He looks around the condo and waves his arms.

"I had help. A couple of friends and Mr. Aleman and his oldest son, Michael, helped me load the U-Haul. Ja'Niece, mom, and Jeremiah helped me unload and unpack."

"Your mom and Jeremiah – those two are thick aren't they? Your mother always had a special spot in her heart for Jeremiah."

"Do you still dislike him so much?" Monia asks.

"Oh no, reflection is a wonderful and forgiving thing. I stopped believing Jeremiah had anything to do with Trotter's disappearance years ago."

"Do you think Mr. Trotter is dead?"

"I sure hope not, but sometimes I'd almost prefer it if he was dead. I loved that man like a brother. I hate to believe he abandoned his family like that. Either way it's pretty bad. I would have never thought Jeremiah would have survived this situation better than Clifford. Clifford is in bad shape. He and I talk every once in awhile. He's got his two boys but he and his wife split some years ago. His dentistry practice is doing well. He's just so angry it's sad. Those boys needed to come together and support each other but they grow further apart with each passing year. I doubt they've seen each other in ten years or more."

"Has Jerry tried to talk to Clifford at all about this recently?"

"Honestly, Chunga, I think Jeremiah had to let it go to keep his sanity. He couldn't continue being Clifford's punching bag. You know Clifford jumped him a couple of times not long after Trot's disappearance and has bad-mouthed Jeremiah nonstop over the years."

Monia cannot help but smile at her father's use of the nickname he gave her as a toddler. "What's up with Miss Sharon?" she asks.

"Money, baby, money. She's got expensive tastes, always has. Although she makes pretty good money, she still needs all the time. Sharon wants the best of everything. Trotter used to constantly complain about her spending. Wouldn't surprise me if that had something to do with his disappearance, trying to keep enough money to give her what she wanted. Sharon was always running up to the city or to LA to shop. She likes to gamble too, but then you know that because your mother gambles with her. But of course

Clarissa doesn't drop money like Sharon. I mean Sharon is nowhere near as bad as some I've seen and she is doing better but she can still blow quite a bit of money. She used to take trips to Reno every couple of months. Now she does bingo and goes to the casino out there in Friant, that Table Mountain. When Trotter was alive or around I should say, he couldn't complain as much about the gambling as the shopping because he liked the gambling too.

"Now that Jeremiah's business is doing so well, Sharon seems to be spending more. I think when he bought that house she knew he had to be making pretty good money. She does not mind laying a guilt trip on him or Clifford whenever she has a chance. Naturally, Jeremiah wants to take care of his mother. She stood by him when the cops wanted him in jail. She was vicious. Hired a lawyer she couldn't afford. Jeremiah just finished paying that debt by customizing that attorney's Benz. Sharon can ask that boy for anything and he'll try to get it for her. Clifford sends her a stipend but I guarantee you, it doesn't come close to what Jeremiah shells out for his mother every year. Now she's saying the house is too much but she doesn't want to sell it. She wants to keep it as an investment and buy a condo or a small house in Monterey or Pacific Grove, no less. I guarantee she's hinting for the down payment.

"What burns my hide is that she never pushed for the insurance company to pay out on Trot's life insurance or tried to get his social security for the boys. She still pays the premiums on the life insurance. They initially denied the claim because she couldn't produce a death certificate. She's got the denial letter. She pays over three hundred dollars a month on full coverage policies for Trot and her. Those policies are about thirty five years old and have grown a lot. She never told me but I'm guessing she borrowed money off those policies to send Clifford through dental school. If she did, it's Jeremiah's money she used to pay off the loans for Clifford's education and Clifford won't even speak to his brother."

"Are you telling me she never had Mr. Trotter declared dead?"

"Never did. She gets survivor's benefits from the Army without a death certificate. How she got the federal government to do that, I don't know. Of course the Feds don't mind giving away money because it comes out of all our pockets. They give away money like lunatics and we all pay."

"Dad, you're such a Republican."

"Wait till you get my age and begin to realize how much money you will need in order to live in the style to which you've become accustomed at age one hundred, you'll turn a little red too; mark my words. Anyway, baby, you've got me gossiping like an old woman. It's good to have you so close again." Darnell smiles at his daughter and squeezes her hand causing her heart to melt a bit. "I hope you'll come by and visit me at my home some time."

"I don't know, Dad. I'll have to think about that."

"Feel like you'd be betraying your mother?" Darnell looks at his child and asks with his hand still on hers.

"Well," Monia hesitates, "Yes, I guess that's it. I know at some point I need to spend some time with you and Jenny but I'm just not ready yet. I hope you understand."

"I do, but I live alone and have since your mother put me out. Me and Jenny spent some time together but that was short-lived. I'm alone and will likely continue to be."

Monia is surprised. She had been waiting on the finalizing of her parent's divorce and the subsequent announcement of her father's nuptials soon to follow. She wants to jump for joy but can't because Darnell looks sad and lonely. Now she realizes she can no longer disregard him. He needs her too. *Damn that was a short-lived glee.*

Chapter 8

Monia had worried about being bored and lonely with only Clarissa for company after her return to Seaside. She could not have been more mistaken. Both her parents call, stop by unannounced, and invite her out every day during the week before she starts her new job. Jeremiah, who considers himself family, also stops by unannounced, once with his daughter, Erin, and once alone. When he stopped in with Erin, Monia persuaded them to stay and have dinner. They demolished the roasted chicken she had planned to eat on for at least three meals and a snack.

Monia also comes to expect a daily call from Ja'Niece to check on Jeremiah and discuss her next planned visit. After the third call, Monia asks, "Why don't you just call him, Ja'Niece? You have his work number."

"A woman can't seem too anxious. For all this modern day woman crap, men still like to feel like they are doing the choosing. I figure I'll give him some time. I can't believe he didn't ask for my number. You think I should just have you give it to him?"

"I don't want to be in the middle of this. I gave you his number; call him."

"Umm, I don't know. He's not real social is he? I looked him up on Facebook, Linkedin, and, Twitter, but nothing."

"I never asked him about it, but I think he may stay too busy for a lot of online time. Did you look for his business? It's Del Rey Auto Repair and Customizing. Check it out. I think you'll be impressed."

"Does he make good money? He looks like money."

"I couldn't tell you what he makes, Ja'Niece. I have no idea."

"You're not much help, you know that?"

"Sorry, but you know I've been through a few situations with you on the love front. I don't want you looking at me funny if things don't work out between you and Jeremiah."

"Okay, friend," Ja'Niece responds sarcastically.

Monia identifies her friend's pattern for romantic relationships in her interest in Jeremiah. Ja'Niece falls in love so quickly and deeply that all her affairs end disastrously. She smothers her men with attention. So, no matter how much they like her fun-loving spirit, bubbly personality, and sexy body, they get bored with

Ja'Niece after a few weeks and start to avoid her. Monia only gets snippets of communication from her friend while all is going well in the relationship. Ja'Niece loves to brag about how good her man is in bed and if you let her she will give you graphic details; what they did on their most recent date; and what nice thing the current lover did or bought for her. She relays this information via text, on Facebook, Instagram, or by way of a speedy one-sided conversation. Once the affair begins to wane, Monia becomes a big cushiony shoulder to whine and cry on. Frankly, Monia is more involved and bored with Ja'Niece's love live than her own. She has no intention of promoting a relationship between her two friends.

--

Clutching the most recent edition of the *Monterey Herald* newspaper, Sharon Sumuels enters her friend Clarissa's home in an agitated state. "They found a body buried in the park," she announces, as she slaps the paper on the counter in front of Clarissa and Monia.

"What park?" Clarissa asks as she hesitantly reaches for the paper.

"Laguna Grande. I called Clifford. He's calling the police to get the information. They would not tell me anything. Said I was hysterical," Sharon tells her friend as she turns and paces a few steps away from the counter and turns and paces back with her hands waving about, never looking at either woman.

Clarissa gives Monia a pointed look which Monia interprets to mean, "This means trouble."

"I don't know why Jeremiah is not answering his phone. He's probably with that damn Pismo woman. He must have my grandbaby with him." Sharon gives the appearance of a woman trying to escape her skin. She sits only for a moment and then jumps up and paces back and forth. "I was so afraid this day would come. Oh gracious. What if it's him?" Now she looks from Clarissa to Monia as if she actually expects an answer.

"Sharon, you need to calm down. Why would you assume it's Trotter? There's no point in getting so worked up. Let's wait and see what Clifford says. Jeremiah is not down in Pismo Beach. He and Erin will be here soon and you don't want her wondering what has you so upset." Clarissa tries to calm Sharon. Mentioning Erin has the desired calming effect, though her concern remains palpable.

Sharon has spent the last twenty years telling herself and everyone else that her husband of twenty years abandoned her and their two children. She never allowed herself time to mourn the man. She was by far too strong to whine for a man who was pathetic enough, trifling enough, just plain sorry enough to leave his family without a word – cruel enough to not provide a dime of support to his wife and teenage sons and selfish enough to allow his own son to live under the cloud of suspicion that hovers over Jeremiah to this day. What woman in her right mind would spill a tear over such a sorry excuse of a man?

Now, if it turns out that Trotter Sumuels has been lying under a pile of earth in Seaside's own Laguna Grande Park all these years, all those pent up tears will have to come out in some form. Also the investigation will kick off in high gear all over again. Jeremiah will, once again, be in danger. Clifford will start up at his brother again. Jeremiah might give up and leave Seaside forever this time, taking Erin with him.

Sharon needs Trotter to be alive – somewhere living out his dreams without her. They were birds of a feather in a way. She had loved the over-indulging fool dearly but she needs everyone to believe he is alive and living elsewhere. She needs to believe it most of all. This body in the park cannot be Trotter if Sharon is to survive the week with her sanity.

Darnell, who was not invited to the intimate family dinner at his supposedly-soon-to-be ex wife's home, is summoned and responds immediately. Sharon does not hesitate to walk into his outstretched arms and lay her head on his shoulder. "It's going to be okay, Sharon. I'm certain the body in the park is not Trotter. Don't get yourself all worked up over nothing." He peeps over Sharon's head and mouths to Monia, "Where is Jeremiah?" who mouths back, "I don't know," with upturned palms and hunched shoulders.

"Can I get you a drink, Darnell?" Clarissa asks with more warmth than she has shown him since she told him to leave their home a year ago.

"Is anyone else having anything?" Darnell asks as he looks at the women.

Sharon slowly shakes her head into Darnell's shoulder and Monia tells her father "Maybe later."

"Just me," Clarissa answers, needing something to numb her senses.

"I'll have a scotch if you've got any." Darnell joins her.

Clarissa never acquired a taste for scotch but she still has the bottle of Dalmore single malt Darnell left when he moved out. She quickly serves up the scotch and heads to the kitchen to put dinner in serving platters and bowls with Monia on her heals.

"Did you invite Dad?" Monia asks Clarissa once they are alone in the kitchen.

"I called him so he could be with Sharon. "They both suffered so much behind Trotter that he knows better than anyone how to calm her."

"Better than Jeremiah or Clifford?" Monia asks.

"Oh yeah, those boys have never really dealt with the loss of their father; neither has Sharon really. Darnell is the only person that has hurt from every angle. He's considered and accepted every possibility and believe me, this mess has caused him many a sleepless night."

"Do you ever get jealous of him and Miss Sharon?"

"No, they've never given me any cause to be jealous. They've been friends a long time and love each other, but they have never shown anything but a lot of honest love."

Monia feels proud and close to her mother at this moment as she walks up behind the woman and hugs her. "Mom, you are the best."

Clarissa pats her daughters hand and tells her that they need to get dinner on the table. No sooner than they walk out of the kitchen with their hands filled with serving dishes, Jeremiah shows up with Erin.

Darnell pulls Jeremiah off to the side and tells him about the body in the park and explains Sharon's angst over the situation.

"Is there any reason that you've heard about that may lead us to believe that body is my father's?" Jeremiah asks with no display of concern about how this situation will affect him.

"None that I can tell, but it is obvious to me that your mother is afraid that he may actually be dead."

"I think you're right. We better join them."

Erin has been standing near her grandmother and can tell she is out of sorts. "What's the matter, Nana?" the child asks.

"Nothing baby. Nana just has a little headache. I'll feel better after I eat something."

"Sorry you look so sad. Your head must feel real bad. You should take leve; that's what my daddy takes."

This medical advice from her six-year-old granddaughter results in a momentary smile and a hug.

The little welcome home party Clarissa hosts for her daughter was intended to be a light-hearted joyous affair, not this somber occasion with only Erin and Darnell enjoying the exquisite spread on the table. Darnell is so pleased to have a seat at the table in the home he shared with his wife and daughter for over thirty years that a bowl of grits would seem delicious and Erin is a hungry child protected by the cocoon of youth and ignorance.

Watching Sharon, Monia can tell the woman should not go home alone and says as much to Jeremiah and Clarissa in the kitchen later in the evening.

Clarissa looks at Jeremiah, who is certainly concerned with both his mother and his child, and declares that she will go home with her friend and stay the night.

"No, Clarissa, I think I'll go with her. She and I need to talk through some of these things. I guess we've both refused to believe my dad could actually be dead and we need to prepare ourselves for that possibility."

"You want me to take Erin home and stay with her tonight?" Monia volunteers.

Clarissa had considered offering to keep the child and is pleased that Monia is willing to take on the challenge. Sharon and Clarissa often laugh with each other about how the loquacious six-year-old saps all their energy with her desire for constant interaction, early rising, and nonstop communications. Both women swear their own children were nothing like Erin, who is well-behaved but spoiled.

Stress visibly melts from Jeremiah's demeanor and his gratitude is apparent when he responds to Monia. "That would be a big help. I don't want to deal with my mother while Erin is with us."

Clarissa watches the two friends and gives a quiet smile. Before Monia's return to the area, Clarissa had not thought of her daughter and Jeremiah together. She's not sure why. God knows she has prayed for a good, kind, and loving husband for Monia. She was also aware of Monia's crush on Jeremiah when she was a girl. Darnell was aware of the crush also and swore the feelings ran both ways. That was one reason he chastised the two so harshly the day Jeremiah brought Monia home from Mal's Market. Back then their five-year age gap was significant. Monia was only fourteen. Of course fourteen-year-olds have sex but it is the parents' responsibility to keep them away from the powerful drug as long as possible. According to Sharon, girls had been dropping their undies like basketballs for both Jeremiah and Clifford. Clarissa felt that Darnell had been right to set a strict boundary that day but wrong in his behavior toward Jeremiah. He should have sat the young man down and talked to him directly about his concerns.

That was almost twenty years ago. This is a new day and the age gap has closed. Clarissa dares to hope that there is something brewing between Jeremiah and Monia who has only dated white men since leaving for college.

Clarissa has never discussed Monia's preference in men. She doesn't care about the color of the man's skin but, as Dr. King put it, "the content of their character," particularly when it comes to her child. The problem with the white men Monia dates is they seem to have no soul, no interest in black people or black culture, and little desire to assimilate. You see, in Clarissa's opinion, assimilation needs to flow both ways in a healthy friendship or a romantic relationship. Each partner should adapt, adopt, and compromise, not to the dysfunctional or the anal shit in their partner's culture but to the valued traditions. Ski trips, group vacations, or cycling here and there should not always have precedence over family barbecues, family reunions, or card party get-togethers.

Clarissa does not know many black folks who can afford group vacations each year, or that go skiing, or cycling. Often times black families are just happy to get a good percentage of the family together for a funeral, a reunion, and best of all; a wedding. And honestly, Clarissa can't think of any family she wants to share a home with for a weekend and certainly not a week. Hell, whose going to clean, cook, buy the food, eat up all the food, get the best room, pay their share, do their part, watch the kids, take the kids, control those bad-assed kids. No, most black folks that Clarissa knows take simple trips and have one to three day gatherings. They simply can't afford more and sure don't want to spend all their time piled up together in one house getting on each other's nerves.

With her insurance agency and Darnell's dental practice, they had always been able to afford nice vacations. They usually remained in the states or went to the islands. Once they went to Canada and once to Hawaii. Clarissa had been planning a surprise Alaskan cruise vacation when the sledge hammer smashed up her marriage. She kept the money for that trip untouched in a separate account, telling herself she'll take the trip one day, maybe with Monia or Sharon.

Monia has had her share of exotic vacations but Sharon hasn't had a good vacation in years. Reno, Vegas, and Table Mountain have been her places of refuge. Each of her sons has offered to foot the expense of an extensive getaway, but Sharon would much rather blow the funds at bingo or in a casino. Shopping has even lost much of its allure for the woman. Clarissa thinks she may be able to convince Sharon to accompany her on the Alaska vacation. Better yet, maybe she'll be able to give it to Monia as a special gift!

--

It is nearly two in the morning when Jeremiah enters his home. He had expected to find Monia asleep on one of the sofas since he hadn't been thoughtful enough to tell her to make herself comfortable in his guest bedroom, but there are no signs of life in the front of the house. Making his way to Erin's room, he finds Monia sound asleep lying next to Erin with a copy of *The Pout-Pout Fish* still in her hand. Jeremiah stands there for a few minutes and watches his daughter and friend sleep peacefully before turning off the light and heading to his own bed.

It seems as if Jeremiah has just closed his eyes when he hears, "Wake up sleepy head," as Monia shakes him awake. She is ready to go home and climb in her own bed.

Jeremiah turns over and stares at her for a moment as he tries to clear his thoughts and figure out why Monia is in his bedroom waking him. He can't help but smile as he realizes the situation is completely platonic. After lying there and stretching, he pulls himself into a sitting position with Monia watching him and becoming slightly distracted by the broad expanse of muscular chest with a nice amount of man hair thinning out into a barely visible triangle over his abdomen. She can't help but wonder if he has anything on under the covers and makes herself pull her eyes from that spot where the covers meet his beautiful skin. Jeremiah watches Monia watch him and wonders what's on her mind.

"I'm getting ready to leave. Erin is still sleeping hard. It took her awhile to go to sleep last night. She kept asking me when you were coming home. I was on the third book before she passed out. Man, those kid's books are good. I may have to borrow a few," Monia jokes.

"I'm sure she won't mind," Jeremiah laughs. "What's your rush? Let me make you some coffee and some breakfast if you have time."

Monia jumps with a gasp as Jeremiah suddenly throws the covers off and quickly swings his legs out of the bed. "What's the matter?" he asks as he looks around to see what startled her.

Monia laughs nervously as she steps back to give him space. "I wasn't sure you had anything on under those covers."

"I'm not that crass, Monia," Jeremiah tells her as he heads off to his bathroom and closes the door behind him.

Monia looks around his bedroom and has the urge to take it all in before leaving. She had taken note of the king-sized bed immediately and wondered why he needed such a big bad. "I bet that spot gets lots of action," she comments under her breathe. She stops wondering about Jeremiah's love life when she hears water and realizes the sound is Jeremiah peeing. Monia immediately leaves his room and closes the door behind her. She feels her cheeks flush and hopes he does not know she heard him. Monia cannot recall ever hearing a man pee – such a simple thing – such an intimate thing. How is it she has a much closer connection to Jeremiah than Marcus or any previous lover. She reminds herself that Jeremiah is like her brother. She sits at his island and thinks about their relationship as she flips mindlessly through her phone.

"I don't smell any coffee," Jeremiah tells her when he enters the kitchen with a loosely tied bath robe hanging on his shoulders and still revealing a good deal of manly chest.

"I thought you invited me to stay so you could make coffee. You want me to go over to Starbucks and pick up a couple of cups."

"Nah, I got ya. My coffee's much better than theirs. What were you thinking about when I came out of the room? Must have been something deep."

"You really want to know?"

"Yeah, I really want to know." Jeremiah gives her a serious look as he turns to the sink.

"I was thinking about how special our friendship is and how odd it is that we haven't seen each other or talked for all these years and we've picked up just where we left off." Monia feels sentimental and a little teary. "I'm so glad you're back here. You're like the big brother I never had."

Jeremiah had stood at the kitchen sink, not looking at her as she spoke. He became excited by her words initially but felt a big let down by the time she finished answering the question. He quietly responds. "I'm happy you're here too. Thanks for bringing my baby home and staying with her. That was a big help." Jeremiah turns and gives Monia a superficial smile.

"It was no problem. You know I've reached the esteemed status of aunt. I am now the honorary Auntie Moanie."

"Auntie Moanie?"

"Yes, Auntie Moanie," Monia confirms the title.

"She can't call you that," Jeremiah tells Monia.

"Why not?" Monia becomes defensive immediately and wonders why Jeremiah won't allow Erin to call her "aunt." "I have no siblings, no other close friends with children. This may be my last chance at auntdom or auntism. I can't believe you would do this." Monia sounds genuinely upset.

"Oh, she can call you 'aunt,' 'auntie,' 'aintee,' 'antee,' 'ant,' 'ainee' or even 'nay nay'. She just can't call you 'Moanie'. Only I get to call you that."

Monia starts to laugh. Jeremiah looks at her with a serious expression and says, "I'm not kidding. So do you want to tell her or you want me to tell her?"

"Oh, you tell her. I wouldn't want to steal your pleasure." Monia sniggles as she sips on her coffee. "Now where is my breakfast? And I do have one more thing to say about that. I thought only family were allowed to call you 'Jerry'?" Monia gives Jeremiah a challenging look.

He starts to respond but his cell phone rings and he answers to find his mother on the other end sounding exhausted. "Your brother called and said he heard from the police. They're certain the body they found is not your father. They're pretty sure it's another guy who has been missing about a year. Now why the hell couldn't they tell us that last night? I can't take much more of this Jeremiah, I just can't."

"Come on, Mom. You should be relieved. You want me and Erin to come over later on?"

"No, I'm going to church. It'll do my soul some good. Come go with me."

Jeremiah avoids New Life Baptist Church like it is the plague but he does allow Erin to attend with her grandmother.

"Can't make it, Mom, but I'll stop by later. You still plan on taking that long weekend in Vegas next week?"

"I do and Clarissa is going with me. I almost talked Darnell into tagging along but he's going to some conference in New Orleans. I'm going to get those two back together yet; watch and see if I don't."

Jeremiah laughs and ends the call, pleased his mother is sounding better. "They've concluded that the body is not my dad," he tells Monia with a thoughtful look.

"Is Miss Sharon feeling better?"

"My mother will not get better until my father turns up, dead or alive."

The last thing Monia wants to discuss is the whereabouts of Trotter Sumuels. It seems this subject that she has given so little thought over the past fifteen years is now taking a front seat in her life. Although the subject had always been important to her family and many of her Seaside acquaintances, she had the luxury of ignoring the disappearance of her father's best friend, her mother's best friend's husband, and one of her dearest friend's father. Now it is as if time has backed up with all of them twenty years older. Everyone seems to have moved on with their lives except Miss Sharon who seems to be in some form of emotional limbo. Clifford has married, divorced, had two sons, and started a thriving dental practice; yet continues to wallow in anger because Jeremiah was the most beautifully favored son of a family with two beautifully favored boys. Darnell dedicated his efforts to growing his practice, got bored, dipped his stick where it didn't belong, and now wants his wife back more than he wants to live. Clarissa, remaining on her steady path through life, got slapped down, decided a little reefer would help her cope, and kept trudging through. Jeremiah has stood tall and told his story, left his home and went into the Army in order to survive, met a woman he found luscious and made a gorgeous child, educated himself, and made jobs for others and lots of money. Monia's life has not changed in anyway by the disappearance of "Mr. Trotter." She teased his boys, said yes ma'am to his wife, went off to school and got her education, and never spent more than seven nights in a row in Seaside until two weeks ago. Now baby girl's got to deal with a serious issue that impacts the lives of those she loves and has for two decades.

"Is it always this bad?" Monia asks Jeremiah.

"What?" Jeremiah looks up from a place deep inside his own thoughts and asks.

"The issues around your dad -- here in Seaside."

"Not this bad but always lurking. It's always there. I've had to learn to live with it. At least I took a break. Mom never had one." Jeremiah looks as if he could cry. "Let's go out on the patio and eat. I don't have your view but it'll do."

Monia grabs his coffee cup along with her own and follows him. The friends talk about the upcoming wedding of Monia's friend Tasha and the "Blues in the Park" which will take place in just a few weeks in the very park where the body was found.

"Are you inviting me to attend these events with you? I was surprised to get an invitation to that wedding but Harold and I have always been cool. He told me he was going to send me an invite after we did some work on his Beemer. I really wasn't planning on attending. I'll be working most of the day but I had thought about showing up for the reception. I don't do much hanging out in Seaside you know."

Monia had thought about attending the "Blues in the Park" but is now leery about taking her mother and his to that particular spot. "Maybe next year for the 'Blues in the Park' thing."

"Yeah, I think you're right." Jeremiah reads her thoughts. "So is it a date for the reception?"

"Sure, Ja'Niece is coming down. It should be fun."

Jeremiah is unscathed by the Ja'Niece update. He has something else he wants to know. "What about Marcus?" he asks as he chumps down on a piece of whole wheat toast and steadily watches Monia.

Monia has not talked to Marcus since he left her home nine days ago. She has received a couple of text messages from him. One thing is certain, he does not miss her or she him. "He's not coming down. I think it's just about over for us. We weren't that solid when we were in the same city. I don't think either of us will be making regular road trips up and down the coast."

"You don't sound too heartbroken. You got somebody else on the line?"

"I'm not fishing, Jeremiah. I'm just starting a new job and working on new skills, getting settled into my new home, and learning the ends and outs of living in my home town again. Who has got time for romance?" Monia sounds slightly irritated and gets up from the table to take her dishes inside. "I've got to get home and get ready for my first day tomorrow."

Jeremiah reaches out and stops her from removing her dishes. "I'll take care of this later."

Monia moves her hand away without looking at him. "Let me get my things."

Jeremiah follows her into the living room, where she collects her purse and a small overnight bag and heads straight to the door. "Thanks again for staying with Erin. It was a big help." He opens his arms to give Monia a hug which she gladly accepts and returns as she places her head on his chest. They stand there enjoying their embrace until Monia looks up at him. She senses that Jeremiah wants to kiss her and she wants him to. He simply smiles, drops his arms, takes a step back, and tilts his head to the side. "Good luck on that job tomorrow. Hope everything goes well."

"Thanks. I'll call you in a few days and tell you about it."

"Yeah, if I don't call you first."

As Monia makes the short drive to her home, she asks herself, "What was that?"

Chapter 9

The first week working in Dr. Navya Singh's office is exhilarating and exhausting. The challenge of working in a different specialty of medicine keeps Monia's intellectual juices flowing. Several mornings a week, she shadows Pamela as she conducts preliminary patient evaluations, routine patient exams, and post surgical exams. Monia's afternoons belong to the doctor who is a small powerhouse of a woman. Both Dr. Singh and Pamela are thorough, kind, and empathetic toward their patients, clear and concise.

Honest and direct communication seems to be Dr. Singh's credo. She pulls no punches with her patients. She requires most participate in psychological counseling before the extreme bypass surgery and encourages group counseling after the procedure.

Monia quickly realizes that the shared clinic with a plastic surgeon is not to afford Dr. Singh more income but to encourage her patient's to make the most of their transformations.

"I want you to seriously consider having this forty pounds of sagging skin removed." Monia listens to the doctor advise one patient. The skin is unsightly and both the patient and Monia have a hard time looking at the sagging flesh as the doctor moves it around in order to conduct a thorough examination of her patient. "At least get yourself evaluated. This skin will be here forever and only become more unsightly as you become older. Let us be honest; that is most important here. You did not have this drastic surgery for health reasons alone. Your health was fairly good. You have done everything just as I suggested with your exercise regiment and eating. Excellent! So now you think you will be satisfied hauling around this flesh you have to tuck in like you do. I don't know, maybe you will be. Only you can decide. I simply know, I do not think so. You must do what is best for you. As I am sure Dr. Sloan will advise you, you should give yourself twelve months before having skin tightening surgery. Will you at least talk to Dr. Sloan or his colleague?"

After such plain speaking, patients find it hard to ignore Dr. Singh's advice. Pamela is just as direct with only a bit more badgering. Monia hopes her bedside manner garners as much patient trust and respect as that given the doctor and Pamela.

The job makes Monia ravenous to learn as much as possible from the reading materials provided by her coworkers. She spends every evening for the next month re-reading, reviewing and re-reading the materials and researching online. Monia learns what techniques the doctor is using or discarding and soon recognizes which are by the book and which are not. It's not long before she begins asking targeted questions and picking her colleagues' brains as to why they accept particular practices or methods. Due to her surgical background, Monia finds herself assisting in surgery sooner than she had expected on a patient the doctor had earlier declared to be Monia's patient. This meant Monia conducted every remaining aspect of the patient's bariatric treatment except the surgery. Dr. Singh had diligently sat in on each session and oversaw Monia's handling of the patient. "You are as sharp as Pamela. I am hitting two for two at selecting my assistants, or how is it in baseball, batting a thousand."

The days are grueling, not so much due to the hours or the number of patients but the quality of care and the efficiency of the clinic that require so much energy. Dr Singh is downright anal about patient care. Her standards are high and the staff love being part of such a well run clinic. At the end of each day, the doctor and her two PAs sit and go over their cases for that day and review at length any surgery scheduled for the next. The review normally lasts one and a half to two hours, though longer periods are not uncommon.

At the conclusion of Monia's forth week, Dr. Singh extends an invitation to her staff to attend a welcoming party for Monia. "Six o'clock next Saturday at my home and be sure to bring a date – adults only please. Bring a best friend, parent, whomever; it does not matter. Just come, eat up all my food, and drink my liquor, but no driving drunk if you please. So bring your designated driver and no excuses, Shirley."

Shirley rolls her large clear shiny eyes and asks, "Why are you picking on me, Dr. Navya?"

"Because you always try not to come and we miss you. You make the party better."

Shirley has to smile at the compliment.

Monia's mind immediately started working at high gear when she heard the words "be sure to bring a date." *A date? Now, that presents a problem. I could call Marcus but he'll want sex and I'm not up to that. Maybe I'll ask Jeremiah.*

Monia immediately nixes Jeremiah also. He stays in touch and recently she had him bring Erin over to spend the night one evening when he was working late and Sharon and Clarissa were at their beloved bingo. Monia likes spending time with Erin. They talk like girlfriends. Sometimes Monia has to put herself in check to keep the conversation on Erin's level because the child is bright and likes to talk about a variety of subjects. But Monia has used a long handled spoon to deal with Jeremiah over the past month or so. She has no intention of becoming part of his dating pool but it seems the more she backs away the closer they become.

She tries to keep their interaction short and light because, damn it, he excites her – always smiling that crooked smile at her and doing shit like breathing and standing there looking at her, and touching her shoulders, arms, or hair – shit like that. He's her friend and she loves him like crazy. She had no idea how much until he reentered her life. When they were kids, he always made her feel special and loved. He talked to her and explained things. He showed her how to beat Clifford at Super Mario, which resulted in her eventually beating Jeremiah. She remembers him working out with her and encouraging her when she decided to run track in the sixth grade. She got mad because he ran her so long and hard but she excelled in the sport.

Monia had loved Clifford too when they were kids but he became mean as he grew older. Clifford always competed with Jeremiah and Monia. Poor Clifford, he wasn't the oldest, the smartest, or the best looking and when Monia was around he wasn't the baby. Jeremiah always gave way to Clifford unless Monia was with them. Then Clifford had to take a back seat to whatever Monia wanted or needed. As young children, Monia and Clifford played together well but they grew older and Clifford went through puberty and Monia became fodder for his adolescent hormones. Monia wonders if she would feel anywhere near the kinship with Clifford that she feels for Jeremiah now that they live so near each other.

She reminds herself that she feels toward Jeremiah as she would toward a brother but he's making her question her feelings and she does not like the uncertainty surrounding him. He's even started pulling on her hair when he talks to her. He has to know he's making her uncomfortable but doesn't seem to care. *I'll ask mom to go with me.*

--

"Hell no! That's my bingo night. Me and Sharon are on a tear. We can't mess with our mojo, darling."

"Mom, Friday is your bingo night. Your daughter needs you and you need to do something other than go to bingo."

"I do something other than go to bingo. I work five days a week and manage my business, I go to church, I take water aerobics and walk regularly, and I live my life as I choose. Don't act like I just sit in this house and wait for the doors to the bingo hall to open. Why don't you ask Jeremiah? I get the impression he'd love to go anywhere with you."

"I probably will ask him but he won't have a sitter if Miss Sharon is going with you."

"He's got a sitter for Erin, a couple of good ones, but the lady who keeps house for him, keeps Erin all the time. Who do you think watches her when he's at work. If he gives her enough notice it won't be a problem."

Monia tries to pout over the phone with her mother, but Clarissa fails to notice or if she does she ignores it. When Monia ends the call, she swishes through her mind one last time to think of who she can invite. Her father maybe, not! She thinks taking Darnell would make her appear desperate. She considers inviting Ja'Niece down but the last time she visited Monia her sole purpose was to see Jeremiah who happened to be unreachable. Ja'Niece had told Monia she was staying until that Sunday but left midday on Saturday after concluding there would be no Jeremiah sighting. Monia has a couple of other school friends in the area with whom she has reconnected but feels leery about inviting either of them to her boss's party.

She finally sucks it up and decides to at least ask Jeremiah. She doesn't call ahead but stops by his home unannounced one evening. Erin's regular sitter, Delores, answers the door and watches Monia suspiciously through the locked storm door. "I'm sorry but Jeremiah is not in. Do you want me to give him a message?"

"That's my Auntie Moanie. She can come in." Erin pushes her way in front of Delores and starts reaching for the storm door lock.

"No, Erin," Delores tells the child with a shake of her head as she removes Erin's hand.

"That's alright, Erin. I'll see your daddy later, okay." Monia smiles at the child and Delores.

"I want you to come in for a while. Daddy won't care." The child looks from Monia to Delores who now looks uncertain.

"No, but I tell you what, you get your daddy to bring you over for dinner in the next couple of days and we'll do those homemade pizzas we talked about, okay?"

"Okay." Erin still sounds sad but slightly pacified.

Monia receives a "**call me**" text from Jeremiah early the next morning and calls him at her first free opportunity.

"You stopped by last night. Did you need something?" Jeremiah asks.

"Nothing important. I guess you were on one of your dates." Monia sounds jealous but quickly changes her tone. "I need a favor. Can you and Erin come over tonight? I promised her we'd make pizza."

"Well that's not much of a favor." Jeremiah laughs. "Sure. What time?"

"Is seven thirty too late. It won't take long for the pizzas, so we should be able to eat by eight fifteen, eight thirty at the latest. You can make the salad while me and Erin put the pizza together."

"Can I bring anything?"

"Dessert, if you guys want any. I've got nothing sweet in the house."

Jeremiah bites his tongue to keep from responding, "Oh, yes you do" and simply says, "See you at seven thirty."

When Jeremiah returned home the night before, he was surprised to hear Monia had stopped by. She has been distant with him for weeks. He knows it was the hug. He finds her attractive and as hard as he tries to stay in his lane and be the big brother she wants, the lure is strong. He catches himself touching her before he's aware of his hands. He tries not to watch her so much. On one occasion, she came right out and told him, "Would you stop looking at me so damn much; you make me nervous." Instead of him having the good sense to stop staring, he flirted and told her, "I can't get over how beautiful you are." When Monia's expression went from critical to embarrassed, Jeremiah added, "You know you were an ugly little girl," and pinched her on the arm. He just had to touch her in some way.

"Stop it!" She had jerked her arm away. "You're worse now than Clifford was when we were kids. You told me he picked on me because he had a crush on me." Monia's voice had trailed off and her eyes lowered when she thought about the meaning of the comparisons between the two brothers' behaviors. Jeremiah had wanted to press her to finish her thought but left her alone.

He likes Monia and knows she is aware of his feelings and likes him too. It's a problem for them both. Their families are tight like blood relatives, closer than most relatives actually. Clarissa, Darnell, and his own mother, Sharon, would castrate him if he messed over Monia, not that Jeremiah is the type of guy that goes around messing over women but sometimes things happen and people stop seeing each other for one reason or another. Jeremiah has been dumped. Erin's mother dumped him for her career, such as it is, and he has dumped women. Once he gets bored or they become too demanding or clingy, he stops seeing them. Jeremiah dates; that's what he does. If anyone asks him, he will tell them that he dates and does not limit his dating to one woman. He is completely open and honest about that. The last thing he wants is to have his closest friends and mother on the warpath because he and Monia have stopped seeing each other. Also, Darnell would not like the idea of a relationship between Jeremiah and Monia because Jeremiah does have a bit of a reputation when it comes to women. He and Darnell have started spending a little time together and he does not want to hinder their growing friendship, but he does like Monia.

Chapter 10

Monia's surprise visit to his home was the second surprise of the day for Jeremiah. Late that same morning he had received a call from Leslie telling him she was in town and needed a place to sleep. When he asked her what brought her up to the Peninsula, she replied that she had come to see him. Jeremiah was a little baffled and not certain how to respond without seeming like an insensitive fool. "Where are you now," he asked?"

"Standing in your office."

Jeremiah decided to break for an early lunch. He always makes a point of telling Leslie when he plans to visit her home. If there is a possibility he may stop by, he checks with her well in advance to make sure it's okay and calls just prior to his visit. He had not been pleased that Leslie showed up on him unannounced. It meant he had to spend the evening with her or she would have been offended. Just the night before he had gone out for drinks with a couple of the guys and thankfully was home by ten. So Leslie's visit took him away from Erin the second night in a row, which is a pattern he tries to avoid. And what if he had other plans for the day or evening? He wanted to tell Leslie off for the surprise visit but their relationship had become so strained he feared her reaction. If they decided to end things, Jeremiah did not want the breakup to be over something as minor as a visit that he considered an imposition.

"So why this sudden unexpected visit? Did you need to talk to me about something?" Jeremiah asked Leslie over lunch.

Leslie was hurt though she tried to put a good face on things. She wanted to spend some time with the man she had grown to care so much for and felt she needed to decide if she was wasting her time on him. It seemed to her that the more involved she became the less interested he was. "My kids have gone off with my parents for a week. I haven't seen you since the last time you picked Erin up from her grandmother, so I thought I'd come and spend a couple of days with the two of you."

"I wish you had given me some heads up that you were coming, Leslie. I could have made plans for Erin to be away or got someone in to stay with her. You know I don't like to have her in the house when we're together."

"Why exactly is that? Could you explain that to me again?" Leslie's patience with Jeremiah's rules was nearly at its limit. "I didn't realize that the only reason you were spending time with me was because I was a convenient stopover when you dropped Erin off and picked her up. I assumed we would still see each other even if Erin wasn't going to visit her grandmother any longer. What's going on?"

Jeremiah had to think what to say. He really hadn't given Leslie much thought recently. He had been inconsiderate of her feelings and the last thing he wanted was to treat Leslie poorly. But he refused to allow her to push him into opening the doors of his home while his daughter was present. "Leslie, I'm not going to take you to my house to stay over."

"Why not? Don't you have a guest room? I could sleep in there."

Jeremiah smiled for the first time since she arrived. "And we'll stay away from each other, right? I wouldn't sleep a wink. I'll get you a room. Where would you like to stay?"

"You don't need to do that. I can get my own damn room." Leslie was pissed and her voice was raised.

"Can I meet you for dinner tonight?" Jeremiah had asked more to pacify Leslie than out of a genuine desire to spend time with her. He was disgusted with his insincerity because at that moment he simply wished she hadn't imposed herself on him.

"If you want to," she answered, sensing their time together was ending.

"I've got to get back but let me know where you're staying and where you'd like to meet for dinner." Jeremiah had walked her to her car and given her a hug.

Leslie had sat in her car holding back her tears as she watched Jeremiah drive away.

Later that evening, the couple met at Epsilon Greek restaurant for dinner and drinks before heading back to Leslie's hotel. They were barely in the room when Leslie started removing Jeremiah's clothing. He put up no resistance. It had been well over a month for him and he needed the release. As they lie in each other's arms later that night, neither felt satisfied. There was something missing and they both knew it but that didn't stop them from going for seconds.

--

Jeremiah had only returned to the Peninsula to live a month earlier when he spotted the beautiful black woman strolling through the Monterey Bay Aquarium accompanied by an equally lovely young woman of Spanish heritage. The lady he had planned to take to the Aquarium that afternoon had called him earlier sounding like death and begged off of the excursion. Jeremiah hadn't been to the much lauded attraction since visiting with his family as a thirteen-year-old. Tired of spending his free time with his mother, he decided to go it alone as a sight-seeing tourist. Once he laid eyes on Leslie Charles and Christina Suarez, he was shamefully pleased his date had backed out.

It had taken him no time to strike up a conversation with the two women. Christina, who preferred to be called Tina because she idolized Tina Turner, had driven up from Los Angeles to spend a few days with her friend Leslie in Pismo beach and then the friends decided to take a girls' weekend away on the Peninsula.

The ladies were friendly, with Tina being only a degree more flirtatious than Leslie. Jeremiah had sensed Leslie's eyes held promises he wanted to explore, so he had been both disappointed and surprised to learn that she was married with an infant son. He was glad he had kept his options open while talking to the ladies because, Leslie, who would have been his choice of the two, was off limits.

After spending the early evening hours having drinks and conversation with the women, he continued to prefer Leslie's company. She was intelligent and witty, whereas, Tina was outgoing, somewhat rude and self-centered. Jeremiah had asked the friends how they occupied their time. Tina answered the question with a question, "For pleasure or for fun?" and giggled.

Leslie had given him a look and replied, "Don't pay any attention to her. I do photography work and have recently started working on a number of visual art pieces. I keep a space in Pismo where I display my work, if you're ever down that way." She had handed him a card along with her smile and a direct look in his eyes. Jeremiah had been overwhelmed with her easy sophistication. She was a woman like none he had ever met, and he reminded himself that she was married.

"I am an actor and a singer. I also do some modeling work, Tina had blurted out to get Jeremiah's attention away from Leslie. What do you do to keep yourself occupied?" She reached across the table where they were seated and clasp his hand. Jeremiah was flattered because there was no doubt the two women were competing for his attention.

"I customize automobiles."

"You're a mechanic?" Tina had asked with a slight look of contempt.

Jeremiah had never been ashamed of his field. He had worked on cars his entire life and could sniff out an auto problem like a vehicular hound, but he had long ago stopped considering himself a mechanic. He had no problem with being called a mechanic but considered the misnomer as far off the mark as calling a doctor a medic. "Let's just say I work on cars," Jeremiah had conceded and handed cards to each of the ladies. Tina had hardly looked at the card but Leslie had taken in all the information and filed it away in her wallet and her memory.

The next morning, Tina had called and invited him to meet for lunch before the ladies headed back down the California coast to their homes in Pismo and Los Angeles. Two weeks later Jeremiah had made the drive to LA and spent several days with Tina. They wasted no time becoming a couple. Once in a while, Tina would come up to the Peninsula but Jeremiah did most of the traveling.

A year after Jeremiah met Tina and Leslie, Leslie and her husband gave birth to a second child, a baby girl they named LisBeth. It wasn't unusual for Jeremiah and Tina to meet in Pismo and spend the night or have a meal with Leslie and her Italian-born husband, Christopher. Both couples seemed to enjoy themselves the most when they were together.

Jeremiah and Tina were perfectly content with the long distance relationship. The absence made for a lot of passion when they were together but things changed when a ranting Tina called Jeremiah with the announcement that she was pregnant and planned to abort the pregnancy. Jeremiah had pleaded with her to keep the child but she complained a child would ruin her career, ruin her body, ruin her life. She declared she had no time for raising a child because she needed to focus on advancing her career. Jeremiah had taken time off and rushed to Los Angeles to talk Tina out of having an abortion. He and Tina's mother, Veronica, and her sister, Danielle, spent days pleading with Tina. Veronica and Jeremiah both volunteered to raise the child and Jeremiah offered to pay for a personal trainer during and after the pregnancy to help Tina maintain her figure.

Worn down, Tina had agreed to have the baby as long as she didn't have to raise the child and Jeremiah would pay for the trainer and provide financial support starting immediately. Everyone thought that once Tina gave birth she would change her mind about letting Jeremiah and her mother raise the child but they were wrong. Tina did keep the baby with her for about six months. She never told Jeremiah that he needed to come and get his child; she just left the baby with Veronica for weeks on end while she partied and pursued her career.

Once Jeremiah realized that he needed to keep his promise and raise Erin, he started putting things in place to get her with him. He was thankful for Veronica, who had quit working a few years earlier and was able to devote all the time needed to the care of her granddaughter. Jeremiah moved Erin to Seaside with him the day after her second birthday. Tina had complained about her daughter living so far away but was relieved that she didn't have to visit with her little girl so often. She made the trip to Seaside several times a year for the first two years Erin lived there but after she got a few television roles, the visits became less frequent.

Not long after Tina and Jeremiah had Erin, Leslie's husband told her he wanted to move back to Italy and demanded that she and the children move with him. Leslie flatly refused to move to Italy and leave her home in the States. She had visited her husband's home several times and observed how the women of her husband's family had their say about everything in the home but were subservient to the men. She could not see herself in that role and did not want such a life for her daughter. She also believed that her black skin would have created problems in the long run. The more Leslie objected to the move the more determined Christopher was to make it happen. The couple fought incessantly, with Christopher threatening to leave and take their children with him. Leslie remained calm and begged him not to do such a thing. She promised him she would bring the children for a visit whenever he requested. Christopher, secretly looking forward to life as an unencumbered bachelor again, finally agreed and left his wife and children for good. Within a year, he and Leslie were divorced and he was remarried.

So Jeremiah and Leslie were left behind by their former lovers and happily sought refuge in each other's more than willing arms. Initially, they spent time together for comfort and friendship. This period fortified their relationship and was invaluable to Jeremiah as a healing process from the multiple horrors of his life. He and Leslie sat out on her patio overlooking the ocean and talked for hours, often into the early morning. One night they talked until daybreak. Jeremiah told Leslie everything there was to tell about his life. It was more than a year before they found themselves in bed together. At first they both declared they wanted an open relationship. Leslie had been dating another man at the time and felt no need to discontinue that relationship when she started seeing Jeremiah and he felt the same. It wasn't long before Leslie decided she wanted to be with Jeremiah exclusively, though he maintained his open relationship lifestyle.

By the time Jeremiah became involved with Leslie, he had long since stopped sleeping with Tina, though she did on occasion trek up to Seaside to see Erin and offer herself to him. After a time she stopped trying to entice Jeremiah. On one visit, she brought one of her boyfriends to his home and expected Jeremiah to allow the man to sleep there during her visit with Erin. Jeremiah flatly refused and nearly had to fight the man to get him to leave. "Listen man, I'm not going to tussle with you over my daughter. I'm just asking you to respect me and my right to decide who sleeps in my home." The word respect resonated with the man and he knew he was treading on dangerous territory. When women are in conflict with each other and use the word "respect" it means just that: consider me, treat me like you want me to treat you. Women seldom use the word tied to a threat. For men in conflict with each other, the use of the word "respect" often holds a threat of physical repercussion. Jeremiah looked at Tina and asked, "Is this what you want for her – me having to fight your boyfriend to get him out of my house?" Turning his gaze back to the large thug who was Tina's newest man, Jeremiah continued. "Because I can tell you right now, there's not gon be no fight."

The men stood there looking at each other while Erin sat in her mother's lap playing with a handheld video game Tina had just given her. "You'd better get a room," Jeremiah told them, still looking at the man.

"We don't have money for a room," Tina had said defiantly looking at her boyfriend.

"Well, I guess you'd better make this a short visit, because it's a long drive back to LA."

"I know you don't expect us to drive back tonight," Tina had pleaded.

Jeremiah looked at Tina and wondered how he had been dumb enough to father a child with the woman. He loved his daughter but felt sorry that she had such a useless mother. "Tina, the only thing I expect from you is that you visit Erin once in a while. Other than that I have no interest or concern in how you manage your life." This was a harsh comment coming from Jeremiah, who, up to that point, had supported Tina in just about every way imaginable, including financially.

The thug had relaxed his aggressive stance and was waiting for Tina to make a decision, not that there were many options available. Tina asked him to wait outside for a minute while she talked to Jeremiah and he stepped outside Jeremiah's rented home. "Jeremiah, if you could just let us stay one night so I could spend some time with my baby?" Tina had pleaded. "Maybe he could sleep on the couch and I'll sleep in the room with Erin."

The small house Jeremiah was living in at the time had only two bedrooms. Since he and Tina no longer slept together, on her recent visits Jeremiah took the sofa and had given her his bed. He wondered if she had expected him to give up his bed for her and the thug and flinched at the sucker he had been for Tina since meeting her. "I don't trust this man in my house, Tina. I don't want him here and don't you ever bring this type of person here again."

"He just looks rough. He's an okay guy, really, Jeremiah. Do you think I'd bring him around my baby if he wasn't?"

Jeremiah wanted to say, "Hell yeah," but cleaned it up. "I don't know what you would do, Tina."

Jeremiah thought for a moment as he looked over at his daughter who had gone quiet since the discussion started and he suspected was well aware of the controversy. "Let me make a call."

Gilbert's son, Chewy, who worked part time for Jeremiah, had recently divorced and was trying to rent out a fully furnished apartment over his garage. Chewy agreed to allow Tina and her friend to sleep in the apartment for two nights as long as Jeremiah guaranteed any damages. Tina reluctantly agreed to sleep at Chewy's. Three days later and after her return to Los Angeles, she ended up in the hospital from a beating by the "okay guy" because she had failed to come up with monies she had promised him.

Immediately following that particular visit from Tina, Jeremiah visited an attorney and started proceedings for full and legal custody of Erin. Tina fought him hard until she landed a lucrative role on a daytime soap opera filming out of New York. In the past two years Tina has visited Erin in Seaside twice but mother and daughter have also seen each other a number of times during visits to Veronica's home in Los Angeles.

Erin seems content with her father and the periodic visits with her grandmother but has that longing for her mother as do all children. Fathers may do their best but they cannot replace mothers no more than mothers can take the place of fathers.

The only conflict Jeremiah and Tina have had since she became a full-time regular on her soap occurred when Tina learned Jeremiah was sleeping with Leslie. She called and literally cursed him out and did the same for Leslie. She also threatened to fight him for custody of Erin. Jeremiah never understood why Tina took his relationship with Leslie so hard. One thing she said during the verbal assault shed light on her rage, "It was her you wanted all along, you bastard." That wasn't true. Yes, he had initially been attracted to Leslie but he fell in love with Tina. Tina was the one who had chosen to leave him and Erin just as Christopher had left Leslie and her children. He and Leslie were rebound lovers and good friends and he thanked God for putting her in his path each and every day.

Now he has this guilt associated with his relationship with Leslie. They cannot remain in this sexual limbo. She wants more but Jeremiah has no more to give her and feels the need to make room for someone else in his somewhat complicated life.

Chapter 11

Monia rushes home after work to get ready for her dinner guests. She realizes that she has butterflies in her stomach and knows her nervousness is about asking Jeremiah to attend Dr. Singh's party with her. She is certain he will not turn her down unless he has a problem finding someone to watch Erin or has another commitment.

Monia hops in and out of the shower quickly, hoping she hit all the hot spots well enough. After dressing in some jeans and a tee shirt she stands before the mirror and considers leaving her hair loose but envisions Jeremiah pulling on her naps and decides to pull it back into a short nappy poof. This means she'll need to wash it in the morning to get those nappy ringlets back. She notices the upturned corners of her mouth and the sparkle in her eyes as she twists the sturdy hair band into place. She tries to wipe the smile off her face but it is perpetual when she thinks of Jeremiah.

Her guests arrive right on time and she and Erin get started rolling out the pizza dough while Jeremiah does his thing with a salad. The three play a quick game of Jenga while the pizzas, one with cheese and one with Italian sausage, mushrooms, onions, and jalapenos, bake.

As they wolf down their pizza and nibble at their salad, it occurs to Monia that she will need to ask Jeremiah about the party in front of Erin.

"What's the big favor you want to ask me?" Jeremiah asks as if he read her mind.

"Favor, who wants a favor?" Erin asks with her eyes stretched wide as she looks from her father to Monia. The child is enjoying herself. She likes this change of pace. Usually, she eats alone, with Jeremiah, or Delores and usually she does nearly all the talking but tonight the three are talking over the top of each other, laughing, and joking.

Monia is feeling giddy as she chit chats with Erin. She's not sure why she's having trouble asking Jeremiah something so simple. "I need a favor from your dad, but I don't know if he'll do it."

"He'll do it. For you he will do anything."

Monia blushes and has to laugh at the child's declaration. Jeremiah smiles and looks slightly embarrassed as he watches Monia.

"Ask him," Erin prods and throws her greasy fingered hands up in the air in exasperation. "Daddy, you'll do it; won't you?"

Now Jeremiah is grinning from ear to ear. I don't know, baby. This may be serious." He leans back in his seat and eyes Monia suspiciously. "I tell you what, Moanie, run it past Erin and see what she thinks." At this point the secret favor has turned into a better game than the Jenga.

Monia locks eyes with Jeremiah and knows she is treading on dangerous territory. This man is her friend but entirely to exciting to play with, no matter how long she has known him. She sits there looking at him and sees the challenge in his eyes. He wants her to play along. She leans over, cups her hand over the child's ear and whispers her question. Erin makes all sorts of faces as she listens intensely, causing Jeremiah's grin to grow even larger. Finally Monia pulls back and looks at the child for her reaction. Erin wipes her ear off and looks at Monia with a furrowed brow and says, "What?"

Jeremiah cracks up laughing as Monia looks as if she just worked a full day for no pay. "Forget about it." Monia gets up from the table and heads to the kitchen.

"Auntie Moanie, I didn't understand. I'm only six. Tell me again," Erin pleads as she follows Monia into the kitchen.

Monia stands at the kitchen counter with her hands on her hips and looks at the little munchkin trying to appease her and can't help but glow with laughter. Jeremiah walks in with his face still lit up and leans on the wall waiting for resolution. Monia looks at him as if to say, "Can you help me out here?"

He shrugs and says "I don't know what you want, Moanie."

Monia takes a deep breath and says. "What it is is." She stops when she sees the sad look that comes over Erin's face. Erin wants this to pass through her and what will it hurt. So Monia thinks about it for a moment and tries again. This time she simply says, "I want your daddy to go to a party with me. I need a date."

With a huge grin, Erin tells her, "Oh, he'll do that. My daddy goes on dates all the time."

Monia's jaw drops as she thinks about Jeremiah telling her "I date." Now she realizes she interpreted that to mean "I have sex partners." Monia looks at Jeremiah and asks, "All the time?"

"Yep. Don't you daddy? He was on one last night and the night before."

The two adults in the room are no longer smiling. "Hey, Pumpkin, why don't you go out front and watch some television while I help Moanie finish in here. That way she can tell me about this date."

"I want to know about the date too. You never let me go with you."

"Me and Moanie will tell you after we talk about it; I promise."

Monia finally persuades Erin to leave the room by bribing her with a red velvet cupcake.

"Now, what is this date you want me to take you on? What's the occasion?" Jeremiah asks. He knows Monia didn't like hearing that he was on a date each of the last two nights but he can't change that. He just wishes this moment wasn't so uncomfortable for him.

Monia really wants to tell him to forget about it. She is angry, no, mad fits better. She wants to throw him out of her house and if it wasn't for Erin she might, but what right does she have to be mad. She puts herself in check and pushes the jealousy and anger to she-knows-not-where. All she knows is that it is no longer visible to Jeremiah. She still feels it, but at least, Jeremiah doesn't see it. "You want some wine?" She asks with a fake little smile. "I think I'll have a glass."

"Yeah, I'll take a glass." Jeremiah's mouth feels unusually dry for some reason.

Monia hands him a bottle of chardonnay from the fridge and a cork screw and then collects two wine goblets from an above cabinet. "Dr. Navya, that's my boss, Dr Navya Singh, is having a small dinner party next Saturday. She says it's to welcome me aboard." Monia accepts her wine from Jeremiah who is still looking somber. "Anyway she insists we all bring someone. It doesn't have to be a date." Monia makes a quote gesture with her fingers when she says the word "date." "But she insists we all bring someone so I thought about you. Are you free? I understand if it's not convenient or if you have other plans." Monia looks down and begins moving an imaginary object around with her toe.

"I'll have to get a babysitter for my girl. I think my mother's got plans."

"Yeah, she and my mom are going to bingo."

Jeremiah smiles now. "So I guess I wasn't your first choice."

Now Monia's smile is real as she looks up at him. "I thought about you first but I did ask my mother. She turned me down cold. Bingo is her man and he comes first."

"So, what about Marcus?"

Monia leans forward and tries to peep into the living room but can't see Erin from her vantage point. Jeremiah moves from the counter he had been leaning on and goes to check on his child who has finished her cupcake and is stretched out on Monia's sofa with droopy eyes.

"She's on her way," he tells Monia when he returns.

"So, you want to think about it or."

"No. It's cool. I just need to make sure Delores is free. I've got a couple of dependable backups if she's not. My old boss's wife watches her for me and their granddaughter comes to the house and sits with Erin when I've run out of other options. Inez is a little young though and I think she's got a crush." Jeremiah catches himself and decides this may not be a good time to rehash stories of the eighteen-year-old who has a big crush on him.

"Like I used to have, huh?" Monia's smile grows and puts her guest a bit more at ease.

"No, hers is dangerous. Her brothers and father would disembowel me if I messed with that girl and I wouldn't blame them." He watches Monia for a moment. "You didn't answer my earlier question." He follows Monia out to her terrace and they both sit down at the patio table.

"What question was that?"

Jeremiah stares now and wonders if she is evading the question or actually forgot. "Where's your friend Marcus? Why aren't you asking him to take you to your boss's dinner party?"

"I never know when he can get away. He's often on call at the hospital. Besides, I think Marcus and I are pretty much finished. I know I was becoming more of a filler for him when he had nothing better going on and, if I'm completely honest, Marcus was just someone to date once in a while when I needed someone. I doubt he and I will spend much time together in the future." Monia purposely placed emphasis on the word "date," wanting Jeremiah to get the full meaning of her statement and he did.

"So it really was not that serious between you two?" Jeremiah wants to pursue this question for reasons he does not quite understand.

"No. I don't know why he hasn't gotten around to sending me a text message ending things but I'm hesitant about ending whatever it is we have myself. Maybe he figures he may want to date me again." Once again Monia childishly puts emphasis on the word "date."

"You got something you want to say to me, Monia?"

"Why would you think that?"

"Because of the way you keep using the word "date.""

Monia takes a drink from her glass but says nothing.

"Maybe I'm just overly sensitive. Tell me about this dinner party. What's the dress?"

"Evening casual. I'm just wearing a nice summer dress with some dressy open-toed sandals. So be comfortable. I don't think you'll need a jacket."

"Where does the doctor live and what time should I pick you up?

"No, I'll drive."

"The Volvo?"

"What's wrong with my car?"

"It's time for a new one. I've got a beautiful Benz on the lot that I bet you'd love. Isaiah just finished the body work last week. I've got three buyers looking at her. They all say the price is too high but we've put a lot of money and time in that baby and I'm not giving her away, but I'll let you have her for a little of nothing." Jeremiah stands up with his half empty wine glass. "The deal is I drive, okay."

"Or what?"

"This is not about ultimatums. You asked me to do you a favor. I agreed. Now I'm telling you, I prefer to drive. You think you can work with me on that one thing?"

"If it means that much to you to drive, I guess it's okay. I still owe you a thank you, don't I?"

"I haven't done anything yet."

"You agreed to go with me. That's something."

"You want to know the best way to thank me, Moanie?" Jeremiah asks her as they enter the kitchen.

Monia looks at him with skepticism. "How?"

"Stop avoiding me. I could really use another friend." Jeremiah places his glass on the counter and walks out of the kitchen without a look in her direction. He gathers up the forty pounds of dead weight that is his child as he prepares to leave.

Monia doesn't know how to respond. She has been avoiding him but not because she dislikes his company. "I don't mean to make it seem as if I don't want to see you, Jeremiah. I always want to see you and I'm glad you live close by."

He gives a chuckle that sounds more like a grunt. "So, call me sometimes," he tells her as he starts to leave. "We had fun. She really did." Jeremiah nods his head toward Erin, whose head is resting on his shoulder. "Save her another one of those cupcakes."

"I will. I had fun too. Thank you guys for coming. I'll put the cupcakes in the freezer." Monia reaches up and gives both Jeremiah and his daughter a kiss on the cheek.

"Bye Auntie Moanie, and thank you for the pizza," Erin stirs and waves her tiny little hand.

Jeremiah gives Monia a loaded look and walks out the door with his most precious bundle. Monia stands on the porch and watches him until he starts the car up. She waves goodbye before entering her home and securing the doors.

--

Monia wears a sleeveless blue and white dress that reaches just below mid thigh showing off what she considers her best feature, her beautifully toned legs. The dress is slightly flared, clings at the waist, and fits to a tee. She has only worn the dress once but it is one of those pieces of clothing that make her blush when she puts it on, not because it's so revealing but because she looks so damn good in it. It hits all the right places in just the right way. Other than a blue sapphire ring and a small clutch, her only other accessory is an evening shawl scarf to fight the chill from her arms on the cool Peninsula night. Her shoes are a pair of two inch blue and silver toned wedge sandals. Since she is wearing hardly any jewelry she spends a good amount of time perfecting her makeup and twisting her hair out to a nice mass. She checks the mirror no less than six times before her date arrives.

As good as Monia looks, she thinks Jeremiah may outshine her. He stands before her looking as if he has given no thought to his attire. *Damn he looks good.* Jeremiah has on a casual medium gray jacket, a blue gray tee, and dark blue pants just a shade darker than the blue in Monia's dress. As usual, he has his locks pulled back. Monia has only seen them free the night he towed her vehicle and the morning after she watched Erin for him. Before now, a man with locks never caught her attention, but she does like them on Jeremiah.

He is a little cool with Monia but does manage to remain engaged in their conversation during the ride to Navya's Pacific Grove home.

Navya lives in a cozy modern home, well situated with a full on view of the Pacific Ocean in all its glory. The waves can be heard slapping against the rocks as they come ashore. Navya and her wife, Gayla, welcome Monia and Jeremiah at the door and immediately make their guests feel at home with the warmth of their greetings. Navya makes all necessary introductions while Gayla rounds up drinks for the guest of honor and her date.

The party is much larger than Monia expected and consists of about thirty, including the hosts, Navya's staff and their guests, Dr. Sloan, his staff and several of their guests, Navya's brother, David, and two of her neighbors. Monia and Jeremiah are nearly the last to arrive.

The party is going so strong that Monia wonders if she was given a later arrival time than some of the other guests. Some of the party goers look and act as if they have been partying for a while. Navya asks Monia, "Now, which of you is the designated driver. Gayla is to keep watch and make sure the DD does not over indulge." She ends this announcement with a boisterous laugh and pats Jeremiah hard on the back. When she walks away Jeremiah smiles and tells Monia, "I like her."

Monia has noticed Shirley cutting her eyes in their direction and wonders why her coworker seems more out of sorts than usual. During the introductions earlier, Shirley had only nodded coldly and Monia noticed that Jeremiah looked at Shirley as if he knew her.

Navya's brother, David, has Jeremiah engaged in a friendly conversation so Monia decides to join Susan and Karen, one of the office medical assistants, and their guests, Susan's husband, Rick, and Karen's boyfriend, Josh. She eases up to the group and listens in on the conversation for a bit until Susan leans over and whispers in her ear. "Did you bring him down from the city with you? I don't thing we grow them like that down here." Susan is grinning and obviously a tiny bit high. Monia simply laughs in response before telling her coworker, "No, he lives here. We grew up together in Seaside. He owns an auto customizing shop on Del Monte."

This catches Rick's ear. "Not Del Rey Repair and Customizers?"

"That's the one."

"I plan on taking my old fifty seven Chevy in there for some work real soon. I hear they do a good job. Everyone I ask tells me that's the place to take her."

"I wish he'd take her to the dump," Susan jokes and causes Rick to look at her with a hurt expression before he and Josh head off to talk to Jeremiah.

Monia, Susan, and Karen migrate over to Pamela and Shirley and their guests. Pamela gives Monia a smile, nods her head toward Jeremiah and the group of men talking cars, and mouths something Monia cannot interpret. It's not long before Jeremiah walks up to join them. As he approaches, Shirley mumbles something unintelligible and moves away, sending a slight chill over the group. Later in the evening when Jeremiah goes to the bar to get Monia a refill, Shirley, who is at the bar waiting for a drink, walks away angrily and leaves her drink behind. Jeremiah calls out to her, "Shirley, you forget your drink," and picks the drink up to hand to her. Shirley looks back, gives him a hateful stare, and tells him, "I don't want it, not now." Many of the party goers watch as Shirley retreats to the terrace in a huff. Jeremiah looks slightly embarrassed and returns the drink to the bartender. This was, without question, a snub aimed at Jeremiah and it pisses Monia all the way off.

Navya and Gayla take turns going out on the terrace to talk with a sulking Shirley. They each ask her what's bothering her and she declares there is no problem and that she is fine. Gayla lights the outside fireplace because the night has gotten chilly, particularly with the strong breeze coming in from the ocean. When Gayla comes back inside, Monia goes out to talk to Shirley and joins her in the seats near the fire.

"Shirley, what's going on? I get the impression you know Jeremiah and seem to have a problem with him."

"Yeah, I know Jeremiah. I've lived in Seaside nearly my entire life, so I know pretty much everything that goes on there. I know all about him and all about his family. Where did you meet him?"

"You forget I'm from Seaside also. I grew up here on the Peninsula and have known Jeremiah my whole life, at least since I can remember. I don't just know about him and his family, I know them intimately."

"I would think that your mother would have told you to stay away from that young man." Shirley tells Monia with even more attitude than usual.

"Actually, my parents are great friends with him and his mother. Our families have been friendly for decades, so I doubt there's much you or anyone else could tell me about Jeremiah." Monia wonders how true this statement is. As close as she feels to her long-time friend, she really does not know much about his life over the past eighteen years.

Shirley sits up a little straighter and looks Monia dead in the face. "So you know about his father's disappearance and the circumstances around that situation?"

"Knew his father well and knew all about him."

"Well, I knew his father well also," Shirley says.

Monia knows Shirley's declaration has important meaning for the woman. Shirley was obviously more than a mere acquaintance of Trotter's. "My father considered himself Mr. Trotter's best friend. They were very close," Monia says.

"Who is your father?"

"Darnell Phillips."

"I never knew anybody with that name and I knew Trot very well."

"They may have moved in different circles but other than his wife and his sons, my father was the closest person in the world to Mr. Trotter and my father loves Jeremiah and is certain he had nothing to do with his father's disappearance. I think people who didn't really know Mr. Trotter that well should not accuse his son based on misinformation."

"Like I said, I did know Trotter well."

"Well, what's really bothering me, Shirley, is that you may indeed have known Mr. Trotter well but you don't know Jeremiah. You don't know anything about him except some small town gossip.

I would not mistreat one of your guests based on some hearsay. I respect you enough to know that if you bring a person into our environment that person is worthy of my respect. I would never show a guest of yours the disrespect you've shown toward Jeremiah this evening. I respect you too much to behave that way to a guest you bring to one of our gatherings."

"How I feel about him really has nothing to do with me and you," Shirley tells Monia, beginning to feel small and petty.

"Yes it does. If you mistreat my friends, if you mistreat my loved ones, then you're mistreating me."

Shirley takes on her totally surly look and continues her attempt to defend her behavior. "Well, I didn't mean any offense to you but everyone knows that boy is no good."

"No, everyone doesn't know that, Shirley, because I don't know that and I've known him my entire life. He's a good friend to me. He's like a brother to me."

"He doesn't act like any brother I've ever seen."

Monia ignores the innuendo. "Jeremiah did me a big favor in coming here with me tonight. I didn't have anyone else to bring and he didn't really want to come but came because I didn't want to show up alone. I think it's so unfair for you to treat him like this and it's unprofessional. I know we are not in a professional setting right now but this reflects badly on our office; I'm embarrassed. This is my first function with you guys and you treat my guest like this. We work together me and you and this does not look good to anyone."

Pamela and Jeremiah observe the intense interaction between Monia and Shirley out on Navya's terrace. They are pretty sure Monia is giving Shirley a piece of her mind and taking some of Shirley's ass in exchange. "I guess I'd better go out here and see if I can get Monia off of your friend," Jeremiah tells Pamela.

"No, you'd better let me go. This is probably about you."

"Damn."

"What is it? Did you used to date Shirley or something?"

"No, nothing like that." Jeremiah gives a nervous laugh. "I think it's something to do with my father."

"Your father, what could it have to do with your father?"

"It's a long story and not a very good one. Ask Monia to tell you about it when you two have some free time. I'm sure Shirley would be happy to tell you but I'd be a bit leery of Shirley's rendition of the story."

Pamela looks at him with a smile as she heads out to the terrace. She likes him; he seems like a good guy. *Lucky Monia.*

Shirley is happy to see Pamela joining them on the terrace. "Listen here, sistas, there are four black people here at Navya's very nice house party and we all know it's hard to tell what I am until I open my mouth. You know we have a reputation for not knowing how to behave in public. Do you two have to isolate yourselves out here and put on a show for the rest of us? Could you at least try and act like you're not out here arguing?"

"We're not arguing," Shirley says

"We're just having a discussion," Monia adds.

"Well it sure is a serious looking discussion and I think you may be making Navya and Gayla a little uneasy and we do want them to invite us back don't we. Frankly I love the abundance of free liquor and good food. So can we talk about this later?"

Shirley and Monia agree without comment and Pamela joins them in a seat near the fireplace. They sit and talk and actually start laughing and having a good time with the much lightened mood. Pamela's intervention is so effective that everyone except Jeremiah concludes there was no cause for concern over the animated conversation the two women were having on Navya's terrace. Soon the entire party has moved out onto the large outdoor space and the evening becomes more relaxed as Shirley's demeanor mellows considerably.

Chapter 12

What was going on between you and Shirley out on the terrace?" Jeremiah asks Monia on the drive home.

For a moment, Monia questions if she should be truthful but sees no benefit in telling Jeremiah the truth and upsetting him. "It was nothing, just something we needed to talk about."

"It looked like you guys were having a pretty serious argument."

Monia smiles at him. "Did it look that way? It was just work stuff. I can get sort of excited at times."

"It was about me, wasn't it?"

"What makes you think that?"

"First of all, because her attitude toward me changed after you guys had that little tiff."

"It wasn't a tiff, Jeremiah; we were just talking."

"Yeah, right. It was about that whole thing with my dad, wasn't it?"

"Well, she said she knew your dad." Jeremiah doesn't comment on this, so Monia continues. "Shirley would have been pretty young when your dad left."

"Yeah, a lot of women knew my dad – all ages, sizes, shapes, and colors. My dad knew lots of women."

"The apple doesn't fall far from the tree, huh."

"Oh, come on, Monia, you know I'm not like that."

"All I know is you date all the time." Monia copies Erin's voice.

"To Erin it seems like all the time because if I'm on a date, I'm not with her or taking her to do something she wants to do. She's got Delores there with her, or she's with my mom, or maybe with yours. If I've got work, I tell her I've got work. If I'm going out to dinner or drinks with the guys, I tell her I've got a date."

Monia simply repeats in a mocking way, "All the time."

"Does that bother you?"

"What?"

"The fact that you think I date all the time."

"No it doesn't bother me. I guess it kind of surprises me but it doesn't bother me. Why would it bother me?"

"Just asking."

Monia gets quiet for a while and Jeremiah knows she's got something on her mind. "What's bothering you Monia? Tell me," he asks.

"What about my dad? Was he like that too? Did he have a lot of women friends?"

Jeremiah can hear the shame in her voice for asking about her father's fidelity. "You know, one thing about my father was that he would talk to us a lot, me and Clifford. He'd tell us all kinds of stuff he thought we should know as men. He'd show us things my mother knew nothing about and take up places without discussing it with her. I guess these were things he felt a woman wouldn't appreciate or understand. I don't really know, but he wanted us to know about the world and what he had knowledge of but couldn't show us, he told us about. One of the most important things he told me was that you can have friends that do things you don't approve of and you don't have to do the things those friends do to maintain that friendship, not if you're really friends. My dad hung out. He hung out hard and tough all the time. He was always gambling and trying to get extra money."

"Are you saying Mr. Trotter was a hustler?"

Jeremiah glances over at Monia and wonders if she is as naive as she sounds. "Aren't we all hustlers in some way, shape, or form, Monia? So yes, my father was a hustler and loved it. He'd come home for dinner just about every night and often slept in the bed with my mother, at least on weeknights when he didn't have a gig, but that cat was a partier; he was out there. Your father was never like that. If Trot got into a situation, I know he'd call your dad and ask for help and, honestly, I think that happened a number of times. No, your dad didn't hang out like mine, no way. Your mother would not have tolerated it. That's what my mother was accustomed to with my father from the get go. When we were stationed in Hong Kong my dad was always out 'moving and grooving' as he used to say. Maybe that's where it all began. Darnell has always been a homebody but they were buds. How they ever got to be so tight, I'll never know but they were tight."

Jeremiah pauses for a moment and thinks about his father and Monia's father and the relationship between the two men. "You want to know the truth about it, Monia? Sometimes I wonder if when your dad forgave me he hadn't learned something about where my dad is.

I never questioned him about it but when I got back here after being away all those years, he had changed toward me. He didn't have those bad feelings anymore. I had been back to visit a few times and he was still cold as the poles but when I moved back he had changed. Sometimes I can't help but wonder if he learned something that changed him."

"I doubt dad knows anymore than you, Jeremiah. I think he realized that you wouldn't do anything to hurt your father."

"Maybe so. I guess I just wish someone knew something about my dad."

"I do too," Monia agrees.

The night is still early when they arrive at Monia's home so she invites Jeremiah in for coffee. They settle in on her terrace with their coffee and talk. "It's a lot warmer here than it was on Dr. Navya's terrace even with that nice fireplace."

"Yeah, you're right," Jeremiah agrees and goes quiet as he watches Monia.

After a few minutes, Monia tells him, "I told you about that staring at me. Why do you stare at me like that?"

"I told you why I stare at you. You're not ugly no more." He gives her that special smile.

"Well, stop it."

The friends sit and chat for a while longer until Monia starts to yawn. Jeremiah reluctantly rises from the table to leave. "I guess I'd better take my leave since I can't think of a reason to stay any longer."

"I would offer to put in a movie but I'd probably go to sleep on you before the first started."

"I'd probably do the same."

Monia walks him to the door but wishes she could keep him with her a little longer. She gives him a hug and he wraps her up in his arms. "Thanks for going with me, Jeremiah. It was a good time."

"It was a good time wasn't it?" Jeremiah agrees.

They continue standing there with Monia's head resting on Jeremiah's chest for a few moments longer, neither wanting to let go. Finally, Monia loosens her arms from around Jeremiah and reaches up to place a kiss on his cheek. Jeremiah turns his head and the kiss lands on his lips. Monia doesn't pull away. She stands there nearly on her tip toes and allows her lips to press against his.

Jeremiah doesn't move either. The only thing touching are their mouths, as they stand there kissing very gently. After several seconds, Monia parts her lips and Jeremiah slides his tongue into her mouth, still not touching her with his hands. It seems like minutes before Monia gets off her tip toes and backs away. "I guess I should apologize for that."

"No need to apologize." Jeremiah steps closer to Monia and kisses her again. This time he wraps her up in his arms.

"I guess you're not ready to go yet, are you?" Monia asks as they pull apart.

"Not if I don't have to. I want to stay awhile but I can't stay the night."

"Why not?" Monia looks Jeremiah in his eyes and makes him reconsider.

"I've got a child, Monia. I don't want Erin to wake up and I'm not there. If I had told her I'd be away all night that would be different."

Monia backs away and asks. "Are you sure you want to stay?"

Jeremiah's answer comes by way of his taking her hand and walking her into her bedroom. He flips on the light as he enters, leads her over to her bed, sits down, pulls her near, and buries his face in her bosom. Monia holds her arms around his head as he gently bites her breasts through her dress. She closes her eyes and enjoys the sensation of his teeth nibbling at her nipples, then feels his hands running up the backs of her thighs to her butt. Jeremiah's fingers creep under the fabric of her thin lace panties and he begins squeezing her closer to him.

Monia stands there looking down at that thick head of dreads and thinks "this is a mistake" but she knows it's too late to stop. She urgently wants to feel Jeremiah inside her. At his urging, she steps back slightly. "I want to touch you," he whispers as Monia feels his large hand creeping up the inside of her thighs. She relaxes her stance to make his way up her full thighs easier. When she feels his fingers touch her sweet spot and then glide inside her and back out she gasps for air and spreads her legs wider. Jeremiah knows just what places to touch and he's not shy. He stops for just a moment and pushes Monia back as he slides down to the floor and sits in front of her. He then has her lift one of her legs and place her foot on the bed, giving him full access to kiss her between her thighs. He bites and runs his tongue along the crotch of her saturated panties before he slips his tongue inside them. "Damn Jeremiah," is all Monia can whisper as he glides his tongue inside her and along her sweet crevice.

Finally Monia can't take it any longer and pulls back from him.

"Come on baby, let me finish then we'll worry about me."

"No." I hope you have a condom."

"You don't have any around?"

"Are you telling me, you don't have any condoms?" Monia sounds panicked.

"Calm down, baby. I got you."

Monia doesn't like the sound of his words. They sound like something he would say to anyone; they sound generic, but she isn't going to dwell on that slight right now. She wants him inside her. She watches him as he stands and goes into her bathroom. He's still fully dressed when he comes out and so is she, except for her shoes.

Jeremiah takes his wallet out of his pocket and pulls out a condom and throws it on the nightstand. "Happy now?" he asks.

Monia looks at him defiantly and asks, "Is that all you have?" as she sits on the side of the bed.

Jeremiah smiles and walks closer to her. Monia very gently runs her fingers over his groin causing him to groan and immediately reach out to remove her dress.

"No," she tells him for the second time and reaches for his belt buckle and starts undoing his pants. Jeremiah watches her, understanding that she likes to have some control. She reaches inside his boxers, frees his hard body and begins to massage the head, then the shaft, looking up at Jeremiah as she touches him.

"Can I at least take off my shoes?" Jeremiah asks.

Monia rises on the bed and moves him around into a sitting position. She kneels in front of him and removes his shoes, socks, shirt, pants, and then his underwear. Then she settles into a kneeling position between his legs and kisses him on the mouth allowing her tongue to talk to his. After a few moments of this, Jeremiah tries to pull her even closer. Monia pulls away and starts kissing him on his neck and chest. Then she kisses his stomach and his navel, running her tongue in and out. By this time he is standing straight up and pointing at his stomach. Monia lowers her mouth and licks the tip of him very gently and then circles her tongue around the head before taking him in her mouth and squeezing him with her lips and mouth. Jeremiah starts to moan, "You're going to make me come, Monia." After another minute, he tells Monia. "Damn, Monia, I don't want to come like this!" He finally pushes her away, snatches her up from her kneeling position, and pulls her dress up over her head. "Damn, girl you're beautiful."

Monia tells herself this is just bullshit but she likes it anyway. Jeremiah pulls her down on the bed and kisses her again. They lie there and kiss until he can't take Monia's hands touching him in all those special places a moment longer. He quickly puts on his protection and pushes her onto her back.

"Not too fast Jeremiah. I want to feel all of you," Monia whispers.

"I'll try to take my time," Jeremiah tells her but thinks it may be out of his control at this point unless they stop, take a cold shower and start over again. It is as if his body has lost all patience. It's jumping all over the place to get inside Monia. He slides into her body and tries to lie still for just a moment to let the pleasure subside a little. Monia doesn't help him maintain control at all. She immediately squeezes her legs around his hips and pulls him in deep. Jeremiah has to let go and within a few minutes he and Monia are drowning each other out with their groans. "Wait for me, baby. Damn, please, oh goodness, oh goodness!" Monia yells and Jeremiah feels the freedom to go all the way. His complete release comes only a few moments behind Monia's and he collapses with his own "damn!"

Jeremiah reluctantly leaves Monia well after two in the morning. After he's gone, Monia lies in her bed and thinks about what a big mistake their lust fest most likely was. She passes out before she drowns in her regret.

--

Monia bounds out of bed on Sunday morning as she remembers a promise to her mother that she will attend Sunday morning worship service. She gets herself cleaned up and out of the house just in time to catch the beginning of the service. She prays service does not go on too long because Reverend Carlton, a dynamic speaker, loves to hear his sermons far more than his congregation enjoys listening to them. The various announcements are worse. Five people will announce the same event repeatedly. Monia tells herself she would be much more faithful in her attendance if the people didn't like to hear themselves talk so much. In her opinion the services are just entirely too long. People have lives and things to do and places to go and need some rest before they start back trying to make a living on Monday.

Clarissa is seated in her usual spot and her face lights up when she sees Monia take the seat next to her. The service is good, long but good. Monia feels a little guilt when the pastor mentions fornicators. She hopes its not written all over her face that she committed a sin the night before – boy was it some good sin. Monia has to wipe the smile off her face when she thinks about Jeremiah and she prays God will not judge her harshly for her fornicating ways.

After service, Monia is surprised to see Erin running up to her with her grandmother not far behind. Erin is waving and yelling, "Hi, Auntie Moanie. Hi, Auntie Clara."

The ladies speak, give each other hugs, and go into their ritual discussion of how well pastor preached and how the choir did sing. Erin interrupts this dialogue with "Auntie Moanie, did you and my daddy have fun on your date last night?"

Both Clarissa and Sharon stop talking and look at each other with bugged eyes before turning their eyes on Monia who remains cool and collected as she hesitates and responds to the child. "Yes, baby, we had a good time. We went to my boss's house for dinner." Monia smiles at the child who is not finished with the subject.

"I tried to stay awake and wait for my daddy because Delores said he'd be home pretty early but I couldn't stay up. It was late when he came in. I woke up and looked at my clock and it said one thirty and I went to my daddy's room and he still was not home yet."

"I'm sorry he got home so late, baby."

"I'm glad you guys had fun, Auntie Moanie. I'm glad he was with you and not somebody else."

"Me too, Erin." Monia tries to hold a light smile and ignore Clarissa and Sharon's inquisitive stares.

After leaving the church, Monia and her mother take off for Sunday brunch at The Breakfast Club, one of Clarissa's favorite local eateries. They talk casually until they get seated and then Clarissa hones in on what she really wants to discuss. "So, you and Jeremiah went to the party together last night?"

"Well yeah, yeah. That was a good suggestion. You suggested I take Jeremiah and he was a good date." Monia keeps her eyes on the menu and answers indifferently.

"Must have been some house party if Jeremiah wasn't at home by one thirty in the morning." Clarissa watches Monia for her reaction but Monia stays cool.

"Dr. Navya has a beautiful home, Mom. You would love it."

"Yeah, must have been some party." Clarissa now gives her daughter a strange smile and lets the subject drop.

As the ladies sit and enjoy their nice leisurely brunch, Monia gets a call from Jeremiah. She starts to ignore it but the compulsion to answer and speak to him wins her over.

"Hey, I'm going to throw some chicken on the grill and make a salad. Why don't you come over and join us this evening for dinner around six?"

"I'm out with my mom right now and we're having brunch. I don't know if I'll really be hungry so soon." Jeremiah doesn't respond and Monia can tell he's disappointed. "You say about six or so?"

"Yeah, if you don't want to eat, you don't have to eat. There's no pressure to eat. I'd just like to see you."

Monia feels all queasy at his words and wishes she was alone and her mother wasn't watching her so hard so she could beam out her feelings. "Okay, I'll see you around six thirty. Will that work?"

"Hey, that's fine."

"I can't stay long because you know I've got work tomorrow and I've had a really busy weekend."

"Yeah, I know."

Monia blushes and says, "Okay, I'll see you then."

"Was that Jeremiah?" Clarissa asks before Monia has the phone back in her bag.

"Yeah, he's barbecuing and invited me over."

"Barbecuing, huh. Weren't you guys together last night?"

"Yeah, I told you he went to Navya's with me. It was nice, Mom. She's got a beautiful home. I don't know if I'd want to be that close to the ocean but if I could afford it, maybe."

Clarissa looks thoughtful for a few moments and then asks about Dr. Singh. "Didn't you tell me she has a wife?"

"Yes, Gayla. This was my first time meeting Gayla. They are really nice people. Gayla works in real estate and apparently makes a lot of money. Dr. Navya says even with what she makes she would not have been able to afford that nice home but Gayla makes so much, it's not a problem."

"Yeah a lot of people dabble in real estate. It is one thing that eventually always goes up. So I guess if that's how you make your living you're pretty set if you know what you're doing. You know I've got a couple of properties around here and your father has a number of properties."

"So, you and dad have separate properties?"

"Yes dear, we have separate properties. We're not a couple anymore, Monia."

"I know that, Mom. You don't always need to remind me of that."

"I don't understand why you would think we have properties together." Clarissa seems agitated now.

"Well you're not divorced yet, actually."

"That's true; we're not, yet. And speaking of your father, he wanted me to tell you he will be out of town next week. He says he tried to get you on the phone last night but you weren't answering. I believe he left you a message. He's going to New York for some dental conference."

"So when did you see dad?"

"Monia, I see your dad more now that you are back in town than I did when we were living together. He always has something he needs to talk to me about or some papers he needs me to sign or something he needs to check on at the house. It's always something with him. I get tired of looking at him."

"I didn't know you guys were seeing each other that much," Monia tells her mother with a questioning look.

"Seems like since you've been back in town, he comes around more often."

"I don't see him that much!" Monia declares in her defense.

"I understand that Monia but I think your father feels like when he touches base with me, he's touching base with you."

"Okay."

"You've managed to change the subject on me. I was asking you about you going to dinner at Jeremiah's. What's going on between you two?"

"What's going on between us is the same thing that's been going on for the last thirty years, Mom."

"Unh, okay. I think Jeremiah really kind of likes you and I think you like him too." Clarissa tells her daughter bluntly.

"I do. I love Jeremiah. I don't keep that a secret from anybody. That's my Boon Coon. Yep, that's my Boon Coon as dad and Mr. Trotter used to say."

"The term is Ace Boon Coon," Clarissa sarcastically corrects her daughter.

"I know, Mom. I'm just modernizing the term a bit.

"So where is your friend Marcus, anyway? I haven't heard you mention his name in weeks. You guys still seeing each other?" Clarissa tries to speak as casually as possible. She attempts to hide the fact that she wants her daughter to be finished with the wishy washy Marcus.

"It's harder to see him now that I live so far away."

"Only a two-hour car ride – I wouldn't say that's so far away."

"Mom you know Marcus and I were never really that into each other. We just hung out sometimes. It's not like he's my boyfriend or anything."

"Humph." Clarissa grunts before asking her daughter a question that has bothered the piss out of her for years. "Monia, what is it about black men that you don't care for?"

Monia looks downright shocked as she scrunches up her face in disbelief. "I never said I didn't like black men, Mom. The truth is black men don't find me attractive. They pretty much ignore me or want to become my buddy. I have lots of black male acquaintances but most of them seem to be interested in the women that look like they just stepped off the stage dancing behind Beyonce or they want white women. I mean I've had a couple of homeboys hit on me but I think I'm not down enough for them and I'm not thin or fair-skinned enough for the professional black males. For some reason I have always found it easier to date white guys."

Now Clarissa looks shocked. "Maybe you're sending out the wrong signals. Have you ever tried to hit on a man, Monia?"

"Mom, why are you asking me all this?"

"Here you are, a beautiful young African American woman with a good job and good sense, beautiful personality, and a great body, telling me that black men don't like you but white men do. I think you just don't know how to show the brothers they have a chance."

"No, Mom. Every time I go out with my friends up in the city, the black men go after my friends, never me."

"Are you talking about your white friends?"

"White, Hispanic, Asian, everybody but me. I've just learned to accept it."

"What kind of places do you go to, Monia? Oh, I get it. You're talking about the clubs that have only a few black patrons, like you, who mostly hang out with people of other groups."

"Sometimes, but even when we go to places that are mostly black, the brothers still fall all over themselves for the white women. That's even more embarrassing than going to clubs that are predominately white and being ignored by the brothers. Black men just don't like me. Like I said, I've gotten used to it. It's so bad that Ja'Niece got to the place that she would not go out with me if any of my girlfriends from the city were planning on going. She said it was too hard to compete for the brother's attention when my girlfriends from the city were with us.

"So Ja'Niece has the same problem with dating black men?"

"Not hardly. Ja'Niece always has a man. She may be just starting up with him or on the verge of breaking up with him but she always has one and she only dates black men."

"Maybe you need to have her give you some pointers."

"That's okay. I've seen her technique for picking up dudes and I'm not that desperate. She was hitting on Jeremiah."

"I think Jeremiah is a bit out of Ja'Niece's league.

"That's not nice, Mom. What do you mean out of her league? He seemed pretty receptive to me."

"Oh, he's a man so he will flirt and lead her on. Men love for women to flirt with them. It lets them know women think they are attractive. Women who are in relationships tend to be more guarded unless they're looking for something on the side. Men can be faithful as hell but still appreciate a woman making a play for them. It doesn't mean anything unless they're ready to step out also, like your father."

Monia looks as if her mother slapped her across the face and Clarissa feels ashamed. "I'm sorry for saying that, baby. I shouldn't talk bad about your dad to you. I'll try to do better."

"I understand, Mom. It must still sting a lot, this thing with dad?" Monia asks.

"Your being here makes everything better, Monia." Clarissa reaches across the table and squeezes her daughter's hand and gives her a reassuring smile. "Now back to one of my favorite subjects. You say I'm being mean by saying Jeremiah is out of Ja'Niece's league but I'm just telling you what I see. Ja'Niece is lovely to look at and I like her but she is superficial as hell. Jeremiah fell in that trap one time with Erin's mother but I don't think that will happen to him again. He has his father's brilliant mind but is much wiser than Trotter will ever be. Jeremiah likes people who have some balance to them. He enjoys a good time but he's a settled family man. Look at how he protects and takes care of his daughter, his business, even his home. Now that woman down in Pismo Beach, to my understanding, is special. That's the one you have to look out for."

"I'm not looking out for anybody," Monia asserts defensively.

"Ooh, sensitive aren't we. I meant she's the one he'll settle down with," Clarissa gives a subtle little smile, "unless he falls for someone else, hard."

"I'll tell Jeremiah you've chosen a wife for him when I see him later," Monia tells her mother in a huff.

"You do that. So is Sharon going over to Jeremiah's? Maybe I can get an invitation too."

"I don't know, Mom. You'd have to call Jeremiah and ask him." Monia sings out these last words in an attempt at covering up her irritation at all the opinions, curiosity, and feistiness her mother is exhibiting.

"Well he didn't invite me so..."

"I'm sure he won't mind, Mom. You want to come?"

"No, girl, I gotta try and watch this waistline. This big meal I'm eating right now is the only big meal I can have today. You might want to be a little bit careful too because it looks like you're easing up a size." Clarissa is now looking at Monia over the top of her lowered glasses with her lips pursed together.

"I am not. I've actually lost a couple of pounds since I got here."

"Um huh."

Chapter 13

When Monia leaves her mother she does a gut check. How in the world could she and Jeremiah make this misstep? Their parents are much too close for this sexual relationship they dallied with the night before. But even more of a problem is the whole "I date" thing. Jeremiah dates all the time according to Erin. Monia knows she will not be happy when he is out with one of his lady friends or he's gone down to Pismo Beach for a visit. *Lord have mercy! What went through my mind when I went to bed with that boy? What the hell came over me? You'd think I had been drinking, but I only had two glasses of wine early in the evening. It wasn't the wine.* Jeremiah is a fine man but Monia knows there is no way for the two of them to have an uncomplicated sexual relationship with each other. She mumbles, "There is no way in hell this will come out anyway but bad."

All the self condemnation does not stop Monia from showing up at Jeremiah's home later that evening. She finds another couple, George and Melissa, and their two children also present for dinner and thinks this is quite a family affair. The children are out back playing in the yard and the adults sit around the television set. Jeremiah seems to be enjoying himself more than usual.

Later, when Monia is out tending to the meat on the grill, Jeremiah walks up behind her and puts his arms around her waist. She jumps at the contact and moves to the side. "Hey, what are you jumping for? Did I scare you?"

"Yeah, yeah you did." Monia moves back to her position in front of the grill and Jeremiah puts his arms around her again but this time he adds a kiss to the side of her neck. Monia looks up and sees Erin looking toward them. "Don't do that Jeremiah; Erin is watching."

"So what if Erin sees me kissing you. Do you think she'll be traumatized or something?"

Jeremiah continues hugging Monia from behind. She looks up at him by tilting her head to the side. "You and I need to talk."

"About what?"

"We'll talk later, when we're alone."

"Am I in trouble?"

Monia has to laugh. "No," is all she says.

They relax and enjoy the remainder of the evening together with Jeremiah's friends. It's such a nice evening and has been such a good weekend that Monia decides to put her talk with Jeremiah off to another place and time.

--

"I tried to get Shirley to tell me why she acted the way she did with your friend," Pamela tells Monia the next evening after they finish up with their end of day review of cases. "I couldn't get a thing out of her. Did she ever tell you anything definitive?"

"Just that she knew Jeremiah's father. You know about his disappearance, right?"

"Disappearance? No, Jeremiah said her behavior had something to do with his father but he didn't elaborate. He did say Shirley's version may put him in a bad light. What happened to his dad?"

Monia tells Pamela the quick down and dirty about Trotter Sumuels' disappearance and the suspicions surrounding Jeremiah. By the end of the tale, Pamela's mouth hangs open. "All this happened in Seaside?"

"Yes dear, in Seaside," Monia confirms.

"Well, you obviously don't believe Jeremiah had anything to do with his father's disappearance."

"No, I don't, but you know I was pretty young when Mr. Trotter vanished. I would never believe Jeremiah capable of hurting his father. My parents and his mother don't believe Jeremiah was the cause of his father's disappearance either."

"You said he has a brother."

"Now his brother is a different story. He hates Jeremiah and won't even visit their mother's home when Jeremiah is present."

"Wow! It's horrible when things like that happen in families. How long did you say the father has been missing?"

"Well, I was about twelve when he disappeared so it must be about twenty years now."

"And there has been no sign of him at all?"

"Not that I'm aware of."

"That's just awful. I wonder why Shirley feels so involved."

"Mr. Trotter was a popular man. He had lots of friends and moved in different circles. He was a gifted musician and donated a lot of time to local charities. He opened for acts once or twice at both the Blues Festival and the Jazz Festival. He was a skilled mechanic and was known to repair cars free of charge for friends who were short of cash." Monia looks around and lowers her voice slightly. "Also, old boy was quite the ladies man and liked to party; maybe that's how Shirley knows him."

"Sounds like he was something. How's the wife doing after all this drama? Sounds like she may have had her own reasons to get rid of that dude."

"According to my mother, Miss Sharon knew her husband and loved him. He had always been a partier and she accepted it for years. But she had gotten tired of him staying out. That's what caused the fight that night, him hanging out more than usual."

--

First thing the following morning, Monia approaches Shirley on a personal matter. "Shirley, I was wondering if you and I could get together for lunch this week; my treat."

Shirley looks at Monia with a straight face that, thankfully, seems less intimidating than usual. "Any particular reason?" she asks Monia straight and to the point.

"I was hoping we could discuss my friend Jeremiah."

"There's really nothing to discuss. You were right; I was being disrespectful toward you as a coworker, but that's not going to change my mind about that boy."

"He's a man now Shirley; he's nearly your age."

Monia waits but Shirley keeps her head down as she writes in a backup logbook and gives no reply. Monia pushes her lightly on the shoulder. "Come on; I said it's my treat. What can it hurt? We need to get to know each other better anyway. After all we're home girls. I need somebody to catch me up on the place other than my sixty year old parents. How bout it?"

Surly Shirley looks up with an open expression; the veil she usually carries over her eyes is raised. "Tomorrow is a slow day. We can go then if you'd like?"

The next afternoon's lunch between the two women proves to be one of the most informative interactions on local affairs Monia has ever had the privilege to enjoy. Shirley knows everyone in Seaside and knows all the business and has no qualms with dishing out the dirt on everyone from the local pastor who got in trouble for misappropriation of government funds to the school teacher who was sleeping with one of her high school students. If Monia can't think of a person's name but has a description, Shirley fills in the gaps. She tells Monia how many times people have been married and to whom, how many children their fellow citizens have and what each child is doing, and how people are related to each other. And of course, she can tell Monia who slept with whose "old man."

The amazing thing about Shirley's information sharing is that there seems to be no malice intended. She just states the facts as she knows or heard them. Not once does she lean in close to Monia over the table or bother to whisper. She is not at all secretive about the gossip or conspiratorial. Her technique is magnificent. Monia doesn't even feel guilty for listening to all the intimate details of other people's lives.

Eventually, Shirley gets around to Monia. "So are your mother and father getting back together?"

Monia is caught off guard by the question and realizes that she does not know the answer. When she moved to Seaside, she was certain that her parents were finished with their relationship but now she finds hope in the fact that they've become friendly. "You know Shirley, I really don't know. Of course I wish they would but I haven't seen any clear indication that reconciliation is coming. I didn't know you knew my parents."

"When you first told me your father's name was Darnell Phillips, I didn't realize Dr. Phillips' first name was Darnell. Your mother insures my cars and has been trying to get me to switch my house over to her insurance for years." Shirley smiles, and then continues. "Dr. Phillips has been my mother's dentist for a long time, but I never knew him and Trot were such good friends. I asked my mother about it and she said they were like brothers and that your father really took it hard when Trot disappeared. I don't know how I missed that." Shirley lowers her eyes as she has come to a subject that causes her discomfort.

"I'm still curious about why you dislike Jeremiah so much. Why do you believe so strongly that he had something to do with his father's disappearance?"

"There was a time that everyone seemed to think that. He was in some trouble around the time his father died and I know he and his father argued a lot about school and drugs and such." Shirley keeps her eyes down; this subject is personal and Monia knows it.

"I know I can't say anything that will change your mind about Jeremiah. I love him dearly. He has had a hard time with all the accusations and speculation about his role in Trotter's disappearance. I will say this though, Shirley, and please think about it. Jeremiah was a dysfunctional seventeen-year-old when Mr. Trotter left. I don't say "died" because my parents have always honored Sharon Sumuels' belief that he is still alive."

"Everybody knows that woman was saying that because she was protecting her son. She would have said anything to protect that boy. That's what mothers do, protect their children. She was mad at Trotter and probably wanted him dead. I wouldn't be surprised if they planned it together."

So this is what Jeremiah has been dealing with all these years. "I guess that negates what I was about to say. I was about to say, I don't think a seventeen-year-old kid would have the where-with-all to kill his father and dispose of the body in a way that it could never be found. But I guess if his mother helped him it would be easier." Monia watches Shirley who nods her head in agreement. Monia thinks this may not have been the best conversation to have over lunch. She feels a bout of nausea coming on.

"And where did your friend get all that money to buy that business? Trotter had money stashed away. He told me." Shirley stops as if she has said too much.

"Shirley, what exactly was your relationship with Mr. Trotter?"

Shirley looks up and the veiled expression is once again lifted allowing the depth of her sadness over Trotter Sumuels to show. "Trotter used to come to my mother's house and play poker with some of the other men and women who liked to gamble. I was in love with him? He was my first. I was eighteen years old when we started up together. We kept it secret for a long time because of my mother and his wife. He got that apartment over on Olympia, the one where Jeremiah spent the night, so we could spend time together. I was pregnant when he died." Shirley sniffles back a tear, picks up a napkin and wipes her eyes and then her nose.

"Where's the child?" Monia asks with bugged eyes and an open mouth.

"I had an abortion. My mother had no idea I was pregnant – still doesn't know about the baby after all these years."

"Did Trotter know you were pregnant?"

"I didn't even know until he had been dead two months. I was dumber than a rock"

"I'm so sorry, Shirley. This has been hard for you, hasn't it?"

Shirley nods. "Trotter treated me like a queen. He told me to go to school and insisted I take good care of myself. He never told me he loved me but he treated me like he did. I got married two years later but no man can live up to Trot. He ruined me for other men. I compare everybody to him. I've been married and divorced three times. I'm tired of trying; I don't even want another man. I've had the best the world has to offer."

An old assed married man with two nearly grown sons, give me a break. Mr. Trotter should have been horse whipped for messing with that young girl. Monia feels ashamed that the man was so close to her father and was the father of her friend. She vows to never mention this history to anyone, not even her mother. Monia wonders if there were other women mourning the disappearance of Trotter Sumuels, could he possibly have other children who Sharon, Jeremiah, and Clifford know nothing of. One thing is for certain; Trotter was a rolling stone. What had he rolled into that got him killed or where had he rolled off to and left so many lives in flux?

--

"Hi, Hon, I've been missing you. How's the new job coming along?

Damn! I need to get in the habit of checking my phone before answering. He's got a lot of damn nerve calling me like we're still seeing each other." Hey, Marcus. The job's good. Learning lots of new stuff."

"I thought I would come down this weekend. It's been a long time and I really want to see you. Miss me?"

He has got to be kidding. Do you really want to burn this bridge, Monia? Marcus has been pretty reliable for an occasional boyfriend. Monia ignores Marcus's question, mainly because she hasn't missed him at all. "I'm tied up for the next few weeks, Marcus. The doc's got me working extra hours and I'm leaving town on Saturday. How's everything going with you?"

"Bout the same here, Hon. I hate to hear you won't be available this weekend. Maybe I'll just come on down anyway. I've got a few items I can work on while you're away. I just need to get away from the city for a few days. I'll leave your place nice and clean when I leave. You won't even know I was there."

Oh this asshole is looking for a free vacation spot. He can be so damn cheap. I had almost forgotten that about him. "Maybe some other time, Marcus. Maybe we can plan to get together in a month or so, after I'm more settled in my job."

"I thought you said the job was going good. If your time is that wrapped up, you must be working pretty hard." Marcus sounds upset. He's not accustomed to Monia putting him off. She has been his reliable partner for years. His tone mellows a bit and he continues. "I talked to Trace the other day and he said your replacement can't hold a candle to you. Said he'd give anything to get you back." Trace is Dr. Tracy Horton, Monia's old boss.

"I'm sure Cheryl Lynn will be fine once she learns the ropes. Tracy is just spoiled and impatient. I hope he's not giving her too hard of a time."

"I'm the one having a hard time, Monia. You sure we can't get together this weekend."

"I've got to go, Marcus. Maybe I'll call you in a couple of weeks." She doesn't wait for a response. Marcus had not heard her voice in weeks and has the audacity to call her for sex. Monia has accepted that her relationship with the man was iffy at best. She realizes that she doesn't even like him much. She wonders why she keeps hanging on and leaving the door open as if they may get back together at some point in time like they did when she lived in the city. Then it was nothing for them to go a month and not see each other or talk, sometimes longer. Their relationship seems so warped to her now. Monia is about ninety percent certain she is finished with Marcus but is afraid to shut the door completely and she does not understand why.

--

The doorbell brings Monia up out of a stupor. She has fallen asleep with more recommended reading from Dr. Singh. The woman is a bottomless pit of knowledge and wants to share every drop of it with Monia. Monia drags to the door to find Jeremiah standing outside. "Damn!" She murmurs before opening the door. She still has on her work clothes and looks a mess. Hopefully, there's no drool dried on the side of her mouth. She opens the door and stands in the doorway without inviting Jeremiah in. He ignores her unfriendly welcome and walks past her into her home. Monia doesn't bother to resist and says sarcastically, "Come on in, Jeremiah. Have a seat. Can I offer you something to drink?"

Jeremiah stands in the middle of her living room and looks around before he settles his eyes on her. "I'm good. I've been calling you for two days now. Why haven't you returned my calls?"

"I've just been so busy. Was it something important you wanted?" Without waiting for an answer Monia heads off to her bathroom to look in the mirror and wash her face. She finds Jeremiah still standing in the middle of the floor when she returns.

"What's going on, Monia. You told me the other day that you and I need to talk. That was three days ago. What do we need to talk about?"

Monia wrings her hands and says, "I wanted to talk to you about our date the other night. That's not something we can keep doing. We had a date and that's that."

Jeremiah looks at her as if she is talking gibberish and says, "What do you mean we had a date? Are you saying you don't want to see me anymore?"

"That's exactly what I'm saying. We're not dating anymore."

"What's the problem, Monia?"

"Listen, Jeremiah, the entire time I dated Marcus."

Jeremiah cuts her off. "What's this about Marcus? I don't want to talk about him."

"Would you let me finish?"

"You said you're not seeing him anymore so what's the point of talking about him."

"I never said I wasn't seeing him anymore."

"Oh, so you are still seeing him?"

"I never said if I was or wasn't seeing Marcus; I'm trying to make a point here."

Jeremiah finally takes a seat and gets comfortable with his knees apart, arms resting on his knees, fingers intertwined, and leaning forward. "Go ahead, make your point."

"The entire time I dated Marcus, I never happened to run into him. San Francisco is not a very large city but it is pretty big compared to this place. I never had to see him unless we planned to see each other. You live two blocks away from me. I cannot get to my job without passing by your house unless I go out of my way. So if you have overnight guests I will know it.

I don't have overnight guests," Jeremiah rebuts Monia's assertion.

"Well if you were to decide to have guests, I would see their car in front of your house or in your driveway. That's not going to work for me."

"Are you saying you'd be jealous?"

Monia takes one step back, puts her hand on her hip, and looks at Jeremiah with a tilted head. "What was the whole 'I don't want to talk about Marcus' thing? That wasn't jealousy?"

"No, that has nothing to do with jealousy. I just see no point in talking about him if you're not seeing him anymore."

"I never said I wasn't seeing him anymore. Look, you and I did the nasty one time."

"Don't call it that, Monia. That's so crass."

"Okay then, we dated one time."

"Are you saying that you don't want to go to the movies with me or dinner with me or anything like that? I thought you and I were such good friends"

"We are friends, Jeremiah. We're family. That's the whole point. We see each other all the time. We spend so much time together when we don't even expect to. Do you expect me to be all happy and friendly when I know you've been with one of the women you date? My mother loves you dearly but she doesn't love you as much as she loves me. Do you know how both my mother and yours would look at me if they had any idea I was a member of your dating pool?"

Jeremiah leans back with a deep sigh. Monia has him in a spot he's not ready to deal with.

"You got your woman down there in Pismo Beach. Everyone knows about her. Word is she is the main woman. Your mother and my parents talk about what a beauty she is, 'so classy'." Monia mimics Clarissa and is not trying to hide her jealousy.

Jeremiah stands and begins to pace the room to relieve his frustration. After a moment of pacing, he sits on a bar stool. "Listen Monia, you act like it's a bad thing because I haven't committed to one relationship. So what if I date a couple of different women? Isn't that what people do until they find the right person to settle in with?

I've got a child and I'm not willing to start a serious relationship with any woman until I know she's the right person for me and will be good for Erin."

"Answer me this, Jeremiah. How many women are you currently dating?"

Jeremiah starts to ask, "Including you?" but catches himself. "That's none of your concern, Monia."

"Well right now, I'm dating me and me alone. I can see how this open dating thing works for you but I cannot see how it works for me. I'm not that desperate for sex that I need to wait my turn in line."

"Oh, and that isn't what you've been doing over the past how many years with your doctor boyfriend up in Frisco?" Jeremiah yells at Monia.

Monia doesn't respond. Both she and Jeremiah stand and glare at each other after that outburst.

"We need to figure out a way to get back to where we were. We're family. I can't be a part of this pool of women you got going and that's all there is to it."

Jeremiah gets up to leave and tells her, "Damn, you must really think I got it going on, girl," as he walks out the door.

Chapter 14

As much as Monia swears that she wants to be Jeremiah's friend, she finds herself avoiding him more than ever. The problem is her parents and Sharon Sumuels keep planning events that bring the two warring friends together. First there was the birthday party that Clarissa had to give Sharon. This event brought out people Monia had no idea still lived in the area. A few out of town friends also came in from San Jose, Sacramento, LA, and even as far as Vegas. Monia's extra bedroom was confiscated by her mother as well as her time on the Saturday slated for the party. By the time that Saturday rolled in, Monia had a list of tasks to fulfill for her mother. The fact that the party was to be a surprise only made the execution more difficult.

As far as Monia knew, Jeremiah's only task was to get his mother to Clarissa's house on time and keep the secret. Sharon knew she was going to Clarissa's for dinner but had no idea there would be a full-fledged party going on in her honor. "Why can't Jeremiah help with some of this stuff? The party is for his mother. What's he doing today?" Monia had asked her mother, still mad at Jeremiah because she had sex with him and afterwards decided she didn't want to be a member of his quasi harem.

"Jeremiah is working today and you know he's got Erin to get ready and everything. He's got enough responsibility already. Now, are you going to be here by four so we can get everything set up?"

"I'll try but you've got me doing all this running around to pickup stuff and then I've got the Jemison's at my place. I thought it was just going to be Miss Rilda and her husband. You forgot to mention they were bringing their daughter and granddaughter."

"It'll give you and Shannon a chance to catch up. Weren't you and she in school together?"

"She was a year ahead of me. We were never friendly or anything. I hate having all these strangers in my house."

"Monia, you're being difficult now. The Jemisons are not strangers."

"Okay, Mom. I'm going to work with you this time but do not plan for anyone to stay with me ever again and I mean it."

Monia managed to get through all her tasks and show her guests some gracious hospitality. She actually enjoyed talking with the Jemison's daughter, Shannon, and thought Shannon's daughter, who had just turned eight, was fun. Monia wished she could call Jeremiah and set up a play date for Erin and the child but hadn't felt comfortable about dialing his number since he walked out of her house in a huff a week earlier. Fortunately, the girls did get to play together at the party that evening.

If Monia thought her day was busy, it was nothing compared to her night. Halfway through the party she wanted to scream at her mother, "I thought you were the one giving this party, not me," but of course she wouldn't dare scream something like that out loud. She did manage to whisper her sentiments to her father, who felt so sorry for his child that he began helping Monia serve, replenish, refill, and take out trash. Clarissa was much too busy entertaining her guests to be bothered with such mundane tasks. The worst part of the evening for Monia was trying to act normal with Jeremiah who ignored her most of the night. Darnell's efforts; however, caused Jeremiah some embarrassment, so he took over the bar duties and started helping where he could, allowing Darnell the leisure to enjoy friends he hadn't seen in years. The busy work had such a positive effect on Jeremiah that he actually made eye contact with Monia.

Sharon was so overwhelmingly pleased about her surprise party that she picked up the phone a few days later and called Monia personally. Monia was shocked to hear Sharon's proper voice on the other end of the phone when she answered even though the caller ID had displayed "Sharon Sumuels." Monia had never received a call from the aloof gambler. "Monia, sweetheart, I simply had to call you and personally convey my thanks to you for the party. You worked so very hard at making it a success and Clara told me she could not have pulled it off if it weren't for you. Thank you so much for that. I've never been more pleased."

At that moment, Monia was pleased also. "You're welcome Miss Sharon. I am so happy you enjoyed the party. That makes all the work more than worth it. It was fun, huh?"

"Yes, dear, it was. I don't know how you'll manage to top it next year." Sharon laughed and Monia thought, "Wow, Miss Sharon made a joke," and giggled along with the lady.

"I am having dinner at my place next weekend as a way of saying thank you. Just us family and I don't want you to bring a thing. I just want you to relax and enjoy yourself, okay."

Monia hesitated because she knew Jeremiah would be at the dinner and even though he warmed up slightly at Sharon's surprise party, he was still pretty cool toward her by evenings end. "What night is the dinner, Miss Sharon?"

"Which night are you free, Monia? I've already checked with Clara and Darnell and they are available."

What about Jeremiah? Maybe he's not available this weekend. Monia went for Friday, which was actually the worst possible night. She was usually bone tired on Fridays. "Well, I've got plans for Saturday," she lied. Her only plans for the upcoming weekend were laundry and lounging.

"Let's make it Friday at seven thirty and Monia."

"Yes."

"I think it's time you start calling me Sharon."

Monia laughed. "Okay, Miss – I mean Sharon. Thank you."

"See you Friday, dear."

When Monia arrived at Sharon's that Friday night, Jeremiah was placing skewered shrimp on the grill to go along with the Texas oven roasted brisket, pancit, fried rice, a beautiful array of marinated vegetables, a tossed salad, fresh Italian bread, and key lime pie with a pecan crust. Sharon had outdone herself.

Jeremiah was past acting like a spoiled child and was back to his old self. He seemed so happy that Monia became annoyed. She was not pleased with the way things stood between them and didn't appreciate Jeremiah's appearance of contentment. Monia did her best to be at ease but knew she was trying too hard. This was exactly what she had feared; she couldn't even find a comfort zone with the man. She hoped that with time they'd get back to a good place.

After everyone except Clarissa had left Sharon's home that Friday night, the two ladies sat and talked for a while. It was the first time they had to discuss all their old friends from the previous week's party. After they had worn the lives of their friends out, Clarissa asked Sharon, "What's going on with Monia and Jeremiah?"

Sharon shook her head and hunched her shoulders, not feeling free to say what she really thought. After all, Jeremiah is her son. It would have been hard to say, "I think they're screwing."

"You think they're screwing?" Clarissa asks, matter-of-factly.

"Well, they may not be any longer, but the way they're acting toward each other lately, I'd say they have."

"I hope this comes out okay for Monia. These young people these days act like sex is just something to do because it feels good. Maybe I'm just old fashioned but I could never understand how you screw someone and remain emotionally unattached. I guess that is what hookers do."

"Clara, that's business. What's going on between Monia and Jeremiah is not business and they were emotionally connected long before they climbed off into bed with each other, if that's what they did. I'm sure Monia will be fine. Jeremiah has always loved her and I'm sure he won't mistreat her. I'm just worried about how this will affect our relationship, all of us. Will they be able to get past it and remain close? It has been so nice these last couple of months with Monia back. It's been like a big holiday except for that whole 'body in the park thing'. I don't want them to get to the place that they avoid each other. That would be disastrous for us. Jeremiah, Erin, you, Darnell, and now Monia are pretty much all the family I have. Clifford and his sons hardly ever come around and when they do, it's only for an overnight. I hardly know they're here before they're gone."

"I guess we just have to wait and see how things develop. What a mess," Clarissa groans.

"It will all be fine, I'm sure." Sharon patted Clarissa on the shoulder as she left to replenish their tea. She prayed under her breath that the situation between their two children didn't turn ugly.

Two weeks later, Darnell Phillips celebrated the twenty fifth anniversary of his dental practice. Of course Monia had to attend and thankfully Darnell's office staff had made all the arrangements and handled the entire event, which only lasted two hours. Darnell then took his staff, family, and friends out to dinner.

Monia ended up seated to the left of Erin with Jeremiah on the child's right. About halfway through dinner Jeremiah glanced over at Monia and asked quietly, "Do you think we can call a truce?"

Erin looked up at her father and asked loud enough for everyone to hear, "What's a truce?" causing both Jeremiah and Monia to laugh.

"I'd like that," Monia responded.

"This means you'll start back calling me sometimes, right?"

"And you'll start back stopping by my house unannounced?"

"Deal," Jeremiah agreed with a smile.

Monia and Jeremiah reached over Erin's head and shook hands.

"What's a truce?" Erin asked again, even louder this time.

--

The wedding reception for Mr. and Mrs. Harold Hampton is one of the best parties the Embassy Suites of Monterey Bay has ever held. Monia and Ja'Niece are joined by their old friends Angelique and Renetta. At Monia's urging, the Jemison's daughter, Shannon, is also back in town for the occasion. The ladies search the room for old friends and take lots of photos. Monia spots Shirley across the room and is happy to see Pamela as her guest. She goes over to sit with them for a while and laugh and talk. Later, Monia spots her old high school boyfriend, Junior McFarland and another boy she had a crush on, Arnett James. The music is good and Monia and the ladies from her table are a bit rowdy.

Jeremiah shows up later in the evening. This is his first time attending a large event like this in Seaside since his return. He has always felt unwelcomed, but Monia has given him courage. She called him and reminded him that he promised to attend the reception and refused to let him back out of the event. He figures if anyone gives him a hard time, Monia will beat 'em up because she sure stood up for him with Shirley.

"Take a seat," Ja'Niece tells Jeremiah after he has roamed the room for nearly twenty minutes speaking to people and finally settling in at Monia's table. He was surprised at the number of warm greetings he received and that he did not notice one snub. He feels some hesitancy about being the only man at a table of five women but decides to just enjoy himself. Ja'Niece gets him on the dance floor almost immediately, making him wish he had lied and declared he didn't dance, but Monia probably would have called him a liar. After dancing with Ja'Niece a second time, he feels an obligatory pull to dance with Shannon, then later Angelique. Thankfully, Renetta latches on to a friend and dances with him and the ladies have no qualms with dancing with each other. Jeremiah is somewhat relieved when Monia turns him down for a dance. By night's end Jeremiah is exhausted but can honestly say he had a good time.

"I'm hungry, Jeremiah. Will you take me to eat?" Ja'Niece asks, not including anyone else in the invitation. She has already told Monia that she wants to get Jeremiah alone, so Monia is not surprised by the slight.

"Jeremiah looks at Monia and asks, "You guys want to get something to eat?"

Renetta and Angelique have left for their hotel. Shannon, who is staying with Monia, looks at her host for her lead. Monia hopes Shannon will accept Jeremiah's invitation but knows that's the last thing Ja'Niece wants. "I'll pass," Monia says flatly, not looking at Jeremiah or Shannon. She does not want to dissuade Shannon if she decides to join Jeremiah and Ja'Niece.

Shannon picks up on the vibe and knows that at least one of the parties going to eat will not welcome her company. "I guess I'll pass too. See you later, Ja'Niece. It was good seeing you again, Jeremiah."

"You too, Shannon." Jeremiah smiles at Shannon and cuts his eyes at Monia who avoids looking up.

"I am a little hungry," Shannon tells Monia on their way to the car, "but I got the impression they wanted to be alone."

Monia cannot hide her sarcasm when she responds to Shannon's observation. "You got the impression they wanted to be alone?" She places great emphasis on the word "they."

Shannon laughs. "Well not so much Jeremiah but Ja'Niece was shooting daggers at me to say 'no' and you wouldn't even look at me, so I figured Jeremiah was just being polite."

"That's my Ja'Niece. I've got plenty of food at home. I went grocery shopping because I knew you guys were coming for the weekend. We'll dig something out of the fridge, if that's okay or I can take you to pick up something. It's up to you."

"The fridge is fine with me."

Monia and Shannon have a little pig out party in front of Monia's television set with a cold roasted chicken, some havarti cheese, olives, and crackers. They drink some wine to wash everything down before Shannon declares she is finished for the night and goes to bed.

Monia stays up for another hour hoping that Ja'Niece shows but finally drags off to bed also. She wakes up late the next morning when she hears someone moving around in the front of her house. She drags herself out of bed and goes out to find Shannon making coffee. "I hope you like your coffee strong," Shannon tells her.

"I do." Monia stretches and then remembers Ja'Niece didn't come in or if she did, Monia didn't open the door for her. She looks in the bedroom that she uses as an office and finds no sign of her friend. She wonders if Ja'Niece slept in the room with Shannon. "Did Ja'Niece come in?"

"I didn't let her in. I guess she got lucky."

Monia turns to go into her bathroom. "I don't know if I'd call that lucky."

There is a strange sensation from Monia's throat to her stomach. Her eyes seem to want to well up with tears but she fights them back. She finishes in the bathroom and gets her phone from her purse to see if Ja'Niece sent her a message but she hasn't. Something tells Monia to check out front for Ja'Niece's car. Ja'Niece had pulled up just as Monia and Shannon were leaving the house so she had left her overnight bag in her car. Monia is surprised to see that Ja'Niece's car is no longer parked in front of her home. Monia is livid. In this day and age, communication is so important and easy. Monia can only assume her friend spent the night with Jeremiah but refuses to make a call to confirm that assumption.

Monia and Shannon go out for breakfast and then visit with Clarissa for a short time. Later on in the day, Shannon takes off to visit with some friends and accompanies them to dinner. Monia breaks down and dials Ja'Niece's number but gets sent straight to voice mail so she sends a text message and tells herself that if she hasn't heard from Ja'Niece by the end of the day, she'll call Jeremiah. Just before dialing his number, she receives a text message from Ja'Niece that reads "**at home, call u soon.**"

This is the last straw; Monia is mad enough to strangle her friend. Ja'Niece has been talking to her for weeks now about coming down for Tasha's wedding and how much fun they were going to have over the weekend. Now, once again, Monia finds herself dumped because of a man. She wants to call Jeremiah and ask him what happened that caused Ja'Niece to leave and return home a day earlier than planned. As much as she wants to find out what happened, she doesn't think she can stand the sound of his voice right now. She might throw up.

Monia determines this is the last time she will allow Ja'Niece to disregard her. She has been left alone in Ja'Niece's apartment while Ja'Niece went and stayed with a man too many times. No matter what their plans, Ja'Niece will dump Monia if a man comes along and it's gotten to the point that Ja'Niece does not want to do anything that does not involve men or a man. She has no ability to have a good time without a man and if there is a man or men around, Ja'Niece has to end the night with one of them. Monia is sick of it; she is tired of this rejection from her friend. *Why is this an issue for you now, Monia? Ja'Niece has been doing this to you since high school and it never bothered you so much before. Ja'Niece does this to all her girlfriends.*

As angry as she is with Ja'Niece, that emotion is dwarfed by her disappointment in Jeremiah. Monia feels it was low of him to sleep with Ja'Niece when he knew Ja'Niece and she were best friends. The thought that she and Ja'Niece have slept with the same man is nauseating, *YUCK!* She wants to go and take another shower.

--

Jeremiah calls a few days later to tell Monia he has three extra tickets to the Friday and Saturday night sessions of the Monterey Bay Jazz Festival and invites her to go with him.

"No, no, I'm not interested in going. Ja'Niece may want to come down and go, though. Have you asked her?"

"Umm, I don't know if she would want to go, I mean, I just thought I'd ask you. I don't need you to try and think up someone to go with me. I can do that for myself. I called and asked you because I thought you would enjoy the performances and I'd like you to come and go with me. I haven't talked to you since the reception. That was a really good time. I'm glad you talked me into going."

"No, we haven't talked have we. I'm glad you enjoyed it," Monia responds quietly.

"What's going on Monia? You sound pissed and I thought we were working on trying to be friends. Seems like every time we talk these days, there's a negative vibe."

"I thought we had fun at the reception."

"Yeah, yeah we did have a good time but I haven't heard from you since then and now you sound like you're angry about something; what is it?"

"Nothing, Jeremiah, nothing, but let me ask you something. Was Erin at home the night of the wedding?"

Jeremiah repeats the question. "Was Erin at home the night of the wedding?"

"That's what I asked; was Erin at your house the night of the wedding reception?"

"Yeah, she was here. She was here with Delores. Why?"

"What happened to the whole 'I don't like sleeping with people when my girl is at home' thing?"

"Well, I don't. What are you getting at Moanie?"

Monia feels a little hesitancy now. She doesn't understand why Jeremiah is sounding so perplexed. He has to know what she is alluding to. "Didn't you take Ja'Niece home with you the other night?"

"No, I didn't bring Ja'Niece to my house that night or any night. No, hell no!"

Monia is quiet on the line but her mind is working. She wants to ask if he took Ja'Niece to a hotel, did they just get it on in the car, or what."

"What concern is it of yours where my daughter is and who I bring to my house and when?"Jeremiah asks.

"Well you talked about it like it was such a big deal that when I thought about it I decided you were right. It's not a good idea to have a bunch of different women sleeping around your house with Erin there."

"So now you're concerned that Erin may learn I sleep with women."

"Well you said yourself that she will probably figure out for herself one day that you sleep around but you didn't want to flaunt it in her face."

Jeremiah laughs sarcastically. "Moanie, I never said that I sleep around."

"Well, okay, however you worded it."

Monia and Jeremiah are bickering and arguing with each other because they are both frustrated and pissed off about their decision to just be friends.

"I can't believe that you thought I brought Ja'Niece here and slept with her."

"Excuse me. I guess I was under the wrong impression."

"Yeah, I guess you were. Ja'Niece and I went and ate. I brought her back to your house and we sat outside for a while and talked. I didn't think I was ever going to get her out of my car but she finally got out and told me goodnight. She did say she had to go over to the convenience store to pick up something. I offered to take her but she turned me down. She drove off before I did. What made you think she stayed over here?"

"She never came back."

"She never came back!"

"She never came back. I have not talked to her since we left the Embassy Suites after the reception."

Jeremiah's heart starts to beat double time. "Tell me you're bullshittin' me, Monia."

"No – well, I mean, she text me. She sent me a text the next evening."

Jeremiah lets out a soft sigh, "Oh, okay, okay good. You scared me there for a minute. I don't need to be the last known person to have seen anyone else."

"No, she sent me a text – unless that was you texting me from her phone."

"Stop it, Moanie. That's not funny."

Monia has to laugh at him at this point "I'm sorry about that."

Jeremiah tells her, "I think you owe me an apology."

"I apologize. I apologize, friend."

"So, now, how about the Jazz Festival?"

Monia thinks about going to the festival with Jeremiah. "Who else are you inviting?"

"Does it really matter, Moanie?"

"Well, you may be taking one of your girlfriends and I really don't want to tag along with you and one of them."

"I don't have girlfriends, Moanie."

"Dates, okay, dates, is that better? Why do I have to be so specific with what I say to you? Okay you don't have girlfriends; you don't sleep around, okay – one of your dates." Monia sounds upset now and is not hiding it.

"Okay, okay, you don't want to go. I'm gone. Talk to later, bye." Jeremiah hangs up the phone and says, "This is what our friendship is supposed to be. Damn. This is rough. Looks like we really did screw things up."

--

The very next day Pamela tells Monia how much she enjoys the Jazz Festival and made a point of going the first three years she was in Monterey but has not been able to afford the event since her niece started college. Pamela explains that her sister is a single parent of three, so Pamela has taken on the responsibility of helping get the children through school, causing her to set pretty strict spending priorities.

Later in the week Darnell asks his daughter if she would like to go to the festival with Clarissa, Sharon, and him. "I've already purchased our tickets but I can swing another set for you if you'd like to go, Chunga. We go every year and have a blast. Your mother and I didn't go together last year. She purchased her own tickets and sat with some other people. Sharon only went one night. I guess she didn't like choosing between me and your mom but Sharon assures me we'll all be sitting together again this year." Darnell is glowing with this news.

Monia goes home after dinner with Darnell and calls Jeremiah. "Do you still have those tickets for the festival?" she asks unceremoniously and without apology.

"I still have two extra tickets," Jeremiah responds.

"Are you still willing to let me have them?"

"No. I invited you to go with me. Are you planning on taking my tickets and inviting someone else? You might be trying to bring one of your boyfriends and I don't want to be sitting next to you and one of your boyfriends." Jeremiah pokes fun at Monia.

She pokes back. "I don't have boyfriends, Jeremiah."

"Okay, why do I have to be so specific with you when I talk? I'm sure you know what I mean."

"That's enough. Are you going to let me have the tickets or not? I'd like to go."

"With me?"

"Yes, with you. Can I have both tickets?"

"Who are you bringing?"

"Does it really matter, Jeremiah?"

"Now you need to stop."

"I'd like to bring my friend Pamela from work. You met Pam at Dr. Navya's party."

"I guess I'll let you have the tickets, but don't piss me off between now and the festival or I'll take them back."

"I'll be good. I promise."

Chapter 15

Marcus has been calling and texting Monia on a regular basis lately. He seems to want to get their relationship back on track and Monia can't understand why. Neither of them have any real passion for the other; theirs has always been a relationship of convenience. Although Monia questions Marcus's motives for trying to renew such a lack-luster affair, she remains uncommitted in her decision to end the relationship completely. She wants to keep her options open when it comes to Marcus. After all, they have shared some good times over the years. There have been times in the past when she told herself she was finished with him, but then something would happen to throw them back together and Monia would be back on the hook. Marcus has always been successful at drawing Monia closer when she starts to pull away and in the past he reeled her back easily. This time, Monia is giving him much more resistance, but Marcus is not one to give up and enjoys a good fight.

Marcus's recent calls are a bit different from the past. He sounds sincere when he says he misses Monia and wants to see her. He has not given her any type of ultimatum, but she doesn't think she'll be able to go much longer without seeing him. The four-year-relationship with Marcus is the longest Monia has had with any man. She wrestles with her decision to let him go. His last call sent Monia on a real guilt trip. "You know my birthday is in a couple of weeks, Monia. I hope you plan on coming up."

Monia had completely forgotten the man's birthday. Marcus loves to have a big celebration so she is certain there is a party planned. "I remember, Marcus. What have you got planned?"

"I was hoping you had something in mind but if not, we can have a few people over and have the food catered in. A cake would be nice."

That was Marcus's hint for Monia to take care of the cake, but she did not want to commit and wondered why he was so set on placing her in the role of girlfriend. "Marcus, I can't promise I will be up for your birthday. You go ahead with your plans and let me know the particulars and if I can make it, I will."

"It's my birthday, Monia. I can't believe that doctor is working you this hard. I mean is her clinic open on the weekends? Why are you putting in all these weekend hours? Can't you ask for some time off to celebrate your boyfriend's birthday? Damn!"

Boyfriend -- where was I when all this happened? Monia wondered. "I'll do my best to make it up but I can't make any promises."

"Monia, are you upset because I wasn't available to help with your move like I promised because you know I would have been there that first day if I could have. I hope you're not holding that against me."

"I'm not upset about that or anything else. I'm just trying to get settled in here and learn my new job. Soon my weekends will be my own."

Monia knows she must either resume her relationship with Marcus or cut him loose. She can't continue to use her job as an excuse for not seeing him when the truth is the thought of being with Marcus is like taking a cold shower.

--

The 2013 Monterey Bay Jazz Festival proves to be, as always, an event with great music and the group of ticket holders walking through the fairgrounds with Monia and Jeremiah are anticipating a romping good time. Jeremiah has brought Gregory, a long-time customer who is now a good friend. Pamela and Gregory hit it off right away.

The group grabs some drinks and takes in a set by Joe Lovano before making their way toward the arena to catch The Buena Vista Social Club. Darnell hurries everyone toward the gate so they don't miss the beginning of the set but Sharon and Clarissa keep running into old friends or stopping to talk to their favorite vendors. This leisurely pace works for Monia and Pamela because they both enjoy looking at all the art and other items for sale.

Monia looks up at Jeremiah who had been sticking close to her but suddenly appears distracted. He and Sharon are both looking in the same direction and cause the others to turn their heads to see what's so interesting. "Jeremiah, isn't that Leslie?" Sharon asks with a slight smile.

"It sure is," Jeremiah answers in a voice barely above a whisper, never taking his eyes off the woman.

Monia's eyes follow Jeremiah's and she spots Leslie immediately without ever having seen her before. The woman is medium height but has the grace of someone taller. She has flawless golden brown-skin and short thick neatly cut natural curls. She is elegantly beautiful. The man accompanying her is nearly as tall as Jeremiah, fair-skinned, ruggedly good looking, and has the appearance of wealth. Monia senses Clarissa's eyes on her and tries to stand a little straighter and appear disinterested as the handsome couple approaches.

"Jeremiah," Leslie declares with a wide smile and a wicked twinkle in her eyes. "What a surprise. How are you?"

"Leslie," Jeremiah responds and leans forward to accept a kiss on the cheek from her. He then turns toward Sharon and says "Mom, you remember my friend Leslie Cardinale from Pismo?"

Sharon graces Leslie with her most reserved smile along with an extended hand. "Of course I do. How are you, Leslie?"

"Fine, thank you, Sharon."

Jeremiah then introduces the others in his group and Leslie introduces her friend to them. A little polite conversation passes before Darnell clears his throat and the friends separate and once again start moving toward the gate to the arena.

"Wow that was awkward." Monia peeps up at Jeremiah and hopes he's not too heartbroken over the lovely Leslie.

"What was so awkward about it?" Jeremiah asks as he reaches for her hand.

Monia responds, "Well, if you want to talk about it, I'm here."

Jeremiah gives her that favorite smile. "Thanks, Moanie." He pulls Monia's hand up to his mouth and kisses it. "See, I knew we'd be friends again."

Monia blushes and looks up at Jeremiah and lets her guard down. He gives her a look that she feels is far too intimate. Monia does her best not to return his gaze but can't help herself. Neither she nor Jeremiah realize they have passed Leslie and her friend as they grin and stare at each other on their way into the gate and that Leslie has observed their actions.

At the end of the evening, Gregory offers to give Pamela a ride home but Monia tells him. "If you want to take Pamela home, Gregory, you have to ask her on a date. She and I came together and we're leaving together. She's my date tonight."

"Your date?" Jeremiah asks.

"Not dates like you have Jeremiah," Monia responds jokingly.

The friends make plans to meet the following evening for the Saturday night session.

Gregory did not bother to ask Pamela if he could pick her up and take her to the fairgrounds for the next evening, so Pamela is once again Monia's date. Sunday is out of the question for the four younger people this year because each has to be at work bright and early Monday morning. By the end of the night they each vow that they will take Monday off from work the following year so they can attend the Sunday evening session of the event. The three senior members of the group make their plans for the final day of the festival and make fun of the "rookies" as they call Jeremiah, Monia, Pamela, and Gregory.

Monia drops Pamela off and finds Jeremiah's car parked outside her home and him perched outside her front door when she arrives. "What are you doing here?" she asks as she approaches.

"Waiting for you," he answers with so much innuendo that Monia thinks twice about letting him inside. She can hardly get the key in the door because he stands so close behind her and the vibes coming off the man are transmitting a powerfully stimulating signal. No sooner than she gets two steps into her house, Jeremiah closes the door and pulls her back to him. He kisses her long and hard on the mouth. Soon his hands start running up under her blouse and reaching for her breast.

"I've got to go to the bathroom, Jeremiah."

"Damn, woman." He releases her as if she has committed some heinous act.

Monia tells herself not to think about what she is about to do. Her conscience reminds her that she promised off Jeremiah sexually but she refuses to listen. She whispers, "Just one more time," as she leaves the bathroom.

Jeremiah is perched on her sofa watching her when she enters the living room. He hopes she doesn't send him home. The whole point of the quick attack was to catch her off guard and get her so hot and bothered that she couldn't tell him no. He had not considered that she would need to go to the bathroom and thus cool down. So when Monia pushes him down on the sofa, stretches out on top of him, and kisses him, he can't help but smile. They lie there and allow their tongues to play intimate games as they gently and then deeply kiss.

Monia pulls away and sits up on Jeremiah with her crotch directly on top of his and one leg dangling off the sofa. "We can't keep doing this, Jeremiah," She tells him as she begins pulling his shirt over his head.

"Why not?"

"Because it's just sex."

"We're best friends aren't we?"

Monia gets off the sofa and pulls Jeremiah to a sitting position. He reaches up and pulls off her shirt and then reaches behind her and unsnaps her bra. He smiles at her breasts as if they can smile back at him, causing Monia to smile also. She pulls him to his feet and starts unbuckling his belt. Jeremiah takes over and pulls his jeans off. Then he goes to work on her pants and gets them off. He sits back on the sofa and begins running his hands gently over Monia's body.

Monia enjoys the touch of his hands as he glides his fingers over every sensitive spot. She feels his fingers inch up her inner thighs and glide inside her panties. Jeremiah runs his fingers in and out of her causing her to part her thighs wider for his touch. After a while, he gets her to lie down and pulls her panties off. He then pulls her legs apart and sits back on the opposite end of the sofa and looks at her. When she starts to raise up he tells her, "Please don't move, Monia. I want to see you." Monia stays still and enjoys him looking at her most personal assets.

Jeremiah removes his boxers, puts on his protection, positions himself over Monia, and kisses her deeply before entering her. Monia reaches around his butt and grabs him to push him inside her deeper but he is determined to last longer than he did the first time they made love. He takes nice slow lengthy strokes inside Monia causing her to whimper and ask him not to stop. After what seems like only a few minutes, Jeremiah pulls himself from Monia hot aching body. "Why you stop?" she whines.

"I just want to last a little longer, baby; give me a minute."

"I don't like you to call me baby," Monia tells him, a little pissed off because he stopped.

"I'll call you whatever you want," Jeremiah tells her as he kisses on her breast and places his hand back between her wet thighs.

Monia spreads her legs for his hand and allows him to touch those nice spots for a while before she stops him. "I want to last too."

Jeremiah kisses her and barely allows their tongues to touch as he starts to climbs back on top, but Monia pushes him away, stands up, and pulls him onto the floor. She straddles Jeremiah and starts to ride him, gliding up and down on his body. She uses her legs to squat over him and gently squeeze herself around him for a few moments and then tightens her body as she lowers herself on him and back up again. Jeremiah grabs his head and groans relishing the wonderful sensations flowing through his body. After only a few minutes of this, Monia can tell he is on the verge of finishing so she abruptly pulls herself off of him and lies down beside him. Jeremiah immediately positions himself over Monia, enters her and starts his stroking again. They jam their overheated bodies together and after some time, Monia clamps her legs around Jeremiah and starts to moan loudly. The sound of her pleasure pushes Jeremiah closer to his own end and when she digs her nails into him, he joins her in a complete release.

Chapter 16

Going with the flow, going with the flow are the words Monia repeats over and over to herself during the week following the Jazz Festival. Yep, she screwed Jeremiah again, four times to be exact. He won't stay away and she can't resist him. He's not just coming around for sex; he is calling or stopping by each day. He's taken her out to eat three times – once for lunch and twice for dinner with Erin. He even asked her if she liked flowers and if she would think he was corny if he sent her some. Monia just smiled and told him she didn't want any flowers. Jeremiah looked a little disappointed and gave her a yellow rose the next day. Corny, right?

Monia is grinning a lot but trying to maintain some balance. That's what the "Going with the flow" mantra is about.

She wakes up in her bed just before daybreak on Sunday morning and feels Jeremiah spooned up against her and hears his steady breathing in her ear. They had a real date the night before – pizza, bowling, and a nice long walk on the beach. Erin is with her Grandmother Sharon so Jeremiah spent the night for the first time. Monia starts to move but Jeremiah pulls her a little closer so she settles in for a few more moments. He is awake now and he kisses her on the back of the neck as his hands start to roam. "What are you doing?"

"Nothing," Jeremiah responds with his hand becoming more active. Just as Mona turns to face him, his cell phone starts to ring. "Damn!" he complains but doesn't move to answer. "They'll call back if it's important."

As Monia scoots even closer to him, the phone starts to ring again. Jeremiah looks over at the phone but once again makes no attempt to move. "It may be your mother," Monia tells him, causing an immediate response. The call has gone over to voice mail by the time he reaches the phone, so Jeremiah checks the caller ID. An immediate frown takes over his face, quickly replaced by a look of concern. Jeremiah lays the phone down, turns and goes into the bathroom without bothering to mention the call to Monia who cannot hide her curiosity. He comes out and starts pulling on his pants just as the phone starts to ring again. He does not look happy. "Yeah," he answers rudely, still not looking at Monia.

"Jeremiah."

"Yeah."

"I need to see you," Leslie speaks over the phone in a barely audible whisper.

Jeremiah raises expressionless eyes from the floor up to meet Monia's before turning and walking through her living room and dining area on out to her terrace. "What's going on Leslie? Are you okay? Where are the kids?"

"I just need to see you right away. It's important. I need you now."

Monia steps out onto her terrace in the cool morning air to bring Jeremiah his shirt. As she returns to the inside, she hears him ask, "You want to meet me halfway?"

"No. I can't make it. You come here." Leslie answers, sounding even weaker.

Jeremiah is concerned about the events taking place in Leslie's life that cause her to call at this hour of the morning. He has never known her to sound so out of it. "Leslie, please just tell me, where are the kids?"

The line goes dead. Jeremiah dials her back but the call goes to voice mail. He stands on Monia's terrace and thinks for a moment. He has no choice but to drive to Pismo and check on Leslie and the children. He could try and reach Leslie's elderly parents but they live two hours farther away than him, up in Oakland, and he'd rather not scare them unnecessarily.

Jeremiah finds Monia in the kitchen making coffee. "Listen, Moanie, that was Leslie on the phone. There's something going on and I don't know what it is. I need to drive down there and check on her and the kids."

Monia doesn't turn around but asks over her shoulder, "What did she say?"

Jeremiah doesn't want to tell Monia that Leslie said she needed to see him. He doesn't think Monia will understand why he would consider that request urgent. "It's not so much what she said, it's how she sounds. She scared me. I think I need to go."

"Okay, Jeremiah." Monia turns around, stands there, and looks at him with her arms hanging at her sides. She looks defeated.

Jeremiah goes into her room and starts gathering up his shoes and jacket. Monia follows him and watches as he prepares to leave her. "Hey, thanks for being so understanding about this. I gotta see what's going on. She doesn't have much family. Her parents are pretty old and live up in Oakland."

Monia cuts him off. She doesn't want to hear it, whatever it is. "I understand. Don't worry about me. You do what you have to do."

He tries to give Monia a kiss before he leaves but she turns her head and the caress lands on her cheek.

"Jeremiah," Monia calls him just as he reaches for the front door.

"Yeah, Moanie."

"You should call the Pismo Beach police and ask them to check on her right away, just to be safe."

"Thanks, Moanie. I'll do that. See you later?"

Monia doesn't respond but heads back into her kitchen and pours out a cup of coffee before heading out to her terrace with the Sunday morning copy of the *Monterey Herald*.

--

Jeremiah places the call to the Pismo Beach Police Department and explains his concern. The 911 operator says she will send a dispatch vehicle by to check on Leslie. He receives a call back from an Officer Davila nearly three hours later informing him that the officer had spoken with Leslie and all seemed fine. The police officer told Jeremiah that he asked Leslie to call him and she assured the officer that she would. Jeremiah is still on the phone with the police officer when he pulls up to Leslie's home.

He knocks at the door and rings her bell but gets no answer so makes his way around to the back, where he finds Leslie on her deck looking out at the ocean and drinking wine. He doesn't bother to speak. "What the hell is going on Leslie? What's the big emergency?"

"I told you; I need to talk to you," Leslie responds without looking up at him. She sits there in the early morning hours wearing a pair of oversized shades and her favorite oversized button down shirt, exposing most of her legs up to her crotch and much of her cleavage. Jeremiah imagines Officer Davila had a great morning if Leslie answered her door like this.

"You called me this time of the morning and had me drive down here and deal with the early morning fog because you need to talk to me. What do you need to say to me that you couldn't say over the phone," Jeremiah asks with great emotion as he tries not to curse. "Where are the kids, Leslie?"

"The kids are with their father in Lucca. If you had been around at all this summer you would know that. They will return after Christmas, if I want them to."

Jeremiah takes a seat. He thinks Leslie must be struggling if she allowed the children to go live with Christopher. He is at a loss as to how he can help. "What do you need, Leslie?"

Leslie finally takes off the oversized shades, looks at him, and asks, "Are you with Monia, now?"

What the fuck?

"I need to know, are you with Monia now?"

Jeremiah doesn't know how to answer the question. Is he with Monia? He and Monia have spent the last week together. He likes her and wants to spend more time with her, intimate close personal time, but to say he's with her – that's a commitment he's not ready to make yet. "Monia and I are spending some time together. Yes, if that's your question."

"Do you realize you have only been down here once since she returned?"

Jeremiah has to stop and think about what Leslie is saying – that he hasn't visited with her since Monia stepped back into his life. Hell, he's been so busy he hasn't had much time to think about Leslie. He's not sure his lack of consideration toward Leslie is about Monia, at least not a month or two ago it wasn't. "Leslie, the entire time we've been together I've dated other people and you've started dating other people again too, so what's the problems now? I've always been open with you about that. I never tried to hide anything from you and accepted your freedom to do as you please. I'm a man. I'm sexual; I have needs. You and I are good friends."

"Good friends! That's what the fuck we are – good friends?"

"What do you want me to do?" Jeremiah throws his hands up in the air.

"I want things to be like they were before."

"You weren't happy with the way things were before between us. You wanted more of a commitment."

"Is that why you aren't having anything to do with me now, because I want more of a commitment from you?"

"No, it's not that."

"Then what is it? Are you telling me it's not about me but it's about her?"

Jeremiah doesn't know what this is all about. He knows it's not about Leslie wanting more of a commitment from him. He knows he's not ready to give up this beautiful woman who has stood by him for years and been his friend for nearly a decade. Leslie has been open and understanding. He doubts that Monia will be willing to accept him having relationships with other women. She might play along for awhile but Jeremiah knows she won't put up with the open relationship for long, even if she did have a similar arrangement with Marcus. He also knows he won't be happy with Monia seeing other men.

Leslie stares at Jeremiah long and hard as his mind considers Monia. "You don't want me any more do you? Do you know what that feels like to me -- for you not to want me? From the first day I saw you, you wanted me. You always wanted me. Now you have no desire for me. How do you think that makes me feel? I've waited; I've been patient; I've been understanding. 'Oh, Leslie, I can't come down this weekend I've got plans. Oh, Leslie, maybe we shouldn't spend so much time together. Oh, Leslie, we can't sleep together when Erin is in the house. Oh, Leslie, we probably shouldn't sleep together when Beth and Jake are in the house either.' I've been very understanding and I've waited. I've waited while you screwed me in every way imaginable and now you tell me we're good friends. And now little miss girl of your dreams moves back home and you have no desire for me any longer."

"Leslie, don't be like this. I've been honest with you from the very beginning and it's not like you didn't have other people too and you know it."

"I know that you've used me. That's what I know."

"I think we've used each other, Leslie. I think you wanted me just as much as I wanted you."

"I'm not saying I didn't want you, Jeremiah. I stopped pretending like I wanted anyone other than you years ago. Our whole relationship has been based on what you want and how you want things. I've sacrificed a lot to be with you."

"What did you sacrifice to be with me?"

Leslie looks at Jeremiah as if she is trying to determine if she should tell him of her sacrifice. "Do you think I would have given up on my marriage so easily if I didn't know I could have you at the drop of a hat? I knew all I had to do was snap my fingers because you were so anxious to get between my legs. I guess that's all I've ever been to you is another piece of ass."

"You need to stop drinking that wine and go to bed or better yet go take a shower. You're drunk."

"I'll take one if you take one with me." Leslie makes a futile attempt at being seductive but only manages to look like a sloppy drunk on the make.

Jeremiah gets Leslie inside her home. She goes into her bathroom, showers, throws up and passes out across her bed. Not sure how much wine she drank, Jeremiah decides to stay with her until she wakes up. He places a call to his mother and explains that he needed to make the trip to Pismo and asks if she will keep Erin with her until the next morning.

Leslie is surprised to see Jeremiah sitting on her sofa when she stumbles out of her bedroom nearly four hours later. She can't remember most of their conversation but she does remember calling him. "When did you get here?" she asks.

"About four hours ago. I thought I'd wait for you to get up before I headed back." Jeremiah watches her and waits to see if there is anything else she wants to say to him. He'd prefer to get all the discussion about his relationship with Monia out of the way now, but Leslie has no desire to talk. She just wants her tea and her bed.

"Sorry, I passed out on you. What did we talk about?"

"Me and you." He doesn't mention Monia.

"That's it?"

"Pretty much."

"How's Erin. I miss seeing her."

"She's doing pretty good. Her grandmother is talking about coming up for a week or so to visit with her. She missed her too over the summer."

"You know Jeremiah I didn't realize that ours was a relationship of convenience. I never thought you'd stop making time for me once you stopped driving through to pickup and drop off Erin. I thought we had more than that."

"Leslie." Jeremiah starts.

Leslie puts her hand up to stop him from talking. "I've got to get some rest; I'm exhausted. Would you lock the door and set the alarm for me on your way out." She stretches out on a sofa and covers herself with a throw.

Jeremiah gets up to leave. "I'll call and check on you later."

"Yeah, and I'll see you when I see you."

When Jeremiah arrives back in Seaside at nearly six that evening, he thinks about going to see Monia but needs his own shower and bed. Also, he's not ready for yet another relationship discussion, this time with Monia. He needs to figure out things for himself for a while before he involves anyone else in the mess that has become his life.

--

Thankful for a very busy Monday, Monia manages to keep her mind on her work and does not dwell on Jeremiah. She had hoped he would stop by to see her when he returned from Pismo Beach but at least he did call late Sunday evening. She didn't answer her phone because she was in the tub and didn't return the call because she hadn't decided how to deal with Jeremiah. She had already vowed off of him once and that didn't work. Jeremiah has become an addiction. Monia finds him irresistible and he is so lusciously delicious to her, she can't imagine staying away from him. Besides, her parents won't let her shut him out. Her father may, but her mother won't.

Jeremiah has given Monia no signs that he is interested in settling down with her or anyone else. What Monia and Jeremiah have is hardly any different from her relationship with Marcus. Monia knew Marcus dated other women but she didn't care, not in the least. Was that because she never saw Marcus except when they were together. That's what she alluded to earlier when she told Jeremiah she couldn't be in his pool of women. But Monia admits that her feelings for Jeremiah are much stronger than any she ever felt for Marcus. She does not want to overreact, so she vows not to argue with Jeremiah or put restrictions on being with him. She tells herself to live her life and let him live his. Monia decides to play it by ear and take it one day at a time, all those clichés. She's open and if she wants to sleep with Jeremiah, she will and if she doesn't want to be with him, she won't. She's not going to make an issue of it. It's not that important, she tells herself. *Just keep going with the flow, Monia, and hold on tight for the ride.*

Monia considers parking her car in the garage to avoid seeing Jeremiah on Monday but decides that would be childish. She has to see him and talk to him at some point. When he shows up, unannounced as usual, he has a heaviness about him. Their interaction is strained and awkward. Jeremiah feels he should explain the events from the day before involving Leslie but he'd rather not. Monia waits for him to tell her what happened between him and Leslie but doesn't want to hear it. After some uncomfortable small talk, Jeremiah gets up to leave. "I just wanted to stop by and check on you because I left in such a hurry yesterday. I would stay longer but I haven't spent any time with Erin the past few days."

Hearing Erin's name causes Monia to smile but she doesn't go to the door with Jeremiah. She doesn't want him to try and embrace her. "Tell Erin hi for me and I'll talk to you later." Monia drops her eyes to the *Essence* Magazine she has been reading as Jeremiah exits her home.

Two days later, Monia's car won't start and she calls Jeremiah for help. He tows the car to his shop and gives Monia a ride to work. She declines his offer to pick her up that evening because she has no idea what time her day will end. After work, Monia gets Shirley to take her by Jeremiah's shop. Shirley agrees to wait for Monia but refuses to enter the business.

"Bad news, Moanie; looks like you need a new engine," are the first words out of Jeremiah's mouth.

"Can you do that here or do I need to get her to a Volvo dealership."

"We can take care of the engine, but you need to consider purchasing a newer car, Moanie. Engine work is expensive and then the car may still not work as well as before unless we overhaul the transmission. By the time we do all that, it may not be worth the money and time spent and you still may not be happy with the car's performance. I mean we can make her run like new but that's really expensive, mainly the man hours we will need to put in to make her purr."

"It would have to be cheaper that buying a new car."

"That's for certain." Jeremiah looks at Monia and knows she wants to keep the Volvo. This presents a dilemma for him. He wishes he had taken the time to consider the situation before he started talking to her about the repairs. He has worked on the cars of women he dated in the past but those were usually minor compared to the work he'll need to perform on Monia's Volvo. His labor costs will be extensive. She can likely afford to pay those costs better than he can afford to eat them but he feels it would be wrong for him to charge her for the repairs. In recent months, both his mother and his accountant have chewed him up for under charging and performing work for free. "Your father was notorious for working on people's vehicles for a little of nothing. I promise we would have been much better off than we were if he had charged half the people for the work he performed. Then he would not have needed to spend so much time out hustling up money to pay bills. He didn't have the overhead of a large shop and employees like you have. If you don't handle your business, you'll lose it and if you don't value your labor, don't expect others to," Sharon had told him recently.

Sharon will expect Jeremiah to take care of Monia's car at a reduced rate but he cannot justify charging Monia anything for the car when he is trying to climb into bed with her every time he gets a chance. He knows that in the grand scheme of things, the labor costs and parts will barely chink his profit margin by the end of the year. He makes up his mind on the spot to eat the costs if Monia insists on fixing the vehicle but he wants her to have a clear understanding of what the repairs would normally run. "We're going to have to keep her here for a couple of weeks, at least. I'll come up with some figures so you'll know what kind of costs we're looking at but we'll work something out. I got a car I can loan you while we work on old Betsy here."

"I'd like to think about what I want to do – do I want to buy another car or get her repaired. I don't want to decide in a hurry. It may be a week or so before I make up my mind. I need to talk to my mom and dad. Will you be able to keep the car here while I decide?"

"Don't worry about the car, Moanie. You just decide what you want to do. I've got a couple of nice cars here you can choose from as a loaner. I hope Clarissa doesn't get too technical about the insurance since we're not working on your car yet. I need her to cover the loaner if you get into an accident."

Monia smiles and tells him "I was thinking about going up to the city this weekend. Can I drive the loaner up there?"

"Going up to the city, what are you going up there for?"

"I'm going to a party this weekend."

Jeremiah moves around the car to get closer to Monia and leans back against the front end. "Party, oh, okay. Who's having a party?"

"Marcus. It's his birthday, so," Monia stops and wonders why she feels so guilty.

Jeremiah's face has gone hard. "I thought you were through with that guy."

"I never said that, Jeremiah."

Jeremiah looks at Monia as if she has lost her mind. *I'm standing here thinking about doing thousands of dollars worth of work on your damn car and eating the cost and you're telling me you're going to take off this weekend to go see Marcus. This is some bullshit.* Jeremiah looks at Monia hard, and then asks, "So what's the deal? Are you still seeing him?"

"Wait a minute. Is this going to be an issue for you – me still seeing Marcus?"

"I just thought you were through with that guy," Jeremiah tells her in a raised voice.

"We're still friends." Monia answers with an equal rise in her voice.

Jeremiah looks down at his hands and wipes them though they are perfectly clean. A couple of his employees enter the garage talking loudly; he looks around at them and says, "Hey!" The two men see the look on their boss's face and immediately turn and head back in the direction they came from.

"Are you still dating this guy?"

Monia gives a sarcastic chuckle. "Jeremiah, he asked me to come up for his birthday this weekend and I'm seriously thinking about going."

"Does this have anything to do with me going to see Leslie last weekend?"

"No, not really. He called and asked me a couple of weeks ago. I just hadn't decided if I would go or not. You know when I first got back here, you and I sat down and had a long talk and you told me that you understood all about open relationships. You said I didn't need to explain anything to you. So why am I having to stand here and explain to you now?"

Jeremiah shakes his head and wipes his hands some more. He is stunned; there is nothing he can say. He doesn't have a leg to stand on. He and Monia do not have an understanding. He has been unwilling to discuss Leslie or the other women he sometimes casually 'dates', nothing. He's been contemplating how he wants to handle his relationship with Monia and has been straddling the fence between commitment and leaving things as they are. What gives him the right to be upset with Monia for going to spend time with Marcus? He can't think rationally or fairly about this situation; he's a typical male.

He stands up straight and looks away from Monia. "Okay, we'll get you in a car and ah, I'll get you the information concerning the repairs as quickly as I can."

"You want me to take the car somewhere else, Jeremiah?"

"Nah, you don't need to take the car nowhere else. I'd rather work on her here. That way I'll be sure she's done right. I can take care of the car better than any shop on this damn Peninsula and probably better than any place in Northern California. I can take care of this damn raggedy-assed car of yours," Jeremiah shouts.

"You don't have to get mad or yell at me."

"Oh, okay. I don't have to get mad. I don't have to yell. Well, Monia I tell you what. I will let you know what it will cost to get this car engine repaired. I said I would take on the responsibility for that and I will. I've got a loaner you're welcome to take or I can take you to pick up a rental car, whatever works for you. Then we can go from there." Jeremiah is angry and can't hide it. He wants to be angry at Monia but knows he's as much the culprit as she.

Monia wishes she hadn't called him to pick up her car. She had no idea the issue with the car would get this complicated. "I think I'd be more comfortable in a rental car."

"Suit yourself. If that's what you want. I'll get you a ride to the rental agency."

"That's okay. Shirley is waiting for me and listen, I'm not expecting any special favors with the car repairs. I expect to pay just as anyone else would -- parts, labor, everything it will cost to get my car up and running. I don't want you to eat any of the costs."

"So you don't want me to eat any of the costs?" Jeremiah repeats.

"No but I would appreciate it if you'd hold back the mark up costs on the parts." Monia says jokingly as she tries to coax a smile out of Jeremiah but he is not happy, not at all and he wants her to know it.

Chapter 17

"I'm sorry to do this to you, Monia. The registration and everything is already paid, the hotel also. I simply cannot go so I need you to accompany Pamela to this conference. It is Tuesday through mid day on Friday. Shirley will take care of your air reservations. I need you to pay close attention and not get distracted by the big city. I don't expect you to remain in your rooms and become hermits in the evening but I want a thorough briefing from you both when you return so take good notes. I hope this will not be a problem for you." Dr. Singh tells her newest physician's assistant.

"Well it's pretty short notice, but it won't be a problem. I've got nothing planned for the week or the weekend."

"What did you decide about your car? Is that boyfriend of yours going to fix it for you or are you going to go into debt with a new one?"

Monia has told Dr. Singh more than once that Jeremiah is not her boyfriend. The doctor just says each time, "Well, he's your friend and he's a boy; that makes him your boyfriend."

"Looks like it's going to be the debt, Navya, so don't fire me any time soon," Monia laughs.

"I promise not to fire you if you go on this trip for me with such short notice," the doctor smiles.

Dr. Singh is recruiting Monia to take her place along with Pamela in attending a four-day Defeating Obesity Conference in New York City. Pamela has been talking with great enthusiasm about the conference all summer. Monia enters her co-workers office after leaving Dr. Singh's to find Pamela giddy with joy. "Girl, we are going to the Big Apple. Shirley hasn't made your reservations yet has she?"

"No. I don't think so. I just found out I was going. I came straight to talk to you. I hope she can get me on the same flight."

"I'm staying until Sunday. You've got to stay over with me. I know some great places to shop and some clubs that have the finest men you ever feasted your eyes on."

"I thought things were getting serious with you and Gregory."

"Ooh, I been meaning to thank Jeremiah for that introduction. I like him and I mean a lot but hey, I plan on taking my bite out of the apple next weekend. Come on and stay over until Sunday with me. The conference ends at noon on Friday. We can sleep in on Saturday and Sunday and get a late afternoon flight back."

"That's cutting it a little close for me, Pamela, but I will stay until Sunday. I just need to get out Sunday morning."

"Okay, that'll work. Ooh, we're going to have so much fun. Bring your most sophisticated party clothes and some casual sexy stuff too."

Casual, sexy, sophistication, huh? I think I have a few things in my closet that will fit the bill.

--

Monia is a little excited about the trip also. She wanted something different in her life and this six-day trip should do it. She had talked herself out of going to Marcus's birthday party the week before, admitting that her only reason for going was to give Jeremiah a taste of his own medicine. She was packing her bag when it finally dawned on her that she hadn't made a hotel reservation and she didn't want to call either of her two girlfriends in the Bay Area to ask to stay at their place overnight. She could not stay with Marcus because he would expect her to sleep with him unless he had someone else attending the party that he liked better, which was unlikely. That was not Marcus's style. If Monia refused to sleep with Marcus, he would have hounded her until he either got his way or she was back at home in Seaside. Monia decided not to set herself up for a bad time just to show Jeremiah how it feels. He's already angry enough with her and acting like his spoiled child self. Also, she knew it would be unfair to show up at Marcus's fortieth birthday party and refuse to sleep with him when that was likely his main reason for inviting her.

--

The conference is educational and boring as a slug race. Monia makes sure she is well rested for each session but still has to fight to keep her eyes open during much of the conference. She does find the Child Obesity Q&A session interesting, not to say none of the other sessions are captivating, but that particular issue is the most informative for Monia. She is very pleased with her knowledge level. There are few topics or methodologies that she does not understand. Doctor Singh and Pamela have trained her well thus far.

There are sessions that are designated as physicians only sessions and cause great joy amongst the few physician's assistance in attendance.

This is not Pamela's first bariatric conference so she knows a number of their fellow attendees and has partied with a few. She tells Monia that one of the docs and two of the other PA's are talking about taking in a club on West 10th Street on Friday night. "They're a fun group. Just be careful of Wayne, Monia. He's been eyeing you and can get a little grabby when he's had too much to drink. We'll take our own cab down and back."

"I'm sticking with you, buddy, so don't lead me astray."

"We'll have a good time and after sitting through all this repetitive crap, we'll need to let off some steam."

Monia agrees.

The conference ends at mid day on Friday. The ladies have a light lunch and go out for a little shopping. They are back resting in their hotel rooms by four. After dinner, they meet up with six other conference attendees in front of the small jazz club, snatch up two tiny tables, and squeeze in together. The first group is the Henry Jackman Trio who rock their set. Monia relaxes and enjoys her share of $10 drinks as she tries to drown Jeremiah from her psyche. The drinks are good and potent and seem to be working. The music is sublime. By the third set Monia is ready to pass out and thinks she could be hallucinating. Pamela gets her back to the hotel where she throws up and eventually falls into a deep fitful slumber.

--

A somewhat haggard Monia begs off from partying with Pamela and two other diehard partiers on Saturday. Monia returns to the small Jazz club on West 10th St. accompanied by her father, Darnell. The music is everything Monia described and brings a smile to Darnell's tired unshaven face. Instead of the Chase Manley Quartet closing out the night as they had the night before, they perform the middle set and just about bring the house down. The piano man is unquestionably a virtuoso and is in rare form. Darnell slips the waiter twenty dollars along with his business card to pass to the pianist. Five minutes later the waiter returns with an odd look on her face and asks Darnell to follow her. Monia starts to go with her father but he tells her to wait for him.

Darnell Phillips enters the small dimly lit office at the very back of the little jazz club. There, grinning at him, twenty years older and twenty five pounds heavier, sitting on a folding metal chair is Trotter Sumuels. Trotter stands and the two men embrace long and hard. They stand back and look at each other for a moment before Trotter asks, "How'd you find me, man?"

"I didn't. Monia did." Darnell takes a seat in another folding chair that is there for his benefit.

"Monia, little Monia. How did she know it was me? I thought my disguise was pretty good." Trotter pats on his expanded abdomen. "Monia couldn't have been more that eleven or twelve years old when I left and I've changed a lot."

"Man, why did you do this?" Darnell looks at his old friend with great despair.

Trotter ignores the question and asks what is most important to him. "Phil, what's going on with my oldest boy, Jeremiah? I can find information about Clifford. I've been keeping up with him since he graduated high school, but I can't find anything on Jeremiah."

"When was the last time you looked? Have you looked online lately?"

"Not in years. I guess I just stopped looking after I couldn't find anything for so long."

"All you've got to do is type in Jeremiah Sumuels in the search engine and Seaside, California."

"He's still in Seaside?" Trotter asks, surprised.

"He left for a long time, lived in LA for a while before going into the Army and serving two hitches in Iraq. He moved back to LA for a bit and then came back to the Peninsula about nine years ago.

"He's okay, though?"

Darnell takes out his cell phone and pulls up Jeremiah's business.

Trotter pulls out his reading glasses and perches them on his nose as he looks at the screen. He sees photos of his old friend Gilbert's garage all spruced up and expanded. "That's Gilbert's place, ain't it?"

"Yep, well it was. It's Jeremiah's place now."

"He bought Gilbert's place? That's a big, reputable business, man." Trotter is shocked.

"Bought him out free and clear; lock, stock, and barrel."

Trotter sits there and reads about Jeremiah's business. He reads the reviews and takes in the entire site. He reads how Jeremiah is considered a premiere customizer in Northern California and how he has expanded the business to include parts and about his plans for increased automobile sales. Trotter feels emotional and his eyes fill with water. "That balling took Clifford all the way through college, didn't it?"

"Sure did. Sharon was really disappointed that Jeremiah refused to go back to school. She held on to the hope that he would play ball and go to college but you know it was too late for that by the time you left. He had missed too much school. He was a damn good ball handler, man."

"Yes, he was, as good as Cliff, if not better. You know, that's how I was able to follow Clifford. His graduation, then the scholarships made it easy to keep up with him. I know where Clifford's office is and his home but I couldn't find out anything about Jeremiah.

The men get quiet for a moment before Trotter states, "My boys turned out pretty good, didn't they, Phil?"

"Yeah, they did. They're good boys."

"Man, I can't thank you enough for all you did for my family. I was too weak to stay there and take care of them like I should have."

"It hasn't been easy, Trot. Those boys needed you. Sharon needed you. We all needed you. How could you just leave everybody like that, man? How could you do that to your family? I mean, I want to say how could you do that to me, but I'm not important, but the boys and Sharon, man. How could you do it? Clifford won't have anything to do with Jeremiah. He pressed the Seaside PD for years to arrest his brother. He jumped Jeremiah twice that I know of because he thought Jeremiah did something to you. It was really bad, man."

Trotter looks as if he's aged ten years in the past twenty minutes. Darnell rises from his seat. "I need to go check on Monia."

"Is she here?"

"Yeah, she caught your set last night and brought me here tonight so I could identify you. She wasn't sure it was you. You mind if I bring her back. I think she'd like to see you."

"Bring her on back, man!"

After Monia and Darnell visit with Trotter Sumuels, the men make plans to meet for lunch the following day. Darnell is not certain Trotter will show up and concerned the man might disappear again, so he tells Monia they should wait to tell anyone in Seaside about Trotter until after their talk the next day. He does not want to get Sharon and her sons' hopes up if the man goes in the wind again.

"I've already called mom and told her. I asked her not to tell Miss Sharon until she talked to you and she agreed that was best."

"Monia, you should have waited. What if it wasn't him?"

"Then you wouldn't have been back there so long, dad. I knew it was him by the look on your face. I'm glad you got to see your friend again and that he's still alive. His sons look just like him."

Darnell smiles at his child. "Maybe I just wanted to be the one to tell your mother, Chunga. I'm looking for anyway I can to get in her good graces again."

--

"Monia sure is a beautiful woman, Phil. She's got a good spirit too, man, a lot like Clarissa. I bet you guys are real proud," Trotter tells Darnell the next day as they sit and talk.

"Yes we are. I don't think four children together could make us more proud." Darnell beams.

"No grandchildren yet? She's not married is she?"

"No, not yet. Her mother's got her eyes set on a prospect though, one of your boys"

This gets a smile out of Trotter. "Clifford?"

"Jeremiah."

"Jeremiah's a lot older than Monia isn't he?"

"Only five years. It was a lot when they were kids but not now."

"That's all, five years. That's nothing. Wow, Jeremiah and Monia. 'Moanie' he used to call her, his little Moanie. He was always crazy about Monia. Clifford was too, but I guess he was too mean."

Darnell likes talking about his daughter but he's anxious for Trotter to explain the past twenty years so he leans back in his seat and says, "So, talk to me, brother."

The musician known as Samuel Terry sits with his old friend Darnell for more than three hours that Sunday and does a brain dump. The story he tells is astounding to him and he feels as if a huge boulder is being removed from his chest as he delves further into the details of his life for the past twenty years.

"Man I owed so much money to Little Willie and I had that young girl begging me to leave Sharon for her."

"What young girl was that?"

"Shirley was her name. I never introduced you to her. She's Annie Jiles's girl. Normally, Willie would hold off on collecting my debts but he wanted Shirley, wanted her bad. That cat and two other dudes I never seen before roughed me up pretty bad just a week or so before I took off."

"Why didn't you come to me, man? You came to me before. You know I wouldn't have turned you down."

"Darnell, you would have needed to mortgage your home and your practice to help me out of the fix I was in. I knew Willie wouldn't mess with my family but he wouldn't have had a problem killing me. He hated me all behind a piece of tail, man. It wasn't only the money."

"You know Little Willie died years ago."

"I know. I read it in the paper online. I keep up with the news around the Peninsula, especially the obituaries."

"So why didn't you come on back home. Did you come straight to New York when you left Seaside?"

"Nah, Nah. I always kept a little money stashed away in case me or Sharon gambled away the house payment or bill money. I had a little over a thousand dollars, nothing much. I took that and caught the bus to LA. I didn't have any trouble finding a job at a repair shop in a part of the city where no one would recognize me, mostly Mexicans in that part of the city. You know I had a few friends in LA so I had to stay real quiet. I made pretty good there and lived real cheap. I only stayed there about year, maybe a little longer. The dude I was working for started getting all these good jobs based on my skills. I taught those guys some things and learned some too. That's where I really changed my look. I started growing my hair out and grew my beard. Always wore glasses though I still didn't need them back then. I do now though. How bout you? Your eyes gone bad too, man?"

"Yeah, I've been in contacts for a while now."

"Anyway, I didn't have any trouble gaining weight, eating all that good Mexican food in LA. I never got so tired of tortillas, rice, and beans, carne guisada, and picadillo. I miss that stuff here but it's getting easier to find good Mexican food here in the city now. When I left LA, man, I took the train to Tennessee and settled in there."

"Did you vanish on those people in LA too?" Darnell asks, showing his frustration at Trotter's matter-of-fact manner of telling the story about abandoning his family.

"Nah, man, I didn't want anyone else looking for me. I told my boss and the family I was renting from that I was leaving. Boss wasn't too happy because he didn't have anybody with my skills. They were good but not that good. When I left I had a craving to play music so I got back in the groove in Memphis. Got some gigs with blues and country groups. I became pretty well known around there. Cats always looking for someone to fill in on a set, you know. I had a number of offers to go on the road but that was way too risky. I get offers here every few weeks or so but I turn them all down. I do just fine picking up work here and there. I stayed in Memphis a little over eight years. Finally, I got bored. The auto shop I was working in during the day, went out of business. There were a couple of fellows who had guaranteed me some session work if I ever made it up this way, so I said why not. By that time I had more money than I knew what to do with. I'm telling you Darnell, living off the grid, so to speak, is a hell of a lot cheaper than getting caught up in all this financial crap they keep shoving at us. Of course giving up gambling, drugs, and women on the side plays a good part too. You always told me that. Too bad I had to get so damn old to learn." Trotter laughs as if he has told a funny joke. Darnell humors him and grins along.

"I've got money stashed away and every dime I don't need is for my boys. I hope they'll accept it. I've been with a nice woman for the past five years. She makes good money and doesn't need mine. She's much younger than me and wants to get married, but I told her that's not possible. She's pretty understanding and easy to get along with, not like Sharon, man."

Trotter takes a break to think about his wife, how fine and sweet she was when he first met her and how rich and deep she became over their years together. "This woman I'm with now is like Sharon was before I gave her such a hard time." Trotter drops his head and shakes it in recollection of the misery he put his wife through. He looks sad when he says, "I sure do miss that woman. Seems like I miss her more every day. I never stopped loving her, not ever and I'm still in love with her. After all these years I still get excited just thinking about her. I started calling that shop where she works a few years after I left. Just needed to hear her voice. Often she doesn't answer, but I keep calling until she picks up. I used to call around the holiday's every year but she got suspicious and called me out. It shocked the hell out of me when that woman said, 'Trotter, is that you? If that's you, you son of a bitch, stop calling here.' I held on a second longer and then hung up. Now I stagger the calls."

"Why do you call the shop and not the house?" Darnell asks.

"I figure if I called the house she would be certain that it's me, and I don't want to scare her by calling and hanging up. She never picked up with another man?" Trotter asks hopefully.

"I'll let you and Sharon talk about that. I don't want to discuss her business." Darnell answers discreetly. The owner of the retail stores Sharon manages has been in love with her for years. Sometimes Sharon is out of pocket for a day or two and Clarissa and Darnell have long believed that Sharon spends time with her boss at his Carmel Valley home.

"Well, it's not like I have the right to complain if she does have someone. I do and have had someone for years now. I want Sharon to be happy, Phil."

The man goes quiet while he regroups his thoughts. "I kept up with the news out of Monterey and I knew they were looking for me and that Jeremiah was a suspect. If they had charged him I would have come back. I wouldn't have let my boy go to jail for that. You have no idea how many times I wanted to call you and make sure he was cleared but I was scared man and I didn't want to burden you with my whereabouts.

"I thought about coming back but I was too ashamed of what I had done to Sharon and my boys, to everyone. I had a lot of people looking up to me, man, and I didn't deserve it but I loved that adulation. I couldn't have faced all those people. I didn't want everyone to know how selfish I was. I'll be honest with you, Phil; I wanted a change so bad I could taste it. I was tired of being saddled with my wife and kids, that house, and my day job. I wanted my freedom and I regret it more than my impending death. I could've gotten that shit straightened out with Willie. Sharon had started complaining about college for the boys and how much money we needed for that and it seemed like it was just one piece of boring shit after another eating up all of my life and my time. I was just fed up to here with all the minutia of life." Trotter takes his hand and lays it out flat at the top of his forehead. "I chickened out, man; I was a coward, and I'm still a coward. Now you understand why I can never go back and face my family, I just don't think I can. I appreciate you being here and not judging me too harshly, at least not now from what I can see. God blessed me with good people in and all around my life but I haven't been a good friend. I will never be able to repay you for being there for my family, man, never."

"So you are not coming out to Cali to see your family."

Trotter knows that his sons and most likely his wife will want to see him and confront him at some point in time but he is not up to making that happen yet. He cannot commit to giving his family that closure. Trotter shakes his head. "I got to process this. I wish I could just fly out there and say "Hey, I been gone but Darnell and Monia found me and now I'm back. If I thought I could and things would work out, I would do that but you know as well as me, that won't work. After what I've done to them, I don't think I can go back and face them. I just don't think I can."

--

The first call Darnell Phillips makes after an entire afternoon with his long lost friend, Trotter, is to his estranged wife, Clarissa, who tells him, "I haven't called Sharon and told her anything yet. I will wait for you to get back and you and I can go and talk to her together."

Darnell agrees with Clarissa's decision and can't help but feel pleased at the alliance he, his wife, and daughter have forged over the Sumuels.

Chapter 18

Monia flies back home on Sunday and feels as if she has had the most exhausting weekend of her life by the time she shows up for work on Monday morning. First chance she gets, she asks Dr. Singh if they can wait a day or two before the debriefing. She explains that her family had a crisis and although she feels well prepared, she'd like some time to review her notes so as not to miss anything. The doctor agrees to the delay and in her normal fashion asks Monia if there is anything she can do to help.

Pamela gives Monia a somewhat cool greeting when they meet each other at work on Monday. When they were last together, Monia was partying hard, laughing, drinking, flirting with one of the other PAs, and enjoying the music. Pamela noticed that toward the end of the last set Monia became pensive and she barely talked on the taxi ride back to their hotel. Monia had called her early Saturday morning and said an important family matter had come up and she wouldn't be able to spend the day or the evening out with Pamela. Although Monia apologized profusely, Pamela remains a little upset with her coworker. Monia was a little too evasive when she called. Pamela wonders if Monia pulled a Ja'Niece on her and found a man she wanted to spend time with.

Monia can't worry about Pamela or explain the situation to her right now. She hopes to give a complete apology and an explanation of her behavior after the Sumuels family learns she and Darnell have seen Trotter Sumuels alive and well, living in New York City.

Monia's brain started working overtime, no sooner than she had awakened the Saturday after seeing the man who resembled Trotter Sumuels in the jazz club. She had lain in the hotel bed and tried to clear her mind and concentrate on what or who she had actually seen that Friday night. She had drunk more than her limit in an attempt at having a good time and not thinking about the ever-present Jeremiah. Roger, the PA she had flirted with, was good-looking, fun, and married, thank God. All thoughts of taking him to bed flew out the window with that bit of information. Of course, his marital status was no deterrent to his attempt to get Monia into bed.

Everyone at their table was having a good time. The conference was over and they all wanted to make the most of their time in the biggest city of them all. The music kept getting better until it reached a climatic point with the piano man swinging out on an original piece composed by the band leader. Everyone had stopped speaking and just listened to that man rock those keys. Monia was so lit that she had to focus. At first she thought, *I'm so drunk that this guy looks just like Jeremiah. I've got to get that man out of my head.* The more she watched the man she noticed that he also bore a remarkable resemblance to Clifford Sumuels. At that point, Monia had sat up straight and tried to sober up but it was useless. She was hopelessly drunk. She ignored Roger and pretty much everyone else for the rest of the set and declined to accompany the group to a dance club after leaving the jazz club. Pamela and one of the other guys had taken Monia back to the hotel and went on to meet the others after getting her to her room.

Monia had told herself that she was imagining things but couldn't let the strong feeling that the piano man was Trotter Sumuels go. That call to her father was a hard one. She had to tell him that she had too much to drink which was a strict taboo with Darnell when it came to Monia. He always told her she would be setting herself up for trouble if she drank too much away from her own home. "That's the perfect opportunity for people to take advantage of you, Monia. Always keep your head clear when you're out at night." Monia's father had repeated that same advice in a hundred different ways since she had become old enough to drink. Also this man was heavier than Trotter, who Monia remembers as a tall slender man, and he played the piano, not the saxophone. Still Monia had a strong sense that the man was Trotter Sumuels.

Monia's first thought had been to call Jeremiah but she quickly decided not to put him through such an ordeal, especially if the man turned out to be someone other than Trotter Sumuels. She considered calling Shirley and asking her to fly up to New York, but the situation would have been traumatizing for her also. She even considered calling Clifford, but he had been the most irrational about Trotter's disappearance over the past twenty years. She had wanted to take a picture, but the club had a strict policy against photographs and recordings of any sort. So she had been left with one recourse. Through the process of elimination, Monia decided the best person for the job was her father, Darnell Phillips. He had known Trotter Sumuels as well as anyone.

Before Monia made the call to her father, she went online to check out the jazz club's website and found the piano man's name, Samuel Terry. When Monia read that name she plopped down in the desk chair. The name was similar to Trotter's with the same initials reversed. She had to call her father.

Darnell had been leery, skeptical, hopeful, and doubtful, all in a matter of minutes during Monia's call for help. He had told Monia he would call her back in order to take time and think about what his daughter was saying and consider his possible actions. He went online and found two photographs of the group the piano man was playing with but the photos were of such poor quality, they were of no use. Darnell found his hands trembling and he got a shot of scotch to calm his nerves. "How certain are you this guy is Trotter?" he asked Monia when he called her back.

"Far from a hundred percent, dad," Monia had whined loudly into the phone in exasperation.

"What do you want me to do, Monia?"

"When I close my eyes I see Mr. Trotter in that piano player, dad. My gut tells me it's him. Yes, he's very different from the man I remember but his mannerisms are so much like Jeremiah's and he looks like both Jeremiah and Clifford. Dad, I'd bet money it's Mr. Trotter. You've got to come right away. This is the bands last night at this club and I can't find where they're playing next. I know I sound crazy but I think we need to find out for the Sumuels; don't you?"

Darnell conceded and caught the flight that would get him to New York City the soonest. When he sat in that little club and confirmed Samuel Terry's identification as Trotter Sumuels Monia had felt vindication. She felt as if she had cured cancer, wiped out world hunger, won the wars on drugs and poverty, resolved all the world's wars, and ended all forms of discrimination. Two days later, after learning that Trotter Sumuels would leave his family in emotional limbo, Monia wished she had never found the man.

Monia feels she is betraying her friend Jeremiah and had wanted to tell him about finding his father in New York but she must respect her parents' decision to allow Sharon Sumuels to tell her sons about their father. She feels Sharon, Jeremiah, and Clifford should be informed immediately of Trotter's whereabouts and that he appears to be living quite well. Monia is thankful that Jeremiah remains distant and upset with her over Marcus. She fears she would not be able to look him in his face and keep such important information from him.

--

On a peaceful Monday afternoon, Darnell picks up Clarissa from her home and drives the four blocks to their friend Sharon's house. They have agreed that Darnell will break the news to Sharon since he has the first hand information.

Sharon is initially pleasantly surprised to find Clarissa and Darnell together at her front door since she holds high hopes that her friends will get back together as husband and wife. They are barely inside her home before she realizes they are visiting her on a serious issue. "Please sit down. Can I offer either of you something to drink?" Her guests decline drinks but both take seats. "What is going on that both of you show up at my house this time of day looking so somber?"

Clarissa looks at Darnell and nods her head for him to tell Sharon their news. Darnell scoots to the edge of his seat and leans in toward Sharon before he begins. "Sharon, Trotter is alive and"

Before Darnell can finish, Sharon says, "I told you all the time that Trotter was alive."

"No, you don't understand. I've seen Trotter; I've talked to him."

Sharon sits up a little straighter and furrows her brow. "When? Where?"

"In New York."

"When were you in New York?"

"Just this past weekend."

Sharon looks at Clarissa and then looks back at Darnell. "I don't understand. I saw you Friday night. You didn't say anything. You were at bingo with me and Clarissa on Friday. You didn't say anything about going to New York."

"Yeah, I know. I received a call from Monia early Saturday morning. She wanted me to fly to New York right away. She said she thought she had seen Trotter but was far from certain. She needed me to come and see the man for myself, so I caught an early afternoon flight out. I didn't want to call anyone until I saw the man. Monia took me to the jazz club she had been at the night before and sure enough there was Trotter, sitting there on the piano playing in a jazz quartet."

"Are you telling me that son of a bitch is alive? All these years that son of a bitch has been alive." Sharon breaks down and starts yelling. "How could he? How could he?"

Clarissa thinks, *All this time she has been saying he was alive but thought he was dead.*

Sharon covers her face and sobs into her hands, "How could he do this to us. Oh my God!"

Clarissa moves next to Sharon on the sofa and tries to comfort her, but she continues to sob uncontrollably into Clarissa's shoulder. She sobs at the relief she feels because her children's father is alive and not dead. She sobs at the pain of being abandoned by the man she loved nearly all her life and bore two sons. She sobs because Jeremiah will no longer live under the suspicion of being "that boy who did away with his father." She sobs to release the anger and because she can't control the tears and the emotions any longer.

Clarissa finally tires of all the crying and starts to move away from her friend. "Wait a minute, wait a minute, wait a minute!" Clarissa says as she reaches for her purse. She pulls out a joint and some matches. Before Darnell realizes what she is doing, Clarissa places the joint in her mouth, strikes a match and fires up. She takes a long drag and holds the smoke in her lungs for a moment before releasing it and handing it to Sharon. "I just need you to take a hit off of this for a minute. Because I need you to calm down."

"Clara, what are you doing? Why are you giving her that?" Darnell asks as he approaches the ladies and reaches for the joint.

Clarissa looks at him as if to say, "You better back up off me," and moves the joint out of his reach. "She needs to calm down and this is the only way I know how to help her. She's getting hysterical. This worked for me when your ass left me."

Darnell backs up a couple of steps and says, "I didn't leave you. You threw me out."

"Well it worked for me anyway, whatever the circumstances, it worked."

Sharon has stopped crying and watches her friends. When Clarissa shoves the burning blunt in her direction, she declares, "I don't want that, Clara."

"Take a couple of hits. All these hysterics ain't doing nothing for nobody. Take a couple of hits," Clarissa demands.

Sharon takes a couple of hits of the reefer and immediately starts to feel the effect. She stretches out on her sofa for a few moments as her tears dry up.

Darnell, always on task, asks, "What do you want to do about the boys, Sharon?"

"Well, they need to know. It's not as if they are little children and I need to keep this a secret from them. They have to know. They have been living in this same hell I've been living with all these years. We have to relieve some of that. I don't know if this news will just throw them into different hell or what but we have to get them out of the one they are in now – this limbo of not knowing if their father is dead or alive. What happened to him? Where did he go? Who killed him or did God only knows what to him? We have to release them from this." Sharon is nearly screaming at this point.

"Wait a minute." Clarissa stops her. "Do I need to give you another hit?"

"No. I don't want any more of that crap." Then something absolutely amazing happens – Sharon laughs and says, "Well, maybe."

Darnell throws his arms up in the air and turns and leaves the room in disgust.

Sharon takes a coupled of more hits off of the relit joint and smiles up at Clarissa. "What was it Richard Pryor said about this stuff? I think it was him. Said 'stuff make you simple.' It'll make you mellow; that's for sure."

Darnell returns with a glass of water for Sharon and repeats his earlier question. "How do you want to do this with the boys?"

"We need to get them both here so I can tell them as soon as possible. Clifford needs to get up here. I'm not going to tell him over the phone. There was a reason you chose not to tell me over the phone and I owe my boys the same consideration. We need to get his ass up here so he can be here and look his brother in the face and apologize after I give him the news."

"How do we get him here quickly without scaring the crap out of him? Darnell asks. "I wouldn't want him driving all that distance like a bat out of hell."

"He needs to fly. He needs to get on a plane today or first thing in the morning and get here." Sharon says as she rises from her sofa and goes straight to the phone. She puts on her mother's voice and calls her youngest son, Clifford. "I need to see you and I need to see you today or first thing tomorrow. I need you to fly. I don't want you to drive. I need to talk to you face to face. These are things I cannot say to you over the phone."

"What is it, Mom?" Clifford asks fearfully.

"I need you to come, Clifford. I need you to come right away."

"Is it Jeremiah? Did something happen to Jeremiah?"Clifford sounds panicked now.

Sharon bites her tongue to keep from cursing Clifford and telling him, "Why the hell are you asking me if something happened to Jeremiah when you haven't done anything but given your brother grief over the past twenty years. How dare you start acting like you care for him now?" But Sharon holds her piece and tells Clifford, "Your brother is fine but I need you here. I need to know exactly what time to expect you. This is of the greatest urgency and I need you to fly. Do you understand me, Clifford?"

Clifford gets off the phone with his mother and immediately dials Darnell's number. Darnell looks at the caller ID and looks at the two ladies. "It's Clifford," He tells them. "Yeah, what's up?" He answers and tells Clifford, "I'm here with your mother. Have you made your reservations yet?"

"What's going on, Darnell? Mom is scaring me."

"Your mother told you that you need to get here. She would not have told you that if it wasn't important for her to see you. You need to get here."

Clifford has never had a call like this from his mother or anyone. Sharon has told him in the past that she wanted to see him and the boys and invited them up for a visit. She has also planned quick visits to his home in San Diego, but she has never before made a direct demand for him to return home immediately with no explanation. Clifford considers calling Jeremiah to find out what's going on but decides not to make the call to his brother. He makes his reservations and calls his mother back and tells her what time to expect him the next day.

Sharon immediately picks up the phone and calls Jeremiah and tells him when he answers, "Jeremiah, I need you here at my house tomorrow at twelve noon sharp. I have something of the greatest urgency to discuss with you."

"What's going on, Mom?"

"I need you here tomorrow and then I'll explain."

"Are you sick? What is it?"

"Jeremiah, I need to do this the way I'm doing it and I need you to understand. There is a reason I'm doing this and I need you to be here at my house at noon tomorrow and I need you to be on time."

Once Sharon completes the calls to her sons she sits down calmly and asks Darnell to tell her everything from the moment he received the call from Monia to his complete contact with her treacherous husband. Darnell tells her what he can recall and ends by informing her that Trotter has no plans to return to Seaside and afford his wife and sons the closure they deserve.

Sharon barely shakes her head as her eyes begin to well up again.

Darnell looks pitiable enough to be the man who abandoned Sharon, Jeremiah, and Clifford twenty years ago when he says, "Sharon, I wasn't going to tell you this but Trotter did say he never stopped loving you. He says he still loves you and the boys with all his heart."

Darnell and Clarissa can barely hear the "Humph," that escapes Sharon's chest. "I understand why you weren't going to tell me that, Darnell, because you know as well as I, that it ain't what a nigga say, it's what a nigga do."

--

Clifford Sumuels gets on the first flight out of San Diego that will get him to San Jose in the early hours of the day. He picks up his rental car and makes the fifty mile drive to Seaside.

Jeremiah pulls up to his mother's home at eleven fifty five in the morning and recognizes Darnell's car but not the other vehicle parked in front of the house. He enters his mother's home and finds his brother, Clifford, who he has not seen in sixteen years sitting with his mother. He nods, "Cliff."

"Jeremiah."

The brothers greet each other frostily. Darnell and Clarissa are seated in Sharon's kitchen and wave a greeting to Jeremiah.

Jeremiah looks at his mother and asks, "What's going on, Mom. Why do you have us both here?"

"Have a seat Jeremiah." Sharon says to her son. Once Jeremiah takes a seat, she continues. "Now that I have you both here, I want you to know that Darnell has seen and spoken with your father this past weekend."

Both men look stunned. They look at each other then back at their mother. Jeremiah says, "Seen dad, where?"

"In New York City, at a jazz club."

Clifford does not utter a word but Jeremiah says, "You're kidding me!"

"No, I am not making this up and you know I wouldn't do something like that. I have not seen him or spoken with him but Darnell assures me that it is indeed you father. He spoke with him on Saturday night for a short while and then met him again on Sunday and it seems they sat and talked for hours."

Clifford finally comes to life and asks, "How long has dad been there. How long has Darnell known he was alive? How did Darnell find him?"

"Darnell didn't find him. Monia found him."

"Monia!" Jeremiah stands up from his seat. "How the hell did Monia find my dad?"

Sharon places her hand on Jeremiah's lower arm and guides him back into his chair. "Monia was in New York this past week for a conference. She stayed over a day or two with friends and went out to the club on Friday night and your dad was in the set. She was not sure it was your father but thought he bore an uncanny resemblance to both of you."

"Why didn't she call me?" Jeremiah asks angrily.

"Because, Jeremiah, she didn't know for certain if it was your dad. Monia was just a child when he vanished and would not have remembered him that well. According to Darnell he has changed significantly. He wears dreads now, like his eldest son and his hair is completely gray. He wears dark tinted glasses in public and has gained about twenty pounds. So I guess he has taken on a whole new persona, except he still plays music and still works on cars just like he did when he left us twenty years ago. Monia wasn't sure but thought the resemblance too great to ignore. She called her father and asked him to fly out to New York immediately. Darnell, knowing Monia would not ask him to do such a thing unless she was fairly certain, caught the first flight out and was at the club on Saturday."

"What did dad say?" Clifford asks in a near whisper, barely conscious as all the horrible circumstances surrounding his father's disappearance swirl around in his mind. "Did he tell Darnell why he did this to us?"

"I have not asked Darnell many questions. I let him tell me what he learned. I called my sons almost immediately once I learned about Trotter."

"Is he coming here?" Jeremiah asks.

"He told Darnell that he couldn't face us." Sharon says quietly.

Jeremiah stands again and looks around. No one speaks for several moments before Jeremiah asks his mother, "What do you want to do, Mom?"

"Jeremiah, frankly, I don't know. I'm numb right now. I know my heart is breaking into yet smaller pieces. I didn't think my heart could break again but those pieces that have been broken for all these years are breaking again."

"You want me to go see him?" Jeremiah asks.

"I wouldn't ask that of you. You have to make that decision for yourself. Same goes for you, Clifford. If I feel like I want to see him, I'll go. We don't know that he will stay where he is. He may have already left now that he has been confronted by Darnell. I thought about it all night long last night. It crossed my mind that maybe Darnell should not have approached him. Maybe he should have waited and let one of us speak to Trotter, but Darnell was very close to him and simply had to. If your father is going to run again he would probably do so even if it was one of us who approached him. We each have to make our own decision as to how we want to deal with the news that he is alive and doing just fine is my understanding, and very concerned about how we are all doing." Sharon stops and seems stricken before she continues. "Maybe you both should talk to Darnell now. I think I'll go and lie down."

"Mom, do you need anything?" Jeremiah asks.

"No, I think I'm just going to rest for a bit."

"Mom, if it's okay, I think I'll stay for a few days."

"That's totally up to you, Clifford. I'll be fine." Sharon walks proudly off to her bedroom.

Clarissa follows her friend to her room and Darnell joins Jeremiah and Clifford in the living room. He sits down with the two young men and recants all the information he shared with Sharon the day before.

Clifford hangs his head as he listens. "I'm having a hard time believing this." He raises his head and looks at Darnell with pleading in his eyes.

Darnell pulls out his cell phone and shows the brothers a photo that Trotter allowed Monia to take of him and Darnell. The two men are posing and looking straight into the camera with Darnell looking solemn and Trotter grinning at the camera as if all is right with the world.

"I don't believe this. He's grinning into that camera like he hasn't screwed up our lives, like nothing has happened, like everything is just fine. I can't believe this," Clifford rants.

Jeremiah doesn't say a word. He sits there and stares. Darnell knows this is dangerous. Jeremiah suffered greatly behind his father's loss and disappearance. He was given no time to grieve and had no one to blame or accuse. His own mother had questioned if he had anything to do with his father's disappearance. The brothers had become estranged based on Trotter's abandonment. "What are you thinking about Jeremiah?" Darnell asks.

Jeremiah raises his eyes to Darnell's face but it is as if he is looking right through the man. "I'm just wondering what I should do?"

"Jerry, I owe you an apology, man," Clifford says in a low humble voice. I've been so mad for so long and so many times I admitted to myself I was wrong but I continued to blame you. I just needed someone to blame. God, man, can you ever forgive me?"

"Might take me some time, Bro." Jeremiah doesn't look at his brother as he rises from his chair to leave. "You gonna be here with Mom?"

"Yeah, I'll be here." Clifford stands and extends his hand to Jeremiah, who shakes his brother's hand before walking out the door. "I'll be back later."

--

Monia has just entered her home from work, put her bag down, and kicked off her shoes when her doorbell rings. She is not surprised to see Jeremiah standing on her porch with his back to the door. As usual, he walks into her home without an invitation. "So how was your trip to New York," He asks as he stands in the middle of her living room looking around, too angry to look at Monia.

"It was revealing."

"Why didn't you call me and tell me you found my father, Monia?"

"Because I didn't know for certain that it was him, Jeremiah. I couldn't call you and tell you I think I maybe, possibly see someone who could be your father and I'm pretty damn certain that it's him but I'm just not sure. I couldn't do that to you. I had to call the person that I knew would recognize him and that I could trust to drop everything and come and talk to the man. I was only twelve when your dad disappeared. I just didn't know."

Jeremiah looks at Monia as he realizes she dealt with the situation the best she knew how. "I just wish you had told me."

Monia's eyes well up but she is determined not to cry. This is Jeremiah's problem and she will do him no good fretting over it worse than him. "I'm so sorry, baby. I'm so sorry. If I had known for certain, I would have."

"When your dad told you it was him, why didn't you call and tell me?"

"Because dad thought Sharon should tell you and Clifford, not me and I didn't know if that was right or not. I just didn't know. All I could do was lean to my father for what he thought was best and he felt Sharon should tell the two of you together and that she should know first. That's what he thought was best and I went along with him. Please don't be angry with me?" Monia walks over to Jeremiah and wraps her arms around his waist and places her head on his chest. Jeremiah stands there stiff as a board and does not return the embrace. After a minute, Monia lets go and steps away from him. He sits down on her sofa, clasps his hands together, and puts them under his chin. "Goddamn it, I don't know what I'm going to do about this! I just don't know what I'm supposed to do. This is all such a mess."

"Why is it such a mess? I mean, he's alive; isn't that a good thing?"

"He abandoned us. Abandoned us and allowed everyone to think that maybe he was dead and that I killed him. He basically said 'I don't care about you guys anymore, I don't want you anymore.' I loved my dad. I loved him a lot. God, did I love that man! He was a good father. I'm not saying he was perfect or that he didn't have bad habits but he taught us so much. He showed us how to live well and take good care of ourselves and how to be good strong men and then he just walked away. How are we supposed to believe in the things he taught us after that? How are we supposed to believe in anything?"

"How is your mom?"

"Not good. We're all so lost now. My father may have been found but I feel lost." Jeremiah gets up to leave. "I've got to go and take care of my girl?"

"Can I come with you?" Monia asks.

"I wouldn't be good company."

"I just want to help, Jeremiah."

"Maybe some other time," Jeremiah leaves as abruptly as he came in.

--

Late the next morning Jeremiah returns to his mother's home and finds Clifford sitting at the kitchen table drinking coffee but there's no sign of Sharon. "Where's mom?"

"She's gone to work."

"Gone to work?"

Clifford looks at his brother matter-of-factly and says, "Said she was going to work, man. Says she can't let this stop her life. Says she's got to keep living. Got up this morning, showered and dressed, fixed breakfast for me and her, and sat here and read the paper and chatted with me. She looked stricken. I tried to stop her but couldn't. She's gone to work." Clifford drinks from his cup. "Want some coffee?"

"Yeah, I'll take a little bit." Jeremiah sits at the table and let's his younger brother serve him. He doesn't feel a strain. You'd think after all the years of separation and all of Clifford's accusations toward him that he would harbor resentment toward his brother, but he doesn't. He's just glad to have his brother back. Hopefully they can have a relationship again. Jeremiah drinks from his cup and smiles. "This is pretty good. Did you make it?"

"Yeah, I did. I need to cut back. That's my only addiction, coffee."

"So, what are we going to do?" Jeremiah asks Clifford.

"I was about to ask you the same thing, brother. What are we going to do?"

The brothers sit quietly and drink their coffee as they take in the splendor of the beautiful Monterey Bay from Sharon's large bay window. "It's beautiful ain't it, man?" Jeremiah asks his brother.

"It is. I never appreciated the beauty of the place growing up here. Looked out at that ocean every doggone day of my life growing up for fifteen years and never appreciated the view."

"I know, me neither until I came back. This is home again, this small little piece of the world, expensive as hell, but I love it."

"How could he do it, man? How could he just up and leave us the way he did?" Clifford asks. "There is nothing that could make me leave my children, nothing."

Jeremiah doesn't respond to the question. He doesn't have an answer. "How are your boys doing?"

"They're good."

"You get to spend much time with 'em?"

"Yeah, I do. Well not as much time as I would like. But you know I've got two boys and man they wear me out. So, yes, I get to spend plenty of time with them." Clifford chuckles.

"I was sorry to hear about your divorce."

"Happens," is all Clifford has to say about that unhappy event for a moment. "It was pretty rough going through it. I wanted to call you a couple of times but I was still trying to be – well. I really meant what I said yesterday when I apologized." Jeremiah can see water on the rims of Clifford's eyes. "I blamed all this shit on you. I just needed somebody to blame and I chose you. Boy, when I make up my mind about something that's how it is. Mom always said I was as stubborn and persistent as a bull terrier and I guess she was right because I was determined that you were at fault for dad not being here."

"That's okay, Bro."

Clifford shakes his head in shame and asks, "When do I get to meet my niece?"

"You and mom come to the house for dinner tonight."

"I'll see if she wants to come, but I'll come in any case. I probably won't stay too long if she doesn't come. I want to spend some time with her. I'm going to stay for a couple of days. I've got some other dentists covering me while I'm here." Clifford looks over at Jeremiah and says, "Man it's nice to have my brother back in my life."

"You know, I keep asking myself why, if I loved him so much, am I not relieved that he's alive?" Jeremiah asks not expecting a response from his brother.

Chapter 19

Shirley is beginning to wonder what has caused Monia to distance herself. The ladies of Dr. Navya Singh's Bariatric Clinic have grown closer since Monia has been on board. Shirley, Monia, Pamela, and Susan have become especially friendly, but for some reason Monia is avoiding her coworkers and keeping her nose low to the grindstone. When Pamela returned from the conference, she alluded to having cause to be pissed off at Monia but never shared any details and seemed only slightly annoyed. Monia's behavior causes her coworkers to question if something truly serious took place while Monia was in New York.

After two full days of no eye contact, no casual conversation, and only pacifying smiles from Monia, Shirley gets Pamela and Susan together and holds a conference. "What the hell happened to Monia while you two were away? Did you hit on her or something?"

Pamela purses her lips together with attitude and rolls her eyes at Shirley before answering. "I like 'em a little bigger and rougher than Monia. She's been acting strange every since we left the club Friday night. We were having such a good time and I must admit Monia was knocking 'em back but I don't think she had as much to drink as I did. After a while she just got quiet and didn't talk any more. We were all going to another club but she wanted to go back to the hotel. Me and one of the other guys took her to the hotel before we went to the next club. She and I were supposed to go shopping the next afternoon, but she called and said she had some urgent business to attend to and wouldn't be able to make it shopping or out with us that evening. I was a little pissed. At first I thought she was dissing me for a man but I don't know what's going on. I wonder if it's got something to do with Jeremiah."

"Why Jeremiah?" Shirley asks.

"She likes him a lot. You can tell," Susan says.

"I'm just wondering if one of us did something to upset her or maybe the Doc did something." Shirley looks from Susan to Pamela.

"I doubt it. She doesn't seem mad or upset. She just seems to be trying to stay away from us. I asked her to join us for dinner at Epsilon on Friday but she said she wouldn't be able to make it. She didn't say why and that's not like her." Susan looks concerned.

"Well if she keeps this up, I'm going to ask her. She may not tell me anything but I'm sure going to ask her," Shirley concludes.

--

Clifford watches his brother carry Erin off to her bed. The child had been so excited about meeting the man who is her father's brother and also her uncle that she begged Jeremiah to let her stay up a while longer. Jeremiah conceded and let his daughter sit in his lap while he and Clifford talked about past history, keeping the dialogue child friendly. It had only taken about fifteen minutes for Erin to snuggle into the pocket created by her father's arm and shoulder and pass out.

The brother's conversation quickly changes and becomes loud, boisterous and full of humor. Sharon had declined Jeremiah's dinner invitation and Clifford had told himself he needed to leave and get back to their mother immediately after dinner. He had arrived at Jeremiah's at seven but he and his brother are just getting to full steam at nine thirty. "So, man, what does Monia look like now? Is she as fine as she was five years ago? That was the last time I saw her."

Jeremiah's smile grows deep as he thinks about Monia. "Yeah man. She's real. She's grown into a nice woman."

"I'm surprised some dude hasn't snatched her up. Darnell probably runs anyone who tries off." Clifford looks at his brother for a moment. "Why did you get so pissed about her not telling you she had found dad."

Jeremiah rubs his chin a few times and says, "We've dated a little."

"Ah, I should have known it. You always did have a thang for Monia."

"What are you talking about, man?" Jeremiah leans back in his seat in protest.

"Man you would let me get away with all kinds of shit but not when it came to Monia. I used to like that girl when we were kids but you kept your big feet in the way. I should have guessed you were waiting for her to get old enough for you."

Jeremiah gets up from the table and heads off to the kitchen. "Dude, you make me sound like a pervert. I can't believe you're still dogging me about my shoe size." Jeremiah returns with two more Rolling Rocks.

"Yeah man, I used to talk about your big feet all the time. Thought I was really putting you down. I was too dumb to know that the ladies like men with big feet until I heard a couple of girls talking about 'Ooh, Jeremiah got big feet and girl did you see his hands.' It still took me a minute to realize the ladies were equating big feet to big other things.

"Man, I was stupid, especially when it came to Monia. I bet you don't remember telling me to leave her alone before you left here. I could do just about anything and you would turn a blind eye. I guess I had laid so many guilt trips on you about dad that you just ignored all my stupidity, but one night I was on the phone with one of Monia's girlfriends. When I got off the phone with her, you heard me tell my boy Harold that I was going to do her and then I was going to do Monia. Man, you walked up to me and looked me in my face and told me, 'You better leave Monia the fuck alone.' I got all flippant and shit and asked you, 'What you gon do about it if I don't? You ain't even gon be around here no mo.' All you said was 'Mess with Monia and find out.' You better believe I left old fine-assed Monia alone too." Clifford giggles. "I used to do shit just to get under your skin and you wouldn't even flinch. Monia was the Achilles Heel, but you left a few days after I realized that. I'd like to think I had better sense than to mess with her. Knowing Monia she probably would have kicked my ass herself. She never took any shit from me. Me and her actually got along pretty good once we got out of middle school but she always loved you. You two should end up together."

"I don't know about all that. We're just spending some time together once in a while." Jeremiah wants to change the subject and does.

The brothers talk until they both begin to yawn. "I better get up out of here. Mom will be wondering what happened to me. Thanks for having me over, Jeremiah. You plan on stopping by mom's tomorrow?" Clifford asks as he heads to the door.

"Yeah, sure. She wants us all to go out to dinner together."

The brothers embrace at the door and pat each other on the shoulder. Although these are troubled times, they are both pleased to be back together. Jeremiah reaches and opens the door for Clifford with both men wishing he could stay longer. They are shocked to find, there, standing on Jeremiah's front porch, Trotter Sumuels. The three men stand there and stare at each other until Clifford says, "Dad?"

"How you doing, Son?" Trotter responds. Turning to Jeremiah, he says, "Jeremiah."

Another moment passes before Trotter asks, "Can I come in?"

Trotter's sons step back inside and make way for him to enter. Once inside with the door closed, Jeremiah embraces his father long and hard. When he lets go, Clifford hugs Trotter also as his eyes well up with tears, yet again.

"I'm sorry about stopping by so late. Once I got here, I couldn't wait until tomorrow. I got your address from Darnell before he left. I told him I wasn't coming out here, that I couldn't face you guys but after seeing him and talking to him I knew I couldn't put this off any longer. I had to talk to you."

"Sit down, Dad." Jeremiah waves his father to a seat.

All three men sit down and Clifford asks, "What happened, Dad?"

Trotter breathes in deep and says, "Can you give me a few minutes, Son? For years I've been trying to figure out what I would say to you boys if God blessed me to see you again – how I would explain what I did to you and your mother. I have no excuses, no explanation that you will find acceptable or that will make this situation any better for you. Admitting I was a sorry excuse for a man – yeah that fits but it's not an excuse and it's sure not a good reason for what I put you through."

Trotter is trembling visibly, so Jeremiah gets him some water. The father takes the glass with his quivering hand and drinks as if this water will save his life. He looks at his sons and sniffles. He feels like he wants to throw up. The boys he left are grown men and require a full accounting for his offense against them. They sit looking at him with unsmiling faces and something verging on hatred in their eyes. Trotter thinks that maybe he should not have come.

Clifford thinks, *Maybe it would have been better if someone had killed this motherfucker*. He looks over at his brother, who returns his gaze. They are astounded. They can't believe the man has shown up and has nothing to say, nothing to make them feel better.

"I know it might have been a mistake to come here when I have so little to offer you boys." Trotter shakes his head. "I wasn't healthy. I've never been healthy. My mind was always just a whirlwind, never stopping. I could never rest. Nothing was ever enough. Everyone thought I was doing so well. I was good at making other people happy but I was miserable. I couldn't stop partying. I couldn't stop gambling. I couldn't stop doing drugs even though I told myself I wasn't an addict. I'd stop for a week, a month, three months but I always started back up again because I always needed something outside myself to make me feel better. The music and the cars worked as long as I was actively engaged but I couldn't work on cars and play music nonstop. Family, sex, women, friends, gambling, church, God; none of that satisfied me. At first your mother understood about who I was and how I did things. She worked with me and talked to me about working through my 'behaviors', as she called them. She was always there for me. She got counseling and tried to get me to go with her. Your mother begged me to get some professional counseling but I was too much of a man for that.

"This is something I never wanted to share with anyone. I never told anyone this. I never wanted to use it as an excuse. I always told myself it wasn't important." Trotter lowers his head for a time and goes quiet. He shakes his head again before he continues. "When I was six years old my daddy disappeared. He just left. Three or four years later we heard he was living with one of my mother's old friends in Greenville, Mississippi. They had taken off together. I don't know. Maybe between that and the shit I experienced in Vietnam – I don't know. I just felt so overwhelmed and so unhappy that I couldn't even sleep anymore. I just left and it seemed that once I was away all the burden and misery lifted, not completely but a lot.

"I don't know how much Darnell told you, but when I was in Memphis I started seeing a counselor, a younger woman. She followed me on up to New York and opened an office there and started counseling. After a while, me and her started dating. I still go to counseling but not with her. She still makes me go though.

"I've missed you guys, but like I said, I don't have an excuse. I don't have anything that will make you feel better about what I did. I've only just gotten better but I'm still just holding on. I tried so long and so hard to be a good father to you boys. I tried hard but I could see it slipping away. Everything I had done, everything I had given you and taught you; I could see it slipping away, because I was losing control. Your mother was losing patience with me and we were fighting all the time. I hit my boy. He had to have stitches" Trotter looks up at Jeremiah as he recalls the fight they had the night he left. "I couldn't sit still and let everything slip away. I didn't want to stay and become the person my father was before he left home. He beat my mother and put her in the hospital. Beat her and put her in the hospital twice that I can remember and I was six years old when he left. My mother died a young woman behind those beatings. I'm not saying the things that happened in my family when I was a kid are any excuse for what I did to you and your mother. I just didn't feel I could be your father anymore. I couldn't pretend like everything was fine when things were going crazy inside me.

"I want you boys to forgive me. More than anything, I want your forgiveness and I want your mother to forgive me. I understand if you can't. I told myself that I couldn't come here and face you but I came because I want you to know I never stopped loving you. I will always love you. If you beat me down right now, I will always love you. You're the most important things I've ever had and I know I've failed you but I'm here because I need you to know I love you."

Jeremiah and Clifford are speechless as they sit and listen to their father, not looking at him or each other. Each in his own head tries to figure out how to respond to this man who seems to be sharing all of his guilt and pain. He just walked in Jeremiah's home less than half an hour ago. He abandoned them for twenty years. His story is so sad and pathetic. How could they possibly let him off the hook with such a sad and pathetic story? There must be something they can do to make him pay for what he's done to them these past twenty years. There has to be something. Can they curse him out? Can they beat him down?

Jeremiah eventually looks up and asks, "Where you staying, Pop?" Trotter had always preferred "pop" to "dad" but the boys preferred "dad."

"I hadn't made any arrangements yet. I'm sure I won't have any trouble finding a place to stay." Trotter speaks just above a whisper.

"You want me to make some calls and get you a place?" Jeremiah feels he'd be forgiving his father too quickly if he opened his home to the man and he does not want Erin asking him questions about her grandfather when she may never see him again. Jeremiah wants time away from his father, his mother, and his brother to think.

"That'd be nice, Son, if you don't mind setting something up for me. Do you think I'll be able to see your mother while I'm here?"

"I guess we'll have to ask her if she's willing to see you, Dad. I don't know. We'll have to ask her," Clifford answers his father.

"Clifford, you're living down in San Diego, huh? How long you plan on being here?" Trotter asks.

"I was going to spend a few days with, Mom. It was pretty rough on her hearing about you. The boys are staying with some friends."

Trotter wants to ask about his grandchildren. He would love to meet them but feels that may be asking too much and it would break him even more if his sons were to refuse his request although he wouldn't blame them for the refusal.

Trotter looks at Jeremiah and tells him, "Jerry, I kept up with the news real close when they were looking at you about my disappearance. I would have come back at the drop of a hat if they had charged you. I knew they wouldn't be able to pin my absence on you with no evidence. I'm sorry you had to go through so much and that I caused so much trouble between you brothers. I wouldn't have let you spend one day in lockup for that, Jeremiah. As bad of a father as I've been, I wouldn't have let you hang for that. I hope you believe me."

Jeremiah gives only a slight nod of acknowledgement.

Chapter 20

"I guess you don't want to see me any longer, do you?" Marcus asks Monia when she answers her phone.

"Hello, Marcus. How are you doing?"

"You know, Monia, it was embarrassing when you didn't show for my birthday after I told all my guests you would attend the celebration. I mean it was my fortieth birthday for God's sake. If you didn't want to spend time with me anymore why didn't you tell me? I don't like being in limbo like this."

"I didn't realize I had you in some type of relationship limbo, Marcus. You and I have always had an on-again-off-again relationship. There have been a number of times when we have gone months without seeing each other. So what's the big deal now?"

"The big deal now is I want to see you. I miss you. You won't let me come down. You won't visit me. How long is this supposed to last? Okay, I give up. What is it you want from me? You want me to beg? What? You're not being fair and I'm not going to keep waiting around for you to decide it's convenient for you to see me, Monia. Damn!"

This is the most passion Monia has ever heard from Marcus and she wonders what has gone awry in his world that he wants to see her so urgently. Monia feels that if the man was really as distraught as he makes out to be, he would have already made the trip down to Seaside to see her with or without her okay for him to visit. If he is as love sick as he says why does she only hear from him sporadically? If he misses her so much, why doesn't she miss him at all? *Oh hell no, this is a ploy.* There is something else going on in Marcus's world and he is using Monia as a way to take his mind off of it. Monia feels she and Marcus have used each other up and she is finished with the pretense of a relationship. She may never have a man of her own. She may "date" all of her life but Marcus does not excite her enough to be in her dating pool. He and she got entirely too comfortable with each other. From here on out, any man Monia "dates" is going to excite her in some way. He'll have to make her laugh and she'll have to like him. She and Marcus aren't even friends. Friends keep in touch. Friends call just to check in and see how the other is doing. Friends don't just call when they want something. Marcus has always been a want something friend who is not really a friend at all. He never once called, texted, wrote, or emailed her just to say, "I just wanted to check on you" or "Let me know if you need anything."

"Marcus, I've got to go. I'm grocery shopping."

"What are you saying, Monia. Are you breaking up with me?"

"Breaking up? Ah, were we ever together? We hung out and saw each other on occasion and I was always available when you needed me not the other way around. If you want to call it breaking up then yes, I am."

"What did I do, Monia? Can't we at least talk about this? I've invested a lot of time in our relationship and I can't believe you're ending it this way."

"Marcus, do you really care? I mean, think about it. I have been someone for you to date when you had nothing better to do."

"That's not true. That is not true! You are very important to me. I don't want to end things like this, over the phone. Let me come down. We can go to dinner and I promise I won't try to stay. I'll get a hotel room. Just let me see you."

"That won't do any good and it makes no sense. I've got to go; I'm in the checkout."

"Can I call you back?"

Monia sucks in some air and lets it out slowly. "No, Marcus. You take care." She hears Marcus call her name as she ends the call. Monia is shaken. She had no idea ending things with Marcus would be so dramatic. Why he made that so hard she doesn't understand. She knows Marcus doesn't love her. He never professed to. Neither Monia nor Marcus ever thought they were in love, so why all the pleading. "Weird," Monia says out loud.

--

"The mail box is full and cannot accept any messages at this time. Goodbye." Monia has tried to call Jeremiah repeatedly on his cell phone throughout the day. It has taken her two days to work up the nerve to call. She wants to talk to him about his father but believes he is still upset with her about Marcus and because she failed to tell him she had found Trotter. Frustration hardly describes her emotion after getting the mailbox full message no less than four times. Finally, she breaks down and calls the shop number. She feels like a middle school student calling the boy she likes at his home for the first time. She tries to sound business like when asking for Jeremiah. "Hello, this is Monia Phillips. Is Jeremiah available?"

"Just a minute Miss Phillips, I believe he's out in the garage," the young office worker says and puts her on hold.

Monia has butterflies in her stomach as she waits. "Miss Phillips?"

"Yes."

"He says hold on a minute. He'll be right with you."

The butterflies grow in size and move faster. "Hello. This is Jeremiah."

"Hi," is all Monia can get out.

"Hi. I guess you're calling for that estimate I promised you. I've got all the figures. I can fax or email it to you but I think we need to sit down and talk about the repairs first and let me explain some things. When can you come by?"

Monia is not calling about the car. She has decided to buy a new one and donate her beloved Volvo to charity but if she tells Jeremiah her decision there will be no need to sit down and talk. "Will Monday after work be okay?" She asks.

"About what time?"

"We usually go long on Mondays. I can probably be there by six, six thirty."

"That'll work. I'll see you then." Jeremiah ends the call without a goodbye.

--

Thursday proves to be a pretty rough day for the Sumuels Family. Trotter agreed to stay closed up in his room at the Embassy Suites until his sons told Sharon he was in town. The sons decide to wait until after dinner to tell Sharon that Trotter wants to see her. By the end of the evening Jeremiah is glad he didn't give Delores a specific time for his return home because Sharon has so many questions about Trotter and does so much speculation about his life over the past twenty years and what he may expect from her that the sons fear for her blood pressure. The end result of all Sharon's ranting is her flat refusal to see Trotter ever again. Clifford and Jeremiah tell their mother that Trotter will return to New York soon and now is the best time to see him but Sharon swears she wants nothing to do with the man. By the end of the evening, Jeremiah cannot get away from his mother soon enough.

Friday night finds Jeremiah sitting in his home pondering how he will cope with Sharon once his brother heads back to San Diego. The humming of his cell phone brings him up out of his deep thoughts.

"Hey. Are you alone or is it just you and Erin there?"

"Yeah, what's up?"

"I thought you might not mind some company. You feel up to it?" Monia asks, fearful of his answer.

"Umm, if you want to come by, I guess that's cool. I guess I could use some company."

"I'm outside your door. I didn't want to ring the door bell."

Jeremiah walks to the door, opens it, and he and Monia stand there looking at each other with their cell phones up to their ears. He smiles for what feels like the first time in days. "Come on in, Moanie. You want some coffee or something?"

Monia is happy to hear him use her nickname again. "Sure, I'll take some coffee." She puts her things down in the living room and follows him into the kitchen. "How are you doing?" she asks.

Jeremiah breathes out hard and shakes his head as he pours out their coffee. "Man, Moanie, this thing is trying to rock my world. I thought my life was shaky over the past twenty years and that it couldn't possibly get any worse. I never gave any serious thought as to how I would respond if he showed up. I don't think my mother or Clifford did either." Jeremiah sets Monia's coffee in front of her and she helps herself to cream and sweetener as he continues. "I prayed to God that he was alive somewhere and that I'd see him again, that we could be together again, but I never thought about the havoc it would cause if the dude actually showed back up in our lives. How we would go on with life, what I would tell Erin, how I would feel about him after he left us the way he did. All my mother's financial crap and her emotions. This is a mess."

"Do you know if he's seen your mother yet?"

"Not yet. We just told her at dinner last night that he's in town and wants to see her. She says she doesn't want to see him. I wish she would. I'm sure she will want to eventually."

"Where is he?"

"Clifford took him to the Embassy Suites on Wednesday and tonight he's with your father. Thank God for your parents, Moanie. They've been my mother's life line all these years."

"No, my mother says you were your mother's life line."

"I know she was mine."

The friends sit and drink their coffee quietly. "Want me to turn on the television?" Jeremiah asks.

"I kind of like the quiet."

"Some music?"

"Umm" Monia responds thoughtfully.

"Okay, nothing. Just me, huh?" Jeremiah gives her that smile. "Thank you for being my friend, Moanie. I know I've been difficult."

"That's what we are for Jeremiah, to be each other's friend."

They move to the sofa where Monia picks up a Maya Angelou tribute issue of *Essence*. She gets close to Jeremiah and flips through the magazine and reads various captioned words of wisdom by the great lady. When she puts the magazine down, Jeremiah thanks her.

Monia leans back on the sofa and watches Jeremiah until she dozes off. Jeremiah goes and takes a shower before waking her. "You spending the night?" he asks as he gently shakes her.

"Can I stretch out here on the sofa?"

Jeremiah reaches for her. "Come and lay down with me. I want you close."

Monia hesitantly accepts his hand. "Erin's here."

"We're not going to do anything, Monia. We're just going to lie down and be close to each other, if that's okay."

"Okay."

"Bring the magazine and read some more to me."

Monia goes back and gets the Essence and climbs in the bed next to Jeremiah and starts to read as he lies there quietly listening. When Monia reads our beloved Maya's, "To those who would try to diminish me, I say you cannot cripple my spirit. You cannot do that. It is not yours to cripple," the tears start to flow down Jeremiah's face. "Oh, Jerry, don't cry," Monia pleads but the tears keep coming one after another. Monia wraps him up in her arms as Jeremiah begins to sob. He cries so long and hard that Monia gets up to get him a box of tissue. He tries hard to stop but can't. "I'm so sorry about this, Moanie. God, Erin doesn't cry like this."

"It's okay, Jerry, let it out. Please let it all out. Erin never had anything like this to cry about."

Jeremiah cries until the tears will no longer flow. When he catches his breath, he says, "I feel sorry for Clifford."

"Why?"

"I don't think he has anyone to cry to like I have."

Monia feels the tears welling in her eyes. Her heart feels heavy for Clifford. "Maybe he has someone back home."

"Maybe; I hope so. He needs someone, Moanie. Thank you for being here for me."

Monia hugs Jeremiah and holds him for awhile before asking, "How about some water?"

"Yeah, I could use some."

Monia gets the water, climbs back into the bed, and turns her back to him. Jeremiah spoons around her.

"Monia?"

"Yeah?"

"I'm about through with all this dating crap. Will you give me a chance?"

Monia turns to face him and says, "I don't think now is the time for me and you to talk about us."

Jeremiah looks in her eyes and knows she's not trying to put him off. She really doesn't think it's a good time to discuss their relationship. "Yeah, I'm feeling pretty vulnerable about now. You might try to take advantage of me."

Monia laughs and turns her back to him. "Don't you think I'm going to forget about the dating thing when some of the pressure from this situation with your father goes away."

"I hope you don't forget, Moanie."

"Good. Let's get some sleep." Monia scoots closer to him and passes out and he soon does the same.

Monia wakes up hours later with daylight peeping through the blinds. She remembers that she's with Jeremiah and smiles; happy she's in his bed and not at home in her own. He's still close behind her but feels strangely different. His arm remains draped across her but just barely. Monia looks down at the little arm lying across her midsection and realizes it belongs to Erin. The child has nudged up between Monia and Jeremiah and gone back to sleep. Jeremiah is asleep with his back to them on the other side of the bed. Monia eases from the bed, places the child's arm down, and covers her. She then tip toes over to Jeremiah and quietly wakes him, pointing to Erin lying next to him sound asleep.

"All the time." Jeremiah whispers. "I ban her from my room and still wake up with her in my bed. I woke up one night and she was crawling on the floor trying to sneak in the bed with me. She comes in very stealthily, little rat. You feel like getting us some breakfast?" he asks as he gingerly climbs from the bed."

"You want me to cook something?"

"No, I don't want you to cook. I'll make some coffee. How about some breakfast tacos? I'll buy if you fly."

"Sure, but I need to brush my teeth."

"There are a couple of new brushes in the bottom drawer in my bathroom."

Monia goes and picks up breakfast. She finds Jeremiah on the phone with his mother when she returns. Sharon tells him that she and Clarissa are going to Gilroy on a quick shopping trip and she wants to take Erin with her so she can buy the child a few things. "I promised her a trip back to the In and Out Burger up there."

"She's still asleep, Mom. Maybe she can go some other time."

"What do you have planned for her to do today other than stay at home with Delores?"

"Well, nothing really."

"You want me to pick her up or will you drop her off?"

Not wanting to argue with his mother, Jeremiah gives in easily. "I'll drop her off, Mom. What time are you leaving?"

"Clara is driving. I think she wants to go at about ten thirty."

"Okay. I've got to get her up and get her cleaned up and her hair combed. I'll get her there as soon as I can."

Jeremiah wakes his daughter and tells her to go wash up so she can eat breakfast.

"Where's Moanie?" Erin whines.

"She's in the kitchen drinking coffee, baby."

"I want to tell her 'hi'."

"You can tell her 'hi' after you finish your shower. Your grandmother wants you to go shopping for some things with her and your Aunt Clarissa."

"Do I have to, Dad? I want to stay here with Moanie," Erin protests.

"Moanie's not going to be here. She's got stuff to do today and I'm going to the shop, so you need to go with your grandmother. She wants you to go with her and she plans to take you to the In and Out Burger."

This information makes the shopping trip a little more acceptable. "Okay."

Erin gets her shower and comes into the kitchen.

"That was a pretty quick shower, Erin. Sit down and eat. Moanie got you a breakfast taco."

Erin waves her hand at Monia as she slides into her seat at the table. "Hi, Moanie. Thank you for the breakfast taco."

"Hi, sugar. You're welcome." Monia smiles at the child.

After a couple of bites of the taco, Erin comes to life. "Moanie, are you my dad's girlfriend, now?"

Monia looks at Erin and then at Jeremiah, who is standing at the kitchen sink rinsing dishes from the night before. He looks uncomfortable and says. "Listen, you eat. We gotta get that hair combed and get you to your grandmother. She is not going to be happy if she has to pick you up."

Monia smiles, winks at Erin, and nods a yes.

Jeremiah gets Erin into the bathroom and starts combing her long tangled hair as Monia stands in the doorway and watches. The child flinches but only a little. Monia can't help but grin at how gentle Jeremiah is as he sections Erin's hair and works from the tips of the hair to the root. She wants to take a picture and put it on Facebook and Instagram for the world to see. He is a good father.

Monia has nothing special planned for the day but expects Ja'Niece to stop by later in the afternoon. She needs to run a few errands and straighten up her house so she reluctantly takes her leave. "Erin, I've got to go, but I'll see you later, okay."

Erin gives Monia a hug and a wave before returning to the table to finish her water and half of an apple Jeremiah insists she eat. When her father returns to the kitchen after seeing Monia out, she asks, "Dad, is Auntie Moanie your girlfriend, now?"

"Listen, Erin. Me and Monia are good friends. We'll talk about it when you come home, okay."

"Okay, but if Auntie Moanie is your girlfriend, then I probably shouldn't call her 'auntie' anymore. She's not my real auntie, is she?"

"Well no, but why are you asking me that? She's like your real aunt."

"Well because if she is my real auntie that would make her your sister, and brothers and sisters don't sleep together, do they?"

"Well, when they're little they do."

"I know. My friend Jessica lets her little brother sleep with her all the time. He's real little like maybe three but you and Auntie Moanie aren't little." The child looks at Jeremiah with a tilted head and a furrowed brow.

"Me and your Auntie Moanie are not brother and sister. You're right; brothers and sisters don't sleep together when they get older. But I want you to finish up so I can get you to your grandmother. Finish!" Jeremiah points to the half eaten apple.

"Is Auntie Moanie going to spend the night with us some more? I like it when she's here."

"We'll talk about it later, Erin."

"Okay, Daddy."

After Jeremiah drops his daughter off with his mother, he heads straight to Darnell's home to meet his brother and his father, two men he has barely had any contact with over the past twenty years and who now take up fifty percent of his time. He'll need to run his shop from a distance today. Clifford will return to San Diego later in the evening and Trotter plans to leave for New York the following day.

Chapter 21

Monia enjoys her second cup of coffee out on her terrace. She tries not to put too much thought into her night with Jeremiah, accepting that she is deeply in love and has been for awhile. Monia thinks he may indeed be vulnerable at this time and may change his mind about dating her exclusively. Her heart feels heavy as she considers how much she is willing to accept to be with Jeremiah because she wants him so badly. She feels ashamed and tells herself not to over analyze their relationship, not to think about it at all; just keep going with the flow. Maybe he meant what he said the night before. Maybe he is finished with the beautiful Leslie. Monia goes into her shower in an attempt to clear her head of all things Jeremiah.

Four hours later, she receives a call from her mother asking her to watch Erin until Jeremiah is free for the day. The ladies have finished their shopping and have business to handle that they cannot manage with Erin. Monia is expecting a visit from Ja'Niece within the hour but has no intention of hanging out with Ja'Niece and her friends so she tells her mother to bring Erin over.

After Erin's arrival, Monia pops in the *Frozen* DVD and she and the child veg in front of her television until the doorbell rings announcing Ja'Niece's arrival. "Who is this little butterfly?" Ja'Niece asks as she gives Monia a casual hug with her eyes on Erin. "Hello, beautiful."

"Hello." Erin speaks politely and continues watching the movie.

"This is Erin. Erin this is my friend Ja'Niece. Erin is Jeremiah's daughter."

Erin looks up at Ja'Niece again to acknowledge the introduction.

"Ooh girl, he got you babysitting. I wish I was here to keep her for him," Ja'Niece says insinuating, much more. "Where is he anyway? I wonder if he's free tonight. Me and my girls are supposed to be hooking up with these guys from DLI we met about two weeks ago but if that doesn't pan out, I sure would like to get with Jeremiah."

Monia pulls Ja'Niece out of the living room and into the kitchen. "Could you tone down your rhetoric? Erin is just a child."

"She don't know what I'm talking about?"

"I said she is a child, Ja'Niece, not deaf. Have a seat. Can I get you some coffee or something?"

"No, I'm fine, girl. I just need to use the bathroom. Be right back."

Monia decides she had better come clean about her involvement with Jeremiah. She figures Ja'Niece will be upset with her but knows it is better to get it out in the open. She prepares herself for the confession but Ja'Niece starts talking as soon as she exits the bathroom and her lips don't stop moving for a full twenty minutes. The only thing that gets her mouth to shut is Erin asking Monia for a snack. Monia knows this is Erin's way of joining the ladies because she doesn't want to be left in the living room alone any longer, even with her favorite movie. She and Erin agree on popcorn and Monia places the bowl of freshly popped kernels on the table.

No sooner than the ladies start munching on the corn, Jeremiah rings Monia's cell phone to check on Erin. Monia leaves the room to talk to him in private.

"I bet that's my daddy," Erin tells Ja'Niece, knowing the woman is interested in her father. She understood the meaning of Ja'Niece's earlier words concerning Jeremiah very well.

Ja'Niece eyes Erin and knows she wants to share. "Oh, really. Does he call Monia a lot?"

"Not so much before but I think he will now."

"And why is that?" Ja'Niece asks, watering at the mouth.

Erin senses that she has something this woman really wants, information. She toys with Ja'Niece. "I maybe shouldn't tell." She looks up with her innocent eyes wide open as if she is asking for permission to share the information she caused her grandmother and Monia's mother to drool over earlier.

Ja'Niece looks over her shoulder to make sure Monia is still in her room. "You can tell me. Me and Monia are good friends. We tell each other everything."

"Monia is my dad's girlfriend. They sleep together."

Ja'Niece's face goes blank for a moment and then her mouth drops open. She didn't know what she expected the child to tell her, but it sure wasn't that Monia is with Jeremiah.

"Maybe you better not tell Monia or your father that you told me that."

"Why not?"

"I think Monia would rather tell me herself. Let her think she told me first. It'll be our secret."

"My dad says I'm not supposed to keep secrets with strangers."

"We are not strangers, baby. I'm Monia's best friend, okay." Ja'Niece is nearly whispering as she hears Monia coming out of the room.

"What are you two talking about?" Monia asks.

"Oh, nothing important but that must have been an important call. You were back there for a while."

"Just Jeremiah checking on Erin." Monia looks at Erin. "Your dad says he'll pick you up at about seven, Erin. You're going to eat dinner with me, okay.

"Cool! Can we make those homemade pizzas again, Auntie Moanie?"

"Not tonight because I have to prepare the dough ahead of time and you had burgers for lunch. We need to eat something a bit healthier for dinner. We need something with vegetables."

"Okay." Erin says sadly.

Ja'Niece has been watching this exchange with disgust. She'd like to think that Erin has it all wrong but that is unlikely. She had been hoping to get with Jeremiah for months and Monia knew it. Monia has had Marcus for years now and never appreciated him and now she goes after Jeremiah. Ja'Niece thinks Monia is not the friend she thought she was. "I've got something to tell you that I can't discuss in front of the child," she tells Monia. Ja'Niece looks serious so Monia tells Erin to go back into the living room and watch television. Erin leaves the room with no resistance.

"So what's this juicy thing you want to share with me? I haven't heard any good gossip in ages," Monia jokes.

"I've had something I wanted to tell you for some time now but I just didn't know how."

"What is it?" Monia asks, slightly concerned.

"You remember my friend Cindy who worked with me when I was at Slauson Rehab?"

"No, I don't remember her by name. What does she look like?"

"Cute little Asian girl."

"Yeah, I do remember her, very pretty with a big personality. She was a lot of fun." The thought of the woman brings a smile to Monia's face.

"Well, she and Marcus are an item."

Monia looks at Ja'Niece and wonders why she is telling her this, where she got her information, and a number of other questions. "Where did they meet?"

"When I had my birthday party, the one you didn't have time to attend, Marcus came down and they hit it off. I noticed that they were talking a lot but I didn't know they had started dating."

"Marcus, who you can't stand, came to your birthday party? You invited him?"

"Oh yeah, girl, because we needed some men and he was more than willing to come so I just sucked it up. He was a lot of fun and we had a blast. We've been hanging out a lot lately."

"Okay, but with all your hanging out with Marcus and your friend Cindy you didn't know they were seeing each other?" Monia appears wounded but it is not what Ja'Niece hopes. Monia had no idea Marcus and Ja'Niece socialized except through her. Now she wonders if all the strife between the two of them was for her benefit.

"Like I said, they talked a lot. I just thought they had become friends but I guess they really hit it off at the party. You know how it is when everybody is having a good time and just the right vibe is going down. People you wouldn't normally expect to get together find their way to each other. Anyway, girl, she pregnant now."

"She's pregnant!"

"Yeah, she pregnant. Says it's Marcus's baby and they're talking about moving in together. That's going to be one pretty baby."

Monia wonders if she is imagining this conversation or the one she had with Marcus just days before. She considers that Ja'Niece is lying but to what end. Why is Ja'Niece telling her this crap and what the hell is Marcus trying to prove? He has been bugging the hell out of Monia to spend some time with him. He had to realize Monia would find out about the pregnancy. Did he assume Monia would not care because she never cared in the past? But Cindy is a friend to Monia's best friend and there's a baby on the way. Monia wishes she hadn't already closed that door so that she could go back and slam it in Marcus's face and kick it a couple of times. Better yet kick him in the balls a couple of times. After scrunching up her face and giving Ja'Niece a great deal of satisfaction at her apparent despair, Monia says, "Give them both my best."

"I will. I hope this is not too upsetting. I wanted to tell you sooner but just couldn't find the words."

"No, Ja'Niece, it's not really upsetting because Marcus and I were never into each other that much. We haven't seen each other since the weekend I moved in here."

Ja'Niece looks surprised. "I thought he was coming down here pretty regularly."

"Where would he find the time to spend with me if he's dating your friend Cindy so hard?"

"Oh, I don't know. I just thought that maybe he was seeing you both."

"No, he may have been seeing someone else but it wasn't me."

"So, you all by yourself again?"

"Jeremiah and I date sometimes."

Ja'Niece had not expected this honesty from Monia. She had thought Monia did not want her to know that she was dating Jeremiah and Ja'Niece preferred Monia not know, she knows. "How long has that been going on?" Ja'Niece asks with a hand on her hip and a disgusted look.

"A couple of months."

"You guys started up before Tasha's wedding."

"We did."

"And you let me leave with him?"

"That was between you and Jeremiah. We had decided not to see each other again. So if things worked out between you two, who was I to stop you?"

"That was dirty, Monia. You should have told me you liked him."

"You're probably right, but would that have stopped you from hitting on him? We were not together." Monia looks at Ja'Niece with no more words. Ja'Niece doesn't answer Monia's question and she does not need to. Monia knows the answer and for the first time wonders if Ja'Niece is a friend she wants to hold on to.

"I wouldn't do some shit like that to you. The least you could do is apologize."

"I'm sorry you're upset."

"Wouldn't you be?"

"I don't know, Ja'Niece, maybe."

Ja'Niece gets up to leave. She is also questioning her relationship with Monia who she has considered her best friend for years. "I gotta go. I'll see you later."

"Bye, Ja'Niece." Monia recognizes that this is a turning point in their friendship. They will either become better friends after this or discard the friendship all together. She'll wait awhile and see what if anything she wants in regards to Ja'Niece.

Chapter 22

"I've got a problem I need to discuss with you." Monia tells Jeremiah with a worried expression on her face.

"Is this something we need to talk about now or can it wait until later?"

"I'd like to get it out of the way."

Jeremiah looks at Erin, who is perched on his lap and tells her to go in the living room so he and Monia can talk.

Erin pouts as she slides off her father's lap. "I'm tired of people talking and I have to leave the room. Every day somebody's got something to say they don't want me to hear. That doesn't make me feel very good. I always have to go and sit all by myself. Why is everybody talking about stuff I don't get to hear?"

Monia and Jeremiah look at each other and know the child is not exaggerating. The past week has been full of secrets and mystery. Jeremiah starts to chastise his daughter but Monia stops him. She's an only child and knows what is like to be sent off alone while the adults talk. "Just a minute. Ja'Niece was here earlier and I made Erin leave the room so we could talk. She didn't complain at all. I would bet your mother and mine made her put on her headphones a couple of times today while they were in the car."

Erin stands there with her bottom lip slightly poked out and nods in agreement. Jeremiah watches his child but does not say anything, giving Monia leeway to handle the situation.

"Erin, if you will just give me a few minutes alone with your father, I will not do this again to you today and It will be a while before I ask you to leave the room again so I can talk to anyone. I promise."

"You promise?" Erin asks and it is easy to see the child is exhausted. No doubt once she gets on Monia's sofa she will be out like a light in five to ten minutes. Jeremiah had planned to pick her up by seven but he was late and it is now well after eight o'clock.

Monia adds her caveats. "I'm not promising that I'll never do it again. I'm just saying I'll take a break from asking you to leave the room."

"You'll take a break?"

"I'll take a break."

"Okay, I'm leaving but don't forget your promise, Auntie Moanie. Don't forget."

"I won't forget."

Jeremiah gives Monia a skeptical look. "You know she's going to hold you to that, right."

"You too."

"No. I didn't make that promise. You made that promise. I'm not in this. Anyway, what is it you need to talk to me about? I've been away from her all day and distracted most of the week. I need to pay some attention to my child. What have you got for me, Moanie?"

"I know how upset you were with me because I failed to tell you I found your father and I understand."

"I was wrong about that. You did the best you could."

"Thank you for acknowledging that but there is something else I haven't told you. It's kind of unimportant in the grand scheme of things but it's important to me."

This has Jeremiah's curiosity up. "Okay. I'm listening."

"You know Shirley, the lady I work with?"

"Yeah, what about her?"

"Remember how she acted when we were at Dr. Navya's party?"

"Sure. You said she acted that way because she knew my dad."

"Jeremiah, she didn't just know your father. She still to this day swears she is in love with him. She told me she's been married three times and that your father ruined her for any other man. She said he was her first."

"Wow! That old dog. I'm finding out more shit about this cat. I mean it's not like I didn't know he played around but damn! How old was she?"

"She says they started up when she was pretty young. I think she said she was eighteen, so they messed around for some years. It's not so much that; it's the whole infatuation thing. To her, your dad is some kind of a hero and she says she knows he's dead and even though she never said it, I think she tells herself he would not have left her unless he was dead. She says if it wasn't for Trotter she wouldn't have gone to school. She gives him credit for motivating her in life because her mother was pretty much into partying and never taught her much."

"Yeah, I know her mother. Her mother has always been a gambler and a partier. She's pretty streetwise, a fast woman."

"I ah, I don't see how I can keep working with Shirley and not tell her that I've seen Trotter. That I've seen him and he's alive and well. She needs to know the truth."

"Tell her."

Monia looks surprised. "I thought you guys wanted to keep the fact that we found him quiet."

"Yeah, well it's not going to be quiet long. That's one reason I was so late getting here. Clifford put off leaving until tomorrow so we could get some of this stuff ironed out. We all went to the police department today, your dad; mine; Clifford; and me. Dad gave the police his name and told them to stop looking for him."

"What!"

"Is it a few minutes yet?" Erin yells from Monia's living room.

"Not quite, baby, just a little bit longer," Jeremiah yells, and then whispers loudly to Monia. "Moanie, they were stunned shitless. That old fat cop that used to harass me so much before I left here – he doesn't mess with me since I came back because he's old and out of shape and I'm – you know." Jeremiah pats his abs and smiles in jest. "Anyway, that cat apologized to me today. The whole thing was pretty rough on my dad. I hate to admit it but I've been feeling sorry for him almost since the moment he got back. I think they were trying to find something they could charge him with. Today was a rough day for the dude. I hope this is not just the beginning for him when it comes to paying for stuff but he's got a lot to answer for. He seems to be up to the task and says he wants everything cleared up. Says he wants the freedom to come back to Seaside whenever he gets ready and wants to be able to look people in the face. Man I think I'd leave this place and never show my face again but that's what he says he wants."

"So I can tell, Shirley?"

"Yeah, go ahead and tell her. The public affairs officer down at the Seaside Police Department agreed to hold off on releasing the news to the media until late tomorrow. It should be in Monday morning's paper. Trotter needs to contact his father. He hasn't been in touch with my grandfather in over twenty years. They were never close. My grandfather left his family also and my dad always blamed my grandfather for my grandmother's early death but he feels he should let him know he is still alive. He's also got people around here he feels like he should talk to before it comes out in the news. Who knows; Shirley may be one of those people. So you might want to tell her right away."

"What about your mother, Jeremiah? Is she still refusing to see him?"

Jeremiah gives a sarcastic "Humph," and says, "Oh she saw him."

"She saw him?"

"Yeah, Moanie, ah, yeah, we were at the police department all afternoon. We only left there about two hours ago. Your mother called me and asked where we were because she hadn't seen my father yet and wanted to see him. I told her we would be in the bar at the Embassy for a while. Your mother showed up a little later and," Jeremiah stops for a moment and inhales deeply before continuing, "my mother came with her. When my father saw my mother walking toward him, he stood up to greet her with tears running down his face. My mother walked up to him with this peaceful expression on her face. I have never seen a person slap the shit out of anybody so hard in my whole life. I've seen dudes hit each other hard but, damn, she hit him so violently, I felt it. He had to go and wash the blood out of his mouth."

"Oh God! You are kidding me!"

"Wish I was."

"Then what happened?"

"Clarissa sat down with us and ordered drinks for her and Sharon while Sharon went off to the bathroom. When she came out, she asked my father to join her at another table. I have no idea what they talked about. They were still there talking when I left. Your parents and Clifford were sitting at another table reminiscing and crap like it's some type of reunion. They told me to bring you down. I told them 'Nah, we got Erin.' We can visit tomorrow."

"Well, I could go," Monia tells him with a sly smile.

Jeremiah looks at her. "I guess you could."

"Or do you want me to stay here with you?"

Now he smiles. "I know one thing. We're both going to be in a lot of trouble if we don't get in there with that little girl or bring her in here with us."

"You're right." Monia agrees.

They find Erin in her usual position passed out on the sofa. They cover her and go and lay across Monia's bed. Jeremiah is ready to fool around but Monia has more questions. "Last night you said something about your mother's financial crap. What did you mean?"

"You know Monia, I was probably overreacting. After my father left I became a little obsessed with our finances but my mother was always on top of things. She has been investing money for years. I think she got started after talking with the old guy who owned the clothing stores she manages, not the son who's got a thing for her but the father who died recently. She started hiding money away from my father right after they bought their home. She was always afraid he would gamble away the mortgage payment. The funny thing was that my dad hid money for the mortgage also. He was afraid mom would shop or gamble the money away." Jeremiah smiles and shakes his head before he continues. "My mother invested my money for me from the time my father left. That's how I was able to buy Gilbert's shop. I had saved lots of money but not that much. I was amazed when she showed me how much money she had made for both of us.

"I sent her the majority of my pay checks when I was on active duty and every month she'd send me a statement. I could see my money growing. I was stationed with a lot of people whose families would blow their money and they'd have nothing to show for their time in the service. It happened more often than not. I lent or I should say gave fellow soldiers money any number of times because some family member was in need and had blown all the money. It was an epidemic of financial irresponsibility.

"Clifford got a scholarship to play ball but it was Sharon's investments that got him through dental school. You know when she tried to collect on dad's life insurance the company denied the claim. The Army stopped Dad's retirement check but gave her survivor's benefits. It wasn't much but she saved half of that money and invested the other half. The Social Security Administration tried to give her dad's social security way back then. She refused and said she would wait until she reached her retirement age and collect her own social security. Mom said she did not want the government coming back and trying to collect money they had overpaid her. Now, I'm thinking the Army is going to owe my dad all that back retirement pay. Mom may have to pay back the survivor's benefits but the retirement back pay will cover the loss easily. Besides she has grown that money tenfold if not more. My mother is a wizard when it comes to handling money. Yeah she likes to gamble but she always told me, 'You don't gamble with your bill money, baby,' and she never did."

--

Shirley is shocked to receive a call from Monia the next afternoon. Monia was distant and cool all week at work and no one knew why. Now here she is calling Shirley and asking to stop by on a Sunday. This is the first time Monia has called her at home. The ladies have had lunch together and went on a couple of outings with the other ladies from the office on weekends but those events were always discussed and arranged at work. So this call from Monia is out of the norm. Shirley is gracious and tells Monia to come on by.

Monia starts talking as soon as she enters Shirley's Luxton Street home. "I'm sorry to impose on you on the weekend like this, Shirley. I know you guys have been curious about what's going on with me this week and I owe you an explanation. I owe Pamela an apology too but I need to talk to you first."

"What is it?" Monia sounds so serious that Shirley wants her to hurry and get to the point.

"Last weekend when we were in New York,"

"Yeah, Pamela told me something went down when you guys were in New York." Shirley is loud and agitated. "What the hell happened when you guys were in New York to cause you to be so upset? I know that Pamela can get wild and if she did something stupid, you don't owe her no apology; she owes you one."

"I wasn't upset, Shirley. I was being secretive. I saw Trotter Sumuels last week when I was in New York."

Shirley looks at Monia and squints as she turns her head slightly to the side. "You what?"

"I saw Trotter in New York. We were out at a jazz club having a good time. I was drinking more than I should have been but the piano man was so good that he caught my eye. It was Trotter. At first I thought I was too drunk and had Jeremiah on the brain because he and his father look alike."

"Are you telling me Trot is alive?"

"Yeah, baby, that's exactly what I'm telling you."

"Where is he?"

"He's here in Seaside."

"Did you mention me to him?"

"I haven't had an opportunity to really talk with him, Shirley. My dad flew up and confirmed that the man was Trotter. They sat and talked a long time. At first Mr. Trotter said he wasn't coming back here because he didn't want to face everyone. He showed up a day or two later but the most I've said to him is 'hello.' I haven't talked to him, really I haven't"

"What's his family saying?" Shirley sits there looking confused.

"They're just trying to figure everything out and work through the mess. There are a lot of hard feelings and all kinds of crap."

"Why did you wait so long to tell me this, Monia?"

"His family had to know first, Shirley, and then they had to decide how they wanted to handle things. He just went to the police department yesterday. I didn't feel I had the right to tell you until they told me it was okay. That's why I couldn't look at you all week." Monia fights back tears. "I know how important Mr. Trotter was to you. But listen Shirley, according to my dad, he has a woman in New York who he's been with for a long time and seems to really care for. I just thought you needed to know that he is alive and left Seaside on his own."

Shirley presses the areas above and below her lips together in an attempt to suppress her tears and maintain her composure. After a moment, she says "Oh Monia, you are so sweet to come and tell me this. Thank you, thank you! I can get on with my life now."

"What do you mean?" Monia prays that Shirley does not assume she will have a life with Trotter Sumuels.

"Monia, as hard as I was on Jeremiah all these years I always thought that first husband of mine, Willie Burrows, probably killed Trotter." Shirley bows her head and weeps for a moment before looking back up at Monia. "Even after I thought he killed the man, I still married him because he wanted me and he had money. I always felt so guilty about that. This is such a relief. You made me feel so guilty when you confronted me for treating Jeremiah the way I did. I've wanted to apologize but have been too ashamed and full of guilt. I've been guilty my whole life it seems. I divorced Willie because I just couldn't stand to look at him any longer. I didn't feel the least compulsion to mourn him when he died. He was a mean man but I was wrong about him too. I thought he had killed the only man I ever loved. I know now what I've felt for Trotter all these years was more guilt than anything else. I thought he might have died because Willie wanted me. Willie even hinted to me and others that he had killed Trotter. He was a horrible man."

Monia realizes she and Shirley are not alone in the house. She looks up and sees Big Chewy coming out of the hallway.

"Hey, Monia."

"Hey, Chewy."

Shirley looks at Monia and smiles. "Me and Chewy were at Seaside High together, Monia. I was surprised to see him when I dropped you off at Jeremiah's shop that day. Seaside is such a small place, but it's amazing how you can go years and not see people who live only a few blocks away." Shirley addresses Chewy. "Baby, did you hear what Monia and I were talking about?"

"Nah, what was ya'll talkin' bout."

"Trotter Sumuels is alive. He's back in Seaside."

"Jeremiah's dad is alive!"

"Yes he is. Yes he is. It should be in the paper tomorrow." Monia tells Chewy.

"That's good news. I'm glad for Jeremiah. That boy's been waiting on his father a long time."

Monia leaves Shirley's home feeling much better than she felt when she arrived. A call from Trotter Sumuels later that day pleases Monia greatly. "Monia, baby, Jerry tells me you work with an old friend of mine, Shirley Jiles."

"I do. Her name is Shirley Conroe now."

"Can you put me in touch with her? Do you mind?"

"No sir, I don't mind at all." Monia gives the man the number and hopes Trotter's call to Shirley permanently closes the door on Trotter Sumuels for her friend.

Chapter 23

Jeremiah is surprised to see Leslie's name come up on his caller ID. He has not talked to her in weeks. Determined not to hold on to relationships with women he has slept with in the past, he considers not answering but only for a short moment before he takes the call. As he picks up, he remembers an evite he received from her for an upcoming exhibit opening in the city. Leslie has been working on the art pieces for the exhibit for over a year and the opening is a big deal. Other than their children and their relationship, the exhibit has been Leslie's main topic of conversation for the past twelve months. She has shown Jeremiah many of the pieces and asked for his opinion. He felt the work was exquisite but he's no expert. Jeremiah had planned to attend the opening and surprise Leslie with a quiet get-away for just the two of them as a congratulatory gift. He had also planned to take Sharon and Clarissa up to the city, put them up in a nice suite, and treat them to a gourmet dinner and the exhibit. What a night that would have been. Leslie would have been pleased; she had frequently asked him to bring Sharon for a visit. But by the time Jeremiah had received the invitation everything had changed between him and Leslie. He had forgotten all about her big opening up in the city. When he read the evite, he had felt that sick feeling in the pit of his stomach. He felt like he was abandoning one of his closest allies.

"I'm calling because I haven't received a reply to my evite for my opening next month. Did you get it?" Leslie asks pleasantly. She sounds as if nothing has changed in their relationship.

"Yes, I did. Boy that came around quick didn't it? Congratulations, this is a big deal." Jeremiah hesitates.

"I'm excited. Will you be able to make it up?" Now Jeremiah can hear the urgency in her voice. He prays she has not put too much hope in his attending the event.

"I don't think I'll be able to make it, Leslie."

The phone is quiet for a full ten seconds that seems more like ten minutes to Jeremiah. "Why not?" Leslie asks quietly.

"I don't think it would be a good idea for me to come up there, Leslie. I'm seeing someone pretty seriously now."

"You have always been seeing someone – me and several other women at the same time. What's the big deal now? What's the difference?"

"I'm not seeing anyone else. We're serious."

"So I guess what you and I have is not serious. Was I just someone to play around with, Jeremiah?"

"No, of course not; you and I had an understanding."

"Are you telling me that your new girlfriend is such a child that she will be jealous if you come to my opening? Why don't you bring her with you, that way she can keep watch on you and make sure you behave?"

Jeremiah can't get rid of the anguish he feels over Leslie; she has been a good friend for a long time and he has used her poorly. He was well aware that she wanted more from him early on in their relationship but he made it clear that he was not ready for anything serious, so Leslie played the game by his rules. She was there whenever he needed her and made him feel special. He has been able to talk to Leslie about his problems when he had no one else to complain to. He loves her but not in the way she wants. As much as he wishes they could remain friends, it's not possible and he would be deceiving himself to try. Leslie is a beautiful and sensual woman and would continue her pursuit of him sexually. Their relationship as friends and lovers may have worked for a time but switching back to friendship only will fail for certain. "Leslie, there's a lot going on here that you don't know about and I'm not going to bore you with it. Like I said, I doubt I can make it to your opening."

"Are you telling me that you and I can no longer be friends?"

Jeremiah tries to think of something to say that doesn't sound harsh or cliché. He could go cowardly and tell her that Monia would not approve but the truth is Jeremiah does not want to remain connected to Leslie as much as he wishes he could. There is emptiness in their relationship that makes him sad. Something important is missing and he does not want to revisit that void. "Not like in the past, Leslie. You've been a good friend to me and I know I haven't been good to you. You said it yourself the last time we talked. I had everything on my terms. I'm not making any excuses. I see no healthy way for us to remain friends."

"You know what Jeremiah. I'd like to say good luck in your new life with your new imbecilic girlfriend, but I won't. You are a self-centered son of a bitch and, yes, I am referring to your goddamn mother. I hope you rot in hell."

--

"Hello," Monia answers her phone as she leaves her office at the end of a long workday.

"How are you doing, Monia?" Jeremiah asks.

"I'm fine. How about you? I haven't heard from you in a few days."

"I know. It's been pretty busy around here. You could have checked on me, you know. How's the car working out?

"I have to admit I like the car, Jeremiah. When are we going to talk about the terms?"

"There's no rush. Listen, what have you got planned for this weekend. I'd like to take you to dinner Saturday night."

"I'm free. Where are we going?"

"I'm not sure yet. I'll let you know when we get there. Pack an overnight bag, okay."

Monia smiles. "Okay."

--

"This is the most beautiful place I've ever sat and had a meal, Jeremiah, and living here on the Peninsula, that's saying a lot. I never heard of The Pacific's Rim. You'll have to bring me back here." Monia reaches across their window front table and squeezes Jeremiah's hand as a gesture of thanks.

"I'm glad the meal was good and the service is on point. Some of the reviews weren't that stellar in those departments but all the reviews indicated that this place has the best view around. I hoped you'd like it."

"I do." Monia takes a breath and looks out at the now shiny reflections of the moon off the barely visible waters of the Pacific Ocean.

"May I refill your glasses," the Sommelier asks.

"Thank you," Jeremiah responds with a casual glance at the woman, who has been peeping at him all evening.

"The service is attentive, isn't it?" Monia asks once the lady leaves their table, causing Jeremiah to blush. "I think she may like you a little bit. I understand; I had a crush on you for years."

Jeremiah stops himself from telling Monia that it happens all the time. Women do love the dreads. He's seriously considering getting rid of them. He sits there for a while and watches Monia without speaking. He hasn't thought about what to say to her. He does not want to argue and he needs her to take him seriously. He's not willing to compromise. Jeremiah reaches for Monia's hand. "You and I had a conversation a few weeks ago, just after my dad showed up and I told you I was finished with the dating game. Do you remember that conversation?"

"Yes, I remember." Monia's voice is a little shaky.

"And do you remember what else I said?"

"You said you were vulnerable."

"No, before that. I remember the conversation, Monia, and I know you remember it too." Jeremiah is so serious that he looks stern.

"You asked me if I'd give you a chance," Monia responds, barely able to get the words out she's so nervous.

"Right, right. So how about it? Will you give me a chance?"

"I thought that's what I've been doing, giving you a chance."

"Yeah, maybe you have been giving me a chance, Monia, but I'm not interested in this open relationship thing any longer."

"Are you saying you don't want to date anyone but me?" Now Monia has a serious look on her face.

"I'm saying a little more than that, Monia." Jeremiah dips his head down and looks at her steadily.

"What?"

"I don't want you to date anyone else either. I want you to stop seeing Marcus."

Monia breathes a sigh of relief. Jeremiah had gotten so serious that she feared what he had to say. "Oh, Jeremiah, I closed that door a long time ago. Do you know the last time I saw Marcus?"

Jeremiah stretches his eyes, a little upset as he recalls their last conversation about Marcus. "No, when was the last time you saw Marcus – when you went up for his birthday party – I don't know. When did you see him?"

"I saw Marcus the weekend I moved into my condo, the weekend you met him. That's the last time I saw him."

"What about the birthday party? I thought you were with him that weekend."

"I didn't go. After I talked to you, I had to admit that I didn't really want to go up and well you know how it is." Monia seems uneasy talking about her decision but goes for it. "I felt if I went up there, he would expect more from me than I was willing to give. That part of our relationship was over. I had to accept the fact that we were friends no longer. Marcus would never allow me to spend time around him on my own terms. I had to cut him loose, besides Ja'Niece says he's going to be a father."

"So you're finished with him?"

"I am. He keeps calling but I'm sure he'll give up eventually."

"Let me talk to him and he'll give up a lot quicker than that."

Monia gives Jeremiah a look that speaks volumes.

"What? You don't want me to talk to him?"

"It's not that."

Jeremiah squeezes Monia's hand. "What then? Something is on your mind."

"What about Leslie. You never told me what happened when you went to Pismo the last time."

"Monia, do you think I could sit here and ask you to stop seeing Marcus, if I was still involved with Leslie?"

"What did she call you down there for? What happened?"

"She wanted to know about you and me. She wanted to know if things would remain the same between her and me. She had drank way too much and needed to sleep it off. I got her to go to bed and stayed there with her until she woke up." Jeremiah gives a little exasperated chuckle and tells Monia, "She told me off and asked me to leave. I didn't sleep with her and I didn't want to. I stayed because I love her and I always will. She was there when I needed someone."

Monia's eyes have gone sad and she looks down in an attempt to hide her hurt feelings. Jeremiah knows she doesn't understand what he is saying about his relationship with Leslie.

"Look at me, Moanie." Monia looks up at him as he leans in closer. "I said I love her. I'm not in love with her. Like you with Marcus, I've declared that she and I cannot be friends. Leslie wants something I can't give her. I don't want to lose you. I don't need another woman as long as I'm with you and I will not allow a relationship with an old girlfriend to come between us. You mean too much to me. I don't want to date anyone else – just you, me," Jeremiah hesitates before continuing, "and Erin. You know she's gotta date with us. I'm sorry but she's not going to let me date you by myself."

Monia and Jeremiah laugh out loud.

"I like her Jeremiah."

"She likes you too, baby. It's a good thing that we were kind of family already."

"Yeah, I think it's a real good thing."

Chapter 24

Trotter knew that his adopted home town of Seaside had changed over his twenty year hiatus but was completely unprepared for the difference in demographics and culture. His beloved Monterey Bay Blues Festival was no more. The black utopia of Seaside, which was more than twenty five percent black when he left, was less than ten percent black upon his return. Most of his old friends had moved on to other cities or states or died off. Seaside had been a happening haven for black folks from the 1950's to the year 2000. The city was small but it had a relatively large and progressive black population. The City of Seaside, California, had been on the map with black folks nationwide. Dr. King and Rosa Parks had both visited the city during the Civil Rights Era. It was a stop on what could be called the west coast's Chitlin' Circuit and stars like James Brown, Ike and Tina, BB King, Bobby Blue Bland, and Etta James played at the Monterey Fairgrounds located just outside the Seaside city limits. Over the years, Seaside boasted black mayors and city managers, though blacks were never the majority population. Seaside even had a black female police officer in the early 1960's. Yes, Trotter returned to a different place from the town he abandoned, but he still loved the small ocean side community. The view was unchanged, the people were still laid back, and you could still ride up and down Broadway.

--

Trotter Sumuels aka Samuel Terry becomes the talk of the town, well actually, the talk of the nation. Now, if Trotter and his family had been average looking people or just plain homely folks, the story of Trotter's disappearance, possible murder, abandoning his family, and reappearance may have received a bit less attention. But the Sumuels are a handsome group and quite resourceful, so Trotter's story is covered in great depth in *The Monterey Herald* newspaper, *The Salinas Californian*, and other local media. Of course with Seaside being so close to the Bay Area, in no time the larger media outlets of San Francisco, San Jose, and Oakland each report on the story surrounding the Trotter Sumuels' mystery.

The story spreads like the proverbial wild fire and takes on numerous angles. The fact that Monia found the missing man playing his virtuoso music in a small New York City jazz club becomes widely known. Since Monia lived and worked in San Francisco, there was a whole segment by a local Frisco television station news team on Monia.

The Los Angeles connection was particularly interesting because both father and the son, who was for years accused of his father's death, sought refuge in The City of Angels. Both men worked in auto repair and auto customizing shops and both earned reputations as the best in the business.

Trotter's story creeps across the country. Don't forget that Trotter is Louisiana born and raised. His musical background was founded in the soulful bayous of that state. Photographs of the little rundown church where he learned to play piano are shown in a *Jet* Magazine article. More important than the music though is the light the story shines on mental illness, domestic abuse, and parental neglect. As much as Trotter attempts to turn focus away from the incidents of his childhood, the circumstances of his young life become too important to the story to disregard. After all, his father put his mother in the hospital twice and abandoned his family first, setting precedence for the son to follow. There are a number of reports about the prevalence of domestic abuse, parental neglect, and abandonment within the glorious state of Louisiana.

Memphis lauds Trotter as its own. He did live in the city for nearly eight years and honed his musical craft and his auto repair skills. The media of Memphis declares that storied city as the savior of the man known there as Samuel Terry. He earned a good living and worked with many well known musicians. If he hadn't been in Memphis, he may not ever have met the two men who sponsored him in the Big Apple. Memphis was where he sought and found the valuable counseling that gave him the tools he needed to cope with the tragedies of his past life. He met his current significant other and turned his life around all while living in Memphis, Tennessee. The media of that city even interviewed the cook at Trotter's favorite soul food restaurant.

New York City media shows little interest in Trotter or his story but that little jazz club exploits the story to the hilt. It becomes known as the place where Trotter can be seen on a recurring basis -- what a windfall. The place did good business without all the Trotter Sumuels aka Samuel Terry hoopla but these days the lines are long and never ending. Once the jazz lovers hear the man behind the story play that piano, they are hooked.

Trotter's story takes on such a life that it affects his family and friends. The LA garages where He and Jeremiah worked gain customers by all the free publicity. Jeremiah's shop has a six month waiting list to get cars in for customizing. Trotter's girlfriend's counseling service has picked up. Sharon has become lauded as a financial wizard based on her ability to invest and put Clifford through dental school and grow a small fortune after being abandoned with two teenage sons. She has been approached by network television to host a weekly show giving financial advice.

Darnell and Clifford's profession of dentistry is one of the aspects of the story the media misses. How the entire media fails to capitalize on the fact that both Trotter's best friend and youngest son are dentists we may never know, especially since so much emphasis is placed on Sharon investing Clifford through dental school. Even though the dental angle is missed, the two men are not given a pass as far as stories go. Darnell becomes famous as the faithful friend who stood in as a role model for Trotter's sons, the man who never judged and loved his friend unconditionally, and the person who identified the missing man and broke the news to the family. Clifford's story is that of the determined younger son who hounded the Seaside Police Department nonstop to bring Trotter's killer to justice, even though Trotter was not dead and the person Clifford wanted arrested for the non-murder was his own brother. It is widely reported that he sacrificed his marriage in pursuit of the cause of justice for his father. Clifford's scholarship, basketball prowess, and academic achievements are thoroughly covered.

Clarissa garners a small amount of attention because she is Sharon's faithful friend, Monia's mother, and Darnell's wife.

After Trotter, Jeremiah receives more attention than anyone. He is portrayed as the fall guy for Trotter's folly, a war hero, and an exceptional single father and entrepreneur. The media wants to know if he holds a grudge, what is the relationship between him and his errant father, and misguided brother. *Ebony* Magazine approaches both Jeremiah and Clifford about gracing the periodicals pages in their "Most Eligible Bachelors" issue. The brothers decline.

The story makes tons of money for Trotter who gets a brand new record deal with Blues Sound Records and he is more than up to the task. Over the years, Trotter has passed up many opportunities to be a group front man and record his own music; his talents have been beyond exceptional for decades. Any number of artists had offered Trotter long term gigs but they always wanted him to travel and perform and that he would not do for fear of being found out. The name Samuel Terry appears on a number of records as a contributing musician. There are even a couple of albums where Trotter sat in as the saxophonist because the regular horn player wasn't up to par for some reason or another. There are a number of interviews given by celebrity musicians telling stories of Trotter's musical prowess and/or his refusal to travel with their groups.

The Trotter Sumuels story has a great impact on the subject of mental illness, domestic violence, child abuse and neglect. Finally giving in and accepting the opportunities to address these issues, during interviews Trotter mentions his struggles with depression and drug abuse along with the trauma of his father's abuse of his mother, abandonment of his family, his time in Vietnam, and the role counseling serves in helping him cope. Sharon and Clarissa sometimes question if Trotter is exploiting the mental health aspect of his story to garner more sympathy. In any case, he has drawn a great deal of attention for these important life problems. His struggles resonate with many people across the country and the charismatic Trotter is just the man to live and tell the story. Little Willie Burrows, Shirley's first husband and the man Trotter owed gambling debts when he disappeared, was long since dead by the time Trotter returned, so not one person has a harsh word to say about the man. The fact that the media interviews every person Trotter has rendered a good deed, and there are many, gives the man a somewhat saintly aura. Empathy becomes the order of the day.

--

As we all know, Americans love celebrity and with all the publicity surrounding Trotter, his family, and friends; old acquaintances, who had fallen by the wayside over the past year or so, get back in touch.

Ja'Niece decides that maybe Monia is not such a bad friend after all. "Monia, girl, why didn't you tell me all that mess was going on with Jeremiah's daddy when I was down there? I can't believe you went to New York and found him all by yourself. How did you know where to look?"

"I wasn't looking for Mr. Trotter, Ja'Niece. I simply happened to visit a club where he was performing."

"You should have told me all that was going on when I was down there, Monia. You're so secretive these days."

"I really wasn't trying to be secretive. It just wasn't my story to tell."

"Well the next time we get together, I want you to give me all the details. When do you think you might be coming up this way? 101 runs both ways you know and you owe me a visit."

"I have no idea, Ja'Niece. I've been staying so busy with everything."

"You're going to have to come up so we can do some shopping. And is it true that Jeremiah's brother's wife left him because of this whole situation with the daddy. Girl, he is fine. Is he still single?"

Monia has to laugh. Ja'Niece will never change. "I don't know Clifford's status. I will let you know when I find out."

"Okay, well, I might be able to get down that way in the next couple of weeks."

"Okay, Ja'Niece; be sure and stop by when you come down." Monia does not want Ja'Niece to assume she has an open invitation as an overnight guest. She wishes she had the gumption to tell Ja'Niece to "Tell yo daddy he owes my man an apology!" but she only chuckles under her breath.

Jeremiah's long time lady friend, Leslie, calls and apologizes to him for her harsh words the last time they spoke. She tells him how pleased she is that his father has been found and that she hopes things work out well for his family. There is no attempt on her part to pave the way for a renewal of their past relationship. She does tell Jeremiah that he will remain one of her dearest friends, thanks him for being there for her over the years, and tells him she will always be available if he ever needs her. Hmm, I guess she does pave the way, doesn't she?

Marcus's call to Monia is a bit more of a fishing expedition. "Hey, Monia, read about your friend's father in a story online and saw it on KPIX the other night. I saw Trace the other day. He asked if I had talked to you. Everybody's interested in this guy's story. Trace thinks he may have seen him perform up in New York one time."

"Oh, really. How is Trace? Tell him I said hello. Is that a baby I hear crying in the background?"

"Ah, yeah, that's my, that's my, ah, that's my girlfriend's, my girlfriend's, yeah my girlfriend's ah babysitting."

"Oh, okay."

"Well, I just wanted to check in with you and say hey. We hadn't talked in a long time."

"Okay, hey. Be sure and tell Cindy I said hello." Monia can hear Marcus choke over the phone. "You take care, Marcus. Bye."

Tina and Leslie rekindled their friendship and not much later, the writers on Tina's daytime soap wrote her out of the script. Leslie had told Tina that her relationship with Jeremiah ended but failed to mention that Jeremiah was involved with someone else. Seeing Jeremiah and his family receive more publicity over Trotter's return than she has received her entire acting career, Tina, in sheer desperation for the spotlight, calls Jeremiah and announces her desire to "move back home."

"What about the acting gig? Is the filming moving to LA?"

"I'm taking a break for a while. I want to spend some time with Erin and you."

"Will you be staying with Veronica or getting your own place?" Jeremiah asks.

"Jeremiah, I'd like to move back up to Seaside with you and Erin."

"Tina, I know Erin would love to have you close by, but you will need to get your own place."

Tina wants to make her usual threats about getting a lawyer and regaining custody of Erin but is tired of that idle threat herself. She tries to think of a way to get back in with Jeremiah, at least long enough to capitalize on the whole Trotter story, but quickly realizes she is wasting her time. Jeremiah won't even agree to start back meeting her family at the half way point so Erin can visit. He tells Tina, "When you get your own place, I'll bring her down for a visit but you'll need to come up here and get her the next time. You've got to do your share if you want to have a relationship with your child. I've made it easy for you in the past and I won't do anything to stop you from seeing her as long as the visit is planned in advance. She misses you but if you don't start giving her more of your time, you're going to regret it."

   Clifford's ex wife, Lisa, has started talking much nicer and gives every indication that she would consider reconciliation, something Clifford does not want. He and his sons are much happier without Lisa living with them. The boys visit with their mother on a regular basis and that seems to work fine. Jeremiah and Erin have visited with Clifford and his sons several times, twice with Monia and twice without. His mother and Clarissa came down and stayed an entire week. He hadn't thought he would enjoy the two senior citizens so much. He showed them a good time and they cooked every dish they thought he and the boys would enjoy. He gained three pounds during their stay. The entire gang is coming down to celebrate his oldest son's birthday in two months. Trotter and his lady friend, Glorietta Williams, plan to fly out from New York also. Clifford has asked his mother if she would be comfortable with Trotter's girlfriend coming along and Sharon responded she'd be fine as long as she could bring her long time boyfriend, David Simon. Also, Clifford met Pamela on a recent trip up to Seaside and liked her. He asked Monia to invite her friend down for the party and Pamela agreed to the visit. Life is good and everyone knows you don't mess with a good thing.

Chapter 25

Old friends come out of the woodwork for months to come after Trotter's reemergence but not all call in an attempt at exploiting the Trotter Sumuel's story. One evening after a family dinner at her mother's home, Monia receives a call from her old high school boyfriend, Junior McFarland. She was sitting in Clarissa's living room with her parents, Sharon, Jeremiah, Erin, and an old family friend of Clarissa's named Gwen when Junior's call came through. Once Monia recognized Junior's voice, her eyes went straight to Jeremiah's and she immediately excused herself from the room and went out onto the patio.

Everyone in the room except Erin noticed Monia's guilty demeanor when she recognized the caller. After Monia left the room Sharon looked at Jeremiah and commented, "You better step up your game, Son. You're lagging."

"What game are you playing, Daddy? Can I play?" Erin asked.

Jeremiah shook his head at the child with a dark expression, leading her to believe she had said something bad.

"I thought I was the only one that noticed that lag," Clarissa declared as she walked into her kitchen, followed by the other two women and Erin.

Jeremiah looked at Darnell for clarification but only got a shake of the older man's head and the cryptic advice, "I think it's time you either shit or get off the pot."

Darnell then left Jeremiah sitting alone in Clarissa's living room. Jeremiah wanted to go out to the patio and question Monia as to why she needed to leave the room to speak to the person on the other end of the call. He decided to behave as if the phone call did not faze him because he disliked the role of jealous lover.

There was little cause for Jeremiah's concern. Monia and Junior have remained in touch since graduating high school. During Monia's first few years in San Francisco, she often spent time with Junior and his long time girlfriend, Shelly. The friends' contact became less frequent when Junior followed his lady love to Phoenix for a new job. Junior and Shelly broke up nearly a year ago and his initial calls to Monia after the breakup were to cry on her shoulder. This last call, however, was that of a man on the prowl and Monia was the prey. The friends had not spoken since Monia and Jeremiah became a couple and Monia was surprised by the call. Junior explained that he'd be in Seaside the following week and wanted to know if he could take Monia out to dinner. Monia turned down the dinner date and explained that she was in a serious relationship. Junior kept her on the phone a while longer just to make sure he could not change her mind and to tell her to get in touch with him if and when she felt free to see him. Monia ended the call as graciously as one can under such circumstances.

After the call, Monia reentered her mother's home and found Jeremiah and Erin leaving. Jeremiah thanked Clarissa for the dinner and said his goodbyes to all, including Monia. Normally he would have asked her to come over or they would have at least discussed their plans for seeing each other. Monia suspected Jeremiah was upset and no sooner than she got home and settled into her bed, he called. He started off with a little small talk and had so much difficulty keeping up a casual conversation with Monia over the phone that he finally asked, "Who was it that called you earlier?"

The question took Monia by surprise and at first she wasn't sure which call he meant but quickly realized it was the call from Junior. "Just an old school friend," she answered.

"Okay. Does your old school friend have a name?"

"Yeah, it was Junior. You remember Junior McFarland. He had an older brother who went on to play pro ball. I think his brother was about your age."

"Yeah, I know who Junior is, Haven's little brother." Jeremiah also remembers Monia dancing with Junior at Tasha and Harold's wedding reception and Ja'Niece saying that Junior was Monia's old boyfriend before she went away to college. Jeremiah remembers Junior very well. "So is this somebody you talk to pretty often?"

"You know Jeremiah; if I didn't know better, I'd think you are a jealous man."

"Well, if you think I'm not a jealous man, Monia, you'd be wrong because I am. I don't know; maybe I'm wrong for getting concerned when you leave the room to talk to another man."

"I hate that bothered you. You think we can get together and talk about it tomorrow face to face instead of over the phone."

"Yeah, you're probably right," Jeremiah concedes.

"You want me to come by tomorrow evening?"

"I'll get Delores to come and stay with Erin and I'll come over there. Will that work?"

Monia knew he wanted to talk seriously because he didn't want Erin to hear or interrupt their conversation. Usually they spent most of their at-home-time-together at Jeremiah's home so Erin can simply go to bed and he doesn't have to wake her up and carry her home. Delores was not staying with Erin nearly as often because the child was with Jeremiah and Monia most evenings.

"You want me to cook something? I've got some nice steaks in the freezer."

"Why don't I just pick something up; don't worry about cooking?"

"That's nice; okay." Jeremiah's behavior was getting stranger and stranger. He always preferred home cooked meals and had never turned one down before.

--

The following evening, the night was far too cool to sit outside so Monia set her living room coffee table for dinner. Jeremiah arrived with Thai food which was a nice change of pace. He and Monia sat and ate on paper plates, talked, and drank wine as if they had all the time in the world. After they seemed to run out of light and easy things to discuss, Monia broached the subject of Junior McFarland. She sat down on the floor in front of Jeremiah and leaned back into his chest as he wrapped his arms around her. "Jeremiah, there really is no need for us to discuss Junior. He was just calling. He's called me a couple of times before but I hadn't heard from him in several months. He said he was going to be in the area and asked me out to dinner. I told him no because I'm seeing you."

"So that's why you felt you had to leave the room?"

"I couldn't very well sit there and talk to him about that in front of your mother, my parents and everyone else, including you. Of course I had to leave the room for that conversation, Jeremiah."

Jeremiah doesn't say anything and the quiet is uncomfortable for Monia. "I can't believe you are this jealous."

"I never considered myself a jealous man, Monia."

"So what's going on? You don't trust me or something?"

"Yeah, I trust you; I trust you plenty." Jeremiah squeezed her a little tighter. "You ever think about us living together?"

Monia tried to remain calm. She had always felt living with a man was an all around bad idea but she did not have the best judgment in regards to Jeremiah. "I guess it has crossed my mind. It would be kind of convenient."

Jeremiah laughed sarcastically and loosened his hold on Monia. "Is that the only reason you think about it, because it would be convenient?"

Reason reared its ugly head and Monia had to back track. "Well, Jeremiah, I've never lived with a man and I just don't think that's something I'd want to do because when two people live together it's much more difficult to separate if things don't work out. I wouldn't want to do that to Erin. I love her too much for that."

"You tired of me already? Do you see something happening to break us up anytime soon?"

"I hope not," was all Monia could squeak out.

"So you want us to stay together?"

"Well, I wouldn't be with you so much, Jeremiah, if I didn't want to stay with you."

"Forever?"

At this point Monia got really quiet and after a moment she asked, "Are you asking me if I want to stay with you forever?"

"Yeah, that's exactly what I'm asking, Monia. Do you want to stay with me forever?"

"Honestly?"

"Come on Moanie. Don't make this so hard for me?"

"Well, yeah, yeah."

"Maybe we should get married."

No one speaks for nearly a full minute. "Do you want to get married, Jeremiah?"

"Will you marry me, Monia?"

Tears began running down Monia's face. Jeremiah realized he had made her cry and it scared him. "What's the matter, Moanie?"

"I'm happy."

Jeremiah breathed a sigh of relief. "So is that a yes?"

"Oh God yes, that's a yes." Monia turned around to face Jeremiah, straddled his lap, and kissed him long and deep.

--

Jeremiah looks up from his comfortable spot in the corner of the sofa with his legs splayed and watches Monia approach, carrying a huge bowl of popcorn. He knows exactly what she will do but instead of reacting he turns his focus back to setting up his new phone. Monia plops down on the sofa and scoots as close up between his legs as she can get. She turns her head and looks at him as a way of asking him to move his arms so she can lie back onto his chest. Jeremiah knows what she wants but plays dumb. "What?" he asks with a frown. Monia pushes her head back against his hands until he gives in and parts them, telling her, "Don't choke on that popcorn."

"Want some?" Monia holds the bowl back toward Jeremiah. He starts to decline as a way of protesting Monia's recent popcorn obsession but takes a handful because it smells delicious. After gobbling down his corn, he wipes his hand on Monia's tee. "What are you doing?" Monia protests as she leans forward.

"Getting you off of me so I can finish programming my phone." Jeremiah gives her a mischievous hint of a smile.

"I'll move." Monia starts to slide away from her husband who knows he has gone too far. He doesn't understand why he resists his desire to have her near him. Now he feels like a chump as he drops the cell phone on the floor and wraps his arms around her to keep her close.

"I'm just messin' with you, Moanie. Don't get mad."

"Are we going to watch this program or not?" Monia asks as she settles back against him.

Jeremiah grabs the remote and turns on the television. He pulls up a list of recorded programs and finds an episode of the Steve Garvey Show recorded earlier in the day. The first segment of the show includes a psychiatrist named Jane Brasco, Sharon Sumuels, Trotter Sumuels, and Clifford Sumuels. Jeremiah had been invited but declined the invitation to appear. The segment deals with the need for counseling and therapy for psychological issues that affect the American family.

Steve addresses Trotter Sumuels. "Man, I didn't think we were going to ever get you on our show. You have been one busy dude since your story came to light."

"Yes, I have," Trotter agrees.

"For those of you who are not familiar with the story surrounding the Sumuels family, let me enlighten you," Steve tells his audience. He gives a brief synopsis of the story of Trotter abandoning his family and creating a new life and how counseling helped him deal with the stresses of life. Steve then looks at the doctor and asks how the cycles of domestic abuse and neglect and the issue of abandonment perpetuate throughout families. The doctor discusses the obvious outcomes of domestic abuse, abandonment, and neglect. She goes on to mention the importance of seeking counseling when dealing with depression and post traumatic stress.

"Well doctor, I'd like to know the role forgiveness plays in helping a person overcome the trauma of abuse and abandonment?" Steve asks.

"Forgiveness is a wonderful salve for conditions of the heart but often it takes various forms of therapy before one can reach a place of forgiveness, Steve. I think it is important that we as Americans seek counseling sooner rather than later."

"Now, Sharon -- is it okay if I call you Sharon?" Steve gives Sharon his direct serious look which is never serious.

"Of course," Sharon answers.

I see you sitting here with this man who left you alone without a word and with the responsibility of not one but two teenage boys. He went off and basically started a new life for himself, one, that by all accounts, turned out pretty good, made good money, even got himself a new woman. Just tell me this, how have you managed not to take a gun to this man's head?" Cause I'm gon...." The audience goes into a loud roar of agreement. Steve waits for the audience to calm down and continues. "Cause I'm gon tell you the truth. Not one, but all three of the women I married would have killed me or at least maimed me for life." The audience cheers again.

Sharon laughs along and looks at Clifford and then at Trotter. She thinks for a moment before she responds. "I'm not really a religious woman but I do have a relationship with God, Steve. So I have to say God's grace, the support of my sons and good friends, and therapy helped me a lot." Sharon garners a nice round of applause for this and the camera goes to Clarissa and Darnell Phillips, who remain in separation limbo. "I had stopped going to therapy sessions years ago but realized I needed to resume them after Trotter returned."

Steve looks at Sharon and then looks at Trotter and then out at the audience. "I bet you did," he says with emphasis. "Now Clifford, you're the younger son, right and the dentist?"

"That's right, Steve."

"It's my understanding that you gave your older brother hell. Accused him of killing your father and tried to get the police to pick him up and that you and he didn't see each other for nearly sixteen years."

Clifford sits there nodding his head as he rocks the upper half of his body in agreement with Steve's words. "Yeah, I'm still apologizing for all that."

"We invited your brother to come on the show but he declined our invitation. Is there still bad blood between you two?"

"No, not at all. At least I hope not. My brother has forgiven me. I was young, stupid, and looking for someone to blame for the absence of my father." Clifford looks at Trotter and fights to hide his emotions. "He was a big part of me and my brother's lives. I considered my dad the best father a guy could have. We were both very close to him. I guess I was always a little envious of Jeremiah but he loved me so much he let me take out my anger on him. I don't think he really understood it but he kind of took on the role of a parent. I couldn't ask for a better brother. I know I wasn't a good brother to him but I'm certain he was always there for me if I needed him."

"So where is the anger?" Steve asks Sharon.

"Oh, I'm still mad as hell. I don't try and hide it either. I just try to use it in positive ways like exercise and bingo." Once again the audience laughs.

Steve continues interviewing the family and the doctor. He gives Trotter the last words. "I was a sick man. I was sick from the time I was a man child up until today. Now, my sickness is being treated but I will never be cured because the memories don't leave me. I grew up in an environment of violence and neglect. I had two very intelligent parents who both grew up in environments of violence and neglect. That stuff passes on and embeds in our hearts, spirits, and minds. I needed counseling to deal with my sickness. I'm not saying everyone does but I wish I had gotten therapy before things got to the point that I felt the only way I could save myself was by abandoning my family. I was on the verge of suicide when I left Sharon, Jeremiah, and Clifford. I loved them greatly when I left and I continued to love them up to this moment. I had started fighting my wife and the one thing I had told myself I would never become was an abuser. I was abusing her, my sons, and myself. When I looked in the mirror and realized I was becoming my father, I did something else my father had done; I abandoned my family.

"Men." Trotter redirects for a moment, "This message is for women too, but you know," he looks at Steve Garvey and Dr. Brasco as he points to Sharon and says, "women will get help. My wife went and got counseling and asked me to go with her but I refused." Trotter looks back into the camera. "You men out there, don't be so macho. Don't be so gun ho. Get yourself the help you need so that you can be good men and take care of yourselves and your families. Don't be so proud."

Monia feels Jeremiah stiffen behind her. She presses closer to him, sensing his eyes are filled with water because hers are. "That was a good show. It was a good interview. I love you Jeremiah."

"I love you, Monia." Once again, Jeremiah wraps his wife up in his arms. He then begins to rub on her belly.

Erin enters the room and sees her father rubbing on Monia's belly. "Is she moving? I want to feel. I want to feel." Erin climbs up on the sofa and puts pressure on Monia stomach."

"You gotta be careful, baby. Don't push on Moanie's stomach," Jeremiah tells Erin.

"Okay. Can I feel my little sister?"

Monia takes Erin's hand and places it low on her belly and watches the child's face light up.

"I think you can hear her if you listen, Erin."

Erin's eyes grow wide as Monia lifts her shirt. Erin rests her ear against Monia's stomach while Jeremiah rubs along the side of this major point of interest. The three of them lie there in wait for the newest addition to their family and the population of the City of Seaside, California.

About the Author

Cinda Brea is a native of the city of Carthage, Texas, located in the East Texas Piney Woods and grew up in the city of Seaside on the beautiful Central California coast where she attended Monterey Peninsula College. Cinda is retired from the United States Army after 22 years of service. She has degrees in culinary arts and restaurant management from St Philip's College. She is a wife, mother of four, grandmother of four, great grandmother of two pooches, a family member and friend to many. She and her family make their home in San Antonio, Texas. *Friends No Longer* is her third novel.

Novels by Cinda Brea
Romancing Retha
Sylvia's Story
Friends No Longer

Contact Cinda
http://www.cindabrea.com
Follow Cinda on Facebook at: https://www.facebook.com/Cinda's-Books
contact via mailto:cindabrea@gmail.com